NANTUCKET
DREAMS

Sunflower Summer

Pam Hanson &
Barbara Andrews

Guideposts
New York, New York

CHAPTER

One

What on earth are you doing?" Gracie Gold asked when she walked into the roomy kitchen of Misty Harbor Inn on Thursday morning. It was her first day back on Nantucket.

Her sister, Caroline Marris, had filled the room with daffodils. The bright yellow flowers were crowded into half a dozen vases of every shape and size as well as a collection of improvised containers. The worktable was a mass of cut flowers, and in the middle of the chaos sat Caroline, doing something with wire and a wicked-looking pair of shears. She was dressed in an oversized candy-striped shirt rolled up to her elbows and jeans that were either terribly old or terribly fashionable with thin spots and holes in the knees. Caroline's look of intense concentration as she worked on her project made Gracie think of an old movie with a mad scientist.

"Getting ready for the Daffodil Festival," Caroline said, not looking up from the wire. "Hold this in place for me, would you?"

"Did you get all those flowers from our garden?" Gracie asked, ignoring her sister's request for help.

"No, of course not," Caroline said a bit impatiently. "I got up super early and bought them so they wouldn't all be sold before I had enough. I really need another hand here."

Gracie still stood transfixed by the array of daffodils. "Where did you get them?"

"They're on sale at lots of places in town. I know you haven't been here for a month, but have you forgotten we have to decorate for the parade?"

"I thought that meant paper streamers and such. I didn't dream it meant cutting so many flowers," Gracie, an avid gardener, said.

"If there's one thing this island has plenty of in late April, it's daffodils. There, I did it without you," she said, holding up a small wreath of flowers. "Won't Max look cute wearing this in the parade?"

"Oh dear." Gracie couldn't imagine her sister's cocker spaniel tolerating a collar of daffodils, but no doubt the inn's mascot would make his objections known.

Gracie had almost waited another week to come to the island, but Caroline and Sam, the youngest of the three Marris sisters, had urged her to be there for the festival. She couldn't refuse, not when the inn was scheduled to open for guests in just a few short days after a year of polishing their business plan and renovating, repairing, and refurnishing. Gracie was the third owner of the enterprise, albeit somewhat reluctantly, and she felt an obligation to do all she could to make their first season a success.

"What do you think of all the daffodils growing on the island?" Caroline asked, quickly forgetting her moment of irritation as she put Max's daffodil-festooned collar in the large new stainless steel fridge.

"They took my breath away," Gracie said. "Sam drove me around after she met me at the ferry. It's wonderful how the whole community cooperated in planting them. I didn't see a house or a business that hadn't made some effort. Nantucket Island looks like one big garden."

Thanks to the truly gorgeous displays of daffodils, Gracie felt somewhat compensated for having left her home in Portland, Maine, to help at the inn. It had been hard to come to the island when she had spring cleaning, an important book club meeting, and her own garden to tend. She felt a sudden wave of sorrow when she remembered the beautiful gardens her husband Art had made before his death more than three years ago. She never felt closer to him than when she was planting and cultivating the charming layout he'd designed.

Her grown son, Brandon, and his wife Stacy would look after the house and do the yard work while she spent the summer on the island, but she would miss them and her grandchildren. Her daughter Paige was a park ranger at Acadia National Park, and Gracie didn't know when she'd get to see her.

She still had serious doubts about running an inn with her two sisters. Would visitors to Nantucket choose to stay there? Was it too far out on a bluff to attract tourists? Beautiful as the spot was, could they compete with the multitude of hotels, inns, and bed-and-breakfast accommodations available for visitors? This was their first experience with any kind of business, and Gracie feared there could be all kinds of pitfalls in store for them.

Gracie adored both of her blue-eyed, blonde-haired siblings, so like her in appearance but with drastically different personalities. Without Sam's commitment to the inn, they never would have gotten this far. She was organized, almost to a fault, and competent in dealing with legal and practical matters. Gracie suspected Sam had only begun to explore her creative side, but no one could ever fault her for not giving her all to the inn.

Caroline, on the other hand, was the wild card. The oldest, and in her early sixties, she'd lived in England for many years, supporting herself as a travel writer. She was curious and spontaneous, always quick to do things on a whim. She had convinced her sisters to join her in buying the inn, partly because it had been a dream of their mother's. Gracie had been the holdout, reluctantly agreeing to buy the inn only because it was an opportunity to become closer to her sisters.

"Don't you agree?" Caroline challenged her.

"To what?"

"You didn't hear a word I said," her older sister complained. "Honestly, sometimes you tune me out. If we're going to be partners, you have to pay more attention." The warmth of her smile belied her words.

"Good morning," Sam said, coming into the kitchen with her laptop computer and distracting Caroline. "I was out in the carriage house making sure the Packard is clean and shiny for the parade."

"I'm so glad George got it running without spending a fortune," Gracie said. "I was afraid it might just be another money pit." The 1941 station wagon was a surprise bonus with the purchase of the inn, and the sisters knew it would be perfect for picking up their guests. It was bright red with wooden side panels. They hoped it would become an icon for the inn, a reminder that Misty Harbor Inn was back in business.

"Thank heavens you're here," Sam said to Gracie. "We have our hands full getting ready for our first guests next week, and now we have oodles to do for the parade too."

"I was trying to tell Gracie what still needs doing," Caroline said, cleaning up the stems on the worktable. "But her mind was miles away."

"I was just thinking of everything I left undone at home," Gracie explained.

"Time to focus," Caroline said, although Gracie thought she was the last person who should be giving that advice.

"We'll have to get up early tomorrow so we can finish making decorations," Sam added. "Fortunately we have room in the fridge to keep the flowers fresh. We're going to need a lot of garlands for the station wagon. Since we don't have guests yet, we can wait until Saturday morning to fill the urn on the front porch with daffodils."

"Will all the old cars be decorated?" Gracie asked, wondering if it was really necessary. After all, antique car owners went to a great deal of trouble to get their vehicles in perfect condition to display them. "With the Packard, it seems like it would be gilding the lily."

"It's part of the tradition, but we won't overdo," Sam assured her. "Maybe just garlands on the bumpers and around the windows, and, of course, banners on each side to advertise the inn."

"I'm thrilled we qualify for the parade," Caroline said. "Maybe later we can afford vanity license plates so people associate the Packard with Misty Harbor Inn."

"Yes, it's important the locals know we're open for business. You never know when someone may throw business our way, maybe overflow from a conference or relatives visiting the island. And, of course, I'm hoping everyone who came to the open house will tell their friends about the inn too," Sam said, putting her laptop on a counter and opening it. She flipped a lock of her pale, shoulder-length hair away from her eyes, and put her neatly manicured fingers on the keys.

"They will," Gracie assured her. "What's not to like?"

"We're almost ready for business. Have you seen the finished Web site, Gracie?" Sam asked. "Caroline did such an amazing job on it. Hey, can you believe it? Another hit."

"Someone wants to make a reservation?" Gracie asked, looking over Sam's shoulder.

"Yes, a couple wants to honeymoon on the island, and they're impressed by the photographs you put up, Caroline."

"That's exciting," Caroline said. "What could be nicer than having honeymooners as our first guests?"

"There's a catch," Sam said, reading the request on her screen. "They're getting married today. They want to check in tomorrow so they can be here for the parade Saturday."

"But we're not open for guests for another week," Gracie pointed out.

"It would be a shame to turn down newlyweds," Caroline, who had never married, said. "Think of the wonderful memories they'd have here."

"I agree, sort of," Sam said. "Earlier I was going over the things we still have to do, and the list is pretty manageable. We have shower curtains to hang and beds to make up—not the sheets until guests are expected, but the bed pads and spreads. I found some pretty padded hangers to put in the closets, and we have to be sure each room is sparkling clean before anyone arrives."

"What about breakfast?" Gracie asked. "We advertised it as part of the package."

"I've made tentative breakfast menus, but I can improvise if I have to," Sam said. "And if I don't have time to make something, I can buy some croissants or a coffee cake at the bakery. What do you think?"

"I say we open early for them," Caroline said in a decisive tone, cleaning up the leaves and stems left from Max's collar and changing the subject back to decorating. "I'll have enough daffodils to adorn hats for our ride in the parade. If I have time, I'll make collars for the three of us to wear."

"I'm not wearing a collar like the dog's," Gracie protested. "And who's going to drive the Packard?" George was the expert on their 1941 station, but he had left rather suddenly after Caroline turned down his proposal. No one was sure what his plans were now.

"Originally, George was going to drive it," Caroline started, "but…I haven't been able to reach him by phone."

"Well, one of us can do it, I'm sure," Sam said. "George showed me how to drive it, though driving a vintage vehicle can be a little challenging. I'm much more comfortable driving my minivan."

"So all of us are on board with early guests?" Gracie asked. "We should give them an answer right away, although I suspect every place comparable to ours is booked up for the festival."

"We absolutely should have them," Caroline said.

"Are there other things we need to do to be ready for guests?" Gracie asked.

"Yes, but there's not an overwhelming amount of work to do," Sam assured her. "It might be good to have practice guests, so to speak. See how we handle the two of them before we have a full house."

"We could put a vase of daffodils in their room to welcome them," Caroline said. "Maybe I could make a little wreath for their door too."

"No!" Sam and Gracie said in unison. Much as they loved their oldest sister, they knew she could get carried away by enthusiasm instead of staying focused on a single task.

"I did learn how to do lots of things with daffodils in the two-hour class I took to get ready for the festival," Caroline said with a slight pout.

"We don't have time for any new projects," Sam said. "I'll confirm a reservation for the honeymooners if you're both agreeable to having them." She began tapping the keys of her laptop.

"I think we should," Gracie said thoughtfully. "It may be rough breaking even—not to mention making a profit—our first season. We probably shouldn't turn down paying guests just because they're coming a week early."

"It's a no-brainer," Caroline said, starting to put containers of daffodils in the fridge. "I'm excited to have our first guests. Sam and I have been working hard this last month toward that goal."

Gracie didn't miss the implied criticism in her sister's comment. Perhaps they didn't need her help after all if they'd been getting along so well without her. Or maybe she was having opening-day jitters. She'd had nightmares about an empty inn falling into disrepair as their finances sank with it.

"After you confirm their reservation, I'll make a list of things we each need to do," Gracie said.

"You and your lists!" Caroline teased. "Remember when you used to make lists of all the chores you wanted your favorite doll to do? What was her name?"

"Debbie," Gracie said a bit indignantly. "I was only seven or eight."

Sam turned toward her sisters and closed the laptop's lid with a quiet snap. "That was quick! They've already responded to my e-mail, and they'll be here on the first ferry tomorrow morning," Sam said. "About dividing up the work, I think Gracie's idea is good. It would be helpful to list the jobs and decide who'll do what."

Would the first guests like the inn? Would the rooms please them? Gracie had butterflies in her stomach just thinking of all the things that could go wrong, but she was excited too.

"We're officially in business!" Caroline said jubilantly. "Mom never dreamed her three daughters would launch an inn on Nantucket. But here we are."

They hugged each other, and Gracie winked back the tears moistening her eyes. Maybe there was hope the inn would succeed if the three of them learned to work well together. She could only pray and work hard. The rest was in the Lord's hands.

CHAPTER
Two

Caroline hummed to herself as she made banners for the parade late Thursday afternoon, one for each side of the station wagon. Fortunately, there was a big workbench lining one wall of the carriage house where her handiwork could dry. Her sisters were busy working on the list of things to be done before their first guests arrived, and both were happy to let her be in charge of decorating.

She'd been able to buy stencils large enough for her purpose, so all she had to do was spray the cutout letters with bright blue paint on the heavy canvas. She'd rejected green as too much like Christmas on a red vehicle, and yellow might be difficult for the people lining the streets to read. It was hard to keep the paint from spreading under the cardboard stencils, but she was pleased with her first effort. Now, if the second one turned out as well, she'd be satisfied.

Caroline had thrown herself wholeheartedly into the preparations for the festival. It felt good to keep busy. She treasured George's friendship even though she wasn't as ready as he was to take the next step. He'd proposed to her when he came for the official opening of the inn, and she knew he was upset by her refusal. George had a kind and forgiving nature, but now part of her wondered if maybe she'd lost him.

She hadn't meant to hurt him, and he seemed to understand why she wasn't ready to commit herself to something as permanent as marriage. But then he'd left, and Caroline hadn't been able to reach him. She knew he must be very busy, but it was unusual for so much time to pass between calls.

On the second banner, the Y in *Misty* was smeared a little, but she didn't have enough canvas to make another. Probably no one would notice in the excitement of the parade. She pulled off her latex gloves and left the banners to dry, slowly walking back to the inn. She paused to enjoy the lush garden only beginning to show its vast array of colors. She was glad Gracie was here to tend it through the summer. Her middle sister was the one with a green thumb.

"Caroline, you have a call," Sam called from the newly refurbished porch that swept across the back of the house and faced a breathtaking view of the ocean. Her eyes twinkled and she mouthed the words, "It's George."

She jogged toward the stairs and took the cell phone her sister was holding.

"Hi!" she said, slightly breathless from hurrying. "Are you calling to tell me you're coming for the Daffodil Festival? Gracie was just saying she hoped you'd drive the Packard for us!"

She was a bit taken aback by how much she wanted to see him, and not just because they needed his help.

"I've sold a yacht," he said, evading her question. "I have to deliver it to the buyer in Cannes. He's in a hurry to get it."

"All the way to France," she said, more to herself than George. "When do you have to leave?"

"As soon as possible. There's no way I can come to Nantucket before I deliver it."

"Can't one of your employees do it?" She was grasping at straws, reeling from disappointment.

"Ty and Duane will crew for me, but I don't trust anyone but myself on the maiden voyage."

"I understand." She did, but it didn't dull her disappointment. "Our first guests are booked for Friday evening. I—we were hoping you'd be here to celebrate with us."

She didn't mention that the guests were honeymooners. *No need to make him think about marriage just now*, she thought ruefully.

"I don't have much choice, Caroline. I've already booked a return flight."

He spoke softly, but she detected a slight edge in his voice. Was he angry or just disappointed because she'd turned down his proposal? For the first time, she worried about their friendship, which had always seemed deep-rooted and secure. Had she sacrificed it to maintain her independence?

"You will be able to come to the island when you get back, won't you?" she asked, trying to mask her emotions and sound casual.

"Caroline, you know it's my busy season. I'll have to see how things are going when I'm back in the US. I can't make any promises."

This wasn't the answer she wanted, but maybe it was what she deserved. She tried to look at her refusal from George's point of view. Maybe she was lucky he was even speaking to her, but they had such a wonderful friendship. They'd always been able to share their thoughts about everything. She couldn't imagine not having him in her life.

"Call me when you get back," she said. "We can talk—"

A phone rang in the background. "Sorry, gotta go. Got a call on the other line."

"Have a safe trip!" she rushed to say, but the line was dead.

She plopped down on one of the wicker rockers on the porch, relieved Sam had gone inside. She didn't want her sister to see how distressed she was. Thankfully she didn't cry as easily as Gracie did. It was all she could do not to blubber in disappointment.

They could get along without George's help during the festival, but what would she do without him in her life?

I'm being a drama queen, she said to herself. George hadn't really broken off their relationship, had he? He had a business to run, and sometimes that meant delivering yachts to distant buyers. If he sounded a little impatient, it was understandable. After all, a maiden voyage across the Atlantic required intense attention to details, something George excelled at.

The ocean breeze was slightly chilly, but the weather forecast for the weekend was promising: sunny and mild with winds five to ten miles an hour. For late April on Nantucket, it was ideal weather, but that didn't stop Caroline from shivering as she stared across the deep blue undulating waters of the ocean.

She'd always thrived on being a single woman, loving her career and the freedom to live an adventurous life. Would she regret tying herself down on the island with an obligation to make the inn successful? If George did abandon her, would the love of her sisters compensate for the loss of a dear friend?

She wasn't melancholy by nature, but George's call had hit hard. Of course, he had to deliver the extremely expensive boat himself—the owners would expect that—but something in his voice hurt her. No.

It wasn't something in his voice; it was what was missing. He hadn't sounded at all sorry to miss the opportunity to come and see her. He hadn't made any promises about seeing her later in the summer.

Part of her wanted to call him back and offer to go to Cannes with him, if he'd have her, but she had a responsibility here. It had been her idea to buy the derelict inn. She had to help her sisters make a success of it, even if her heart was aching.

She gave herself a mental shake but wasn't ready to go inside and face her sisters with the news. They knew her too well, in spite of the years they'd spent apart. She didn't want to dampen their enthusiasm for the festival and their first guests. They were sure to pick up on her unhappiness.

The sea was calm, a huge expanse of deep blue disappearing into the horizon. On this waning spring day, there were no sailboats in view. The tranquil sea only served to remind her that there was always a risk in sailing a new and untried vessel. She wished she could share the adventure with George instead of worrying about all the things that could go wrong. He could run into a storm, or there could be glitches in the untested boat. *The two of us could make it an adventure*, she thought.

She wandered down the steps of the landlocked porch and made her way into one of the gardens surrounding the inn. They'd had to replace more than one rotten trellis and vine-covered fence, but a surprising number of plants had survived the years of neglect. Now, with new plantings, the gardens of Misty Harbor Inn should be a local showpiece again.

Much as she tried to find peace of mind among the golden daffodils and early-blooming purple and white hyacinths, she couldn't get the conversation with George out of her mind. She was so distracted, she nearly walked into Gracie.

"Oh, you startled me," Gracie said. "My mind was miles away."

"Sorry," Caroline said. "I was just admiring the spring flowers."

"Sam did a great job planting new bulbs," Gracie said, sounding a bit wistful. Gardens, Caroline knew, were one of Gracie's passions.

"Yeah, she did," Caroline agreed. "What are you doing with that sack?"

Gracie was holding an ordinary brown bag, the kind their mother used to use for packing their lunches.

"You caught me," Gracie said with a wry chuckle. "I brought some sunflower seeds to plant here. You know how I love them. The ones in my garden grow taller than me. I like to imagine they're smiling and nodding at me when they reach their full growth."

"Do you think the soil is right?" Caroline asked. "No, I take that back. You'll give them the best care possible. I'm sure they'll bloom by midsummer."

"We'll see," her sister said. "Once they establish a foothold, I'm sure they'll grow like weeds. Sunflowers seem like a good way to remind me of the gardens Art made for us."

"I seem to remember how the back section of the garden was solid gold when they reached their peak."

"We used to harvest the seeds to feed the birds in winter. I'm afraid I haven't been that energetic these last few years. But tell me, how did the banners turn out?"

"Pretty good. Stencils are harder to use than I expected, but they'll show the name of the inn in bold letters. I did get some bad news though." She tried to sound offhand and casual. "George won't be able to drive the station wagon in the parade."

"I'm sorry to hear that. He's still coming for a visit, isn't he?"

Caroline paused. "Not immediately. He has to deliver a yacht to France. The buyer wants it right away, and you know George. He won't trust his employees on a maiden voyage without him."

"I imagine it's a huge responsibility, but I was looking forward to seeing him. He never seems to lose his cool. We would've really appreciated that with all that's going on here."

Caroline nodded, then added quickly, "So how's your list coming?"

"Fine, I guess. Sam is a whirlwind. I got dizzy just watching her dust and polish and put things together. She didn't seem to need my help, so I came out here with my seeds," Gracie said. "Guess it's my way of bringing a bit of home to the inn."

Caroline smiled. "I like the sound of that. Well, I'll leave you to your planting. I haven't taken Max for a walk yet today."

Caroline hurried away from her sister. Actually, it was she, not the dog, who needed to walk the sandy beach below the inn—although her young canine companion certainly could benefit from burning off some excess energy. The cocker spaniel had a mischievous streak, and this would be a very bad time for him to get into trouble at the inn. She hoped their first guests liked dogs, otherwise Max would be underfoot in the kitchen the whole time they were staying.

An hour before she'd been excited about the festival and the honeymooners. Now, for the first time in months, she wondered whether she'd talked her sisters into a financial and emotional disaster. Wasn't it ironic? A phone call from George had changed everything for her.

CHAPTER
Three

I'm not sure I know how to drive such an old car," Gracie said with a worried frown. "I haven't driven a car with a clutch since we traded in our old VW. That must have been twenty years ago."

"It's like riding a bike," Sam said. "Once you know how, it'll come back easily."

"It's such a big station wagon," Gracie protested. "What if I bang a fender or something?"

"You're a much better driver than Caroline," her sister insisted. "She still hasn't gotten used to driving on the right side of the road after so many years in England."

"I'd hate to have an accident picking up our first guests. Talk about a bad start to the season! Why can't you go? After all, George showed you how to drive the Packard."

"I have too much to do here. It's really easier to work through the list myself instead of trying to bring you up to speed on all the things that need doing," Sam said.

"I don't think making up a bed is too challenging for me," Gracie said.

"No, but there's a huge pile of bedding to sort through. Every room has its own sheets, blanket, and spread. I spent a lot of time coordinating everything. Of course, I'll go through it with you later, but right now one of us has to meet the ferry."

"I don't even know how to back the thing out of the carriage house," Gracie said in a last ditch attempt to avoid driving.

"I'll back it out for you and show you everything you need to know," Sam said decisively as she left the room. "Come get me when you need me."

Gracie sipped her cooling coffee and tried not to think of everything that could go wrong on the trip to the ferry. She was still agitated when Caroline came into the room holding a cloth bag and a hand-lettered sign that said: *Mr. & Mrs. O'Hanlon.*

"What do you think?" Caroline asked, laying the sign in front of Gracie on the polished oak kitchen table

"It's good," Gracie said. "They'll be able to spot it the minute they step off the ferry at the dock. I just wish I wasn't the one picking them up."

"You'll do fine," Caroline said, touching up the apostrophe in *O'Hanlon* with a black marker. "It'll be fun meeting our very first guests. I have a couple of things for you. First, you'll want to give them a little tour of the island on the way here. I listed some of the attractions you can point out."

"I'm supposed to be a tour guide too? I'll have all I can do just driving the wagon."

"Just pretend you're seeing the island for the first time. What would you want to know?" Caroline asked, sounding unusually practical.

"I guess I could point out a few things tourists like," Gracie agreed, realizing it could be awkward to drive in silence with the newcomers.

Holding the sign and the list of attractions gingerly by the corners, Gracie turned to leave, but a loud *ahem* from Caroline stopped her in her tracks.

"What?" Gracie asked, peering quizzically at her sister. If she had to go, she wanted to allow plenty of time for a brief lesson from Sam and time to get used to the Packard. Being late to pick up the young couple was not on her list.

Caroline was grinning like the Cheshire cat and holding her arms behind her back.

"*Ta da!*" she said, pulling something out of the bag.

"A cap?" Gracie questioned, wrinkling her nose at a dark heavy-looking hat with gold braiding twisted around the brim. "It looks like something Captain Ahab would wear chasing whales."

Caroline beamed. "Doesn't it just hit the perfect note?" she asked.

"A sour one," Gracie groused. It was bad enough being the inn's chauffeur, but did her sister really intend for her to wear the ugly headgear? "Surely you don't expect me to wear that?"

Gracie felt a sudden pang of guilt at the crestfallen look on Caroline's face, but her sister rallied quickly.

"Of course I want you to wear it! Sam does too. We both thought it was a good idea," Caroline said.

So the two were in cahoots, Gracie thought, reminding herself to tell Sam what she thought of this particular "good idea."

Gracie sighed but took the proffered hat, frowning as she tried to make it fit on her head. "It makes me look like a cabbie with a Napoleon complex," she said, trying to make it feel comfortable.

"Nonsense," Caroline said, "it makes you look like a real chauffeur."

Arguing was useless at this point if she wanted to make a quick exit. Gracie doffed the hat and picked up the sign. "All right, I'll wear it, but I won't like it," she said. "Now I really have to get going."

Caroline looked so pleased it made Gracie feel less grouchy.

"What a great vintage station wagon," the young man exclaimed as Gracie opened the back door for the honeymooners, Erin and Kyle O'Hanlon.

"Thank you," Gracie said, resisting an urge to get rid of the ridiculous hat that kept slipping down over her eyes. "My sisters and I discovered it in the carriage house and thought it would be perfect to shuttle guests back and forth."

Their luggage was sitting on the ground, and she realized it was her job as the chauffeur to load it while they settled onto the Packard's capacious backseat. She blamed it on the silly hat. They probably saw her as a limo driver, not one of the owners. At least all four pieces of luggage had wheels, but they'd brought enough for an African safari.

When the suitcases were loaded, Gracie laid the cap on the seat next to her, started the motor and slowly edged the vehicle out of its cramped parking space.

"Before we go to the inn," she said to the couple cuddling close together in the backseat, "I'll take you on a little tour of the island."

She hadn't had time to memorize the spiel her travel writer sister Caroline had written, so the best she could do was point out places she especially liked. She glanced in the rearview mirror and could tell by the looks on their faces the two of them weren't especially interested in anything other than getting to the inn. But Caroline and Sam both felt a short tour was the best way to start guests' stays, so Gracie would give it a try. After all, this was a practice run for them.

"That is, if you don't mind a slightly longer ride," she added.

"Honey, what do you think?" Erin, a pretty young woman with sleek dark hair, asked her groom.

"I think it would give me time to check my BlackBerry before we get settled in," Kyle said, causing Gracie to glance again into the rearview mirror to see if he was serious. A playful grin played at the corners of his mouth as his bride turned to him in mock horror.

"Kidding," he said.

Erin, apparently slightly mollified, told Gracie to tour away.

"Kyle is in finance, and he's always working," Erin added, nudging him in the ribs. "Always."

"That's not true," he protested. "I did take time to marry my beautiful bride."

The way the two looked at each other made Gracie misty-eyed.

"Did you have a nice wedding?" she asked, blinking back the moisture in her eyes.

"It was fine," Erin said, sounding a bit distressed.

Gracie was beginning to think a silly hat was the least of her problems in this chauffeuring "job." Constantly putting her foot in her mouth made her wonder about her qualifications for the job.

"It was a small wedding, just family," her groom said by way of explanation, but Gracie was still puzzled.

Erin sighed and elaborated. "We paid for our wedding ourselves and deliberately kept it small to save for a honeymoon to Hawaii. Only family and a few close friends were invited, and we just had cake and punch. We tentatively had our trip booked for later in the season, but Kyle's job had interfered," she said.

"So we scrambled for a new destination, and Nantucket was it," he added.

"Not that we're not thrilled to be here," Erin said. "The island looks lovely, and I'm looking forward to seeing all of it. Your tour is a good way to start."

Gracie smiled, appreciating the young bride's tact.

Kyle cuddled closer to his new wife. "Besides, now we have more money to put toward a down payment on a house," he reminded Erin.

"I know," she said.

"Fortunately we bought a cancellation policy for the Hawaiian trip," Kyle explained.

It was time to change the subject, Gracie thought, since she now knew more than necessary about the honeymooners.

"Let me show you some of the sights," she said, making a mental note not to ask future honeymooning guests any questions about their weddings. It was going to be hard hitting just the right professional note with guests, especially since people's stories always fascinated her.

"How big is the island?" Erin asked.

Gracie was happy to slip into the spiel she'd run through her mind on the way to the ferry.

"Nantucket Island is fourteen miles long and three and a half miles wide. Dedicated cyclists can bike around the island in a day," she explained smoothly, beginning to feel at ease with her talk, although driving the beast still took most of her attention.

"At the inn, we provide bike rentals by the half day. Picnic lunches are also available for purchase if you let us know the night before. We'll drive past some picnic areas."

"It sounds lovely, doesn't it sweetheart?" Erin asked her groom, snuggling closer.

"It does darling," he agreed, but Gracie thought she detected a note of preoccupation in his tone. Shrugging it off, she continued with her tour. "There are ten different bike trails on the island, ranging from moderate to difficult."

"Oh, look, a lighthouse," Erin squealed, interrupting Gracie. "Oh, excuse me," she apologized. "I love lighthouses! When I was little my parents took me on a trip to Lake Erie, and we got to go inside one there. I was fascinated. Can we stop?"

"Certainly," Gracie said, bringing the aging station wagon to a stop in an area where she wouldn't get stuck in the sand. She forgot about the clutch and killed the motor, but her passengers didn't seem to mind.

She was tempted to launch into a speech about the history of the lighthouse, but instead she kept silent and encouraged the honeymooning couple to explore the path to the lighthouse. Erin tugged at Kyle's hand to go faster, and soon the two were running toward it.

Gracie's heart constricted as she was hit by a memory of the first carefree moments of her marriage. Her eyes grew misty as she watched the young couple reach the structure. She could see them standing hand-in-hand, his blond hair a contrast to her dark strands as the wind swirled around them. Even at a distance she could tell Erin was trying to pull Kyle farther down the sand while he was trying to edge back toward the wagon.

He seemed to win out, and Gracie watched them heading back— gaily swinging their arms. She took that as a good sign.

They piled into the backseat, the tension from their earlier conversation seemingly dissipated.

"I'm afraid we're getting sand all over the back of the car," Erin said, giggling as Kyle puller her close.

Kyle's BlackBerry buzzed. In the mirror, Gracie saw Erin's shoulders tense.

"I'll check it later, honey," he said, pocketing the device. But the effort it took to ignore it was written all over his face when Gracie glanced at the couple in the rearview mirror.

The mood in the backseat was more subdued as she continued to drive, pointing out picnic areas and historic landmarks.

"There are eighty miles of beaches along Nantucket Sound and the Atlantic Ocean," she said. "Of course, there's also a lot to explore in town, including art galleries along the wharf and a great variety of shops."

"I really hope we can get out for some nice bike rides," Erin said.

Gracie couldn't miss the wistful tone in the young woman's voice. It told her the bride wanted very much to be alone with her new husband.

"We will," Kyle said, and Gracie saw him squeeze his bride's hand. She realized how well the rearview mirror showed what was happening in the backseat.

"The daffodils are so beautiful," Erin said, gazing out the window. "I had a bridal bouquet of carnations and yellow roses. Yellow is one of my favorite colors."

"The Daffodil Festival is tomorrow," Gracie said. "You'll want to get a place on the parade route fairly early if you go. More than a hundred vintage cars will be decorated for the event."

"Are you participating?" Kyle asked, ignoring another insistent beep from his BlackBerry.

"Honey, why don't you just turn that off?" Erin asked.

Gracie shared her feeling. The *beep beep beep* of incoming messages was not only mildly annoying, it distracted her from driving. She needed to concentrate on navigating narrow roads with the huge Packard.

"Are we nearly there?" the young groom asked.

Gracie nodded. "Yes, we are," she said. "It's up on a bluff overlooking the ocean. You'll have a wonderful view from your room."

Now that she'd safely delivered the guests, she had a bad feeling about the parade. Would her sisters want her to drive since George wasn't coming? And would they expect her to wear Caroline's silly hat? She hated the prospect, but at least it was better than wearing a daffodil collar like the dog's.

"I wish you'd left all your electronic gadgets back in the car on the mainland," the bride said.

"Erin, you know I'm working on a big project. I need to be in touch. Anyway, I'm not checking my messages right now," he said, trying to pacify his new wife.

Gracie was relieved they were near the inn. The newlyweds needed some time alone.

"One final thing you might be interested in. The island is a bird-watcher's delight." Privately, Gracie doubted the honeymooners were interested in doing any birding, but one never knew. "The island is home to upward of a hundred and forty different species ranging from robins and finches to Snowy Owls and hummingbirds."

"That sounds interesting," Erin said politely.

"Oh, here we are," Gracie said, suppressing a sigh of relief as she pulled the Packard into the drive beside the inn. In her first run as chauffeur, the island had felt three times as big as it was.

"How lovely!" Erin cried when she saw the inn, perking up considerably. Kyle murmured his agreement as the two got out of the car and started to help Gracie collect their luggage.

In a gesture of goodwill toward her sisters, Gracie had plopped the chauffeur's cap back on her head before leading the honeymooners toward the inn. The inn was officially open, but what part was she supposed to play? Could the inn survive with three owners who didn't always agree?

Much as she loved her sisters, she had a feeling it would be the challenge of a lifetime.

CHAPTER
Four

Sam carried a pile of fresh new bedding into the Emerald Room, her favorite guest room in the inn. She'd selected the deep forest green wall paint and chosen ivory white for the trim, inspired by colonial homes she'd visited some years ago in Alexandria, Virginia. But instead of trying to reproduce a historic room, she and Caroline had tried to take the best of the past and blend it with modern touches. After all, the inn itself mixed colonial roots with dashes of 1950s sensibility. *The lighting fixtures and a glass-based bedside lamp certainly reflect our eclectic touch*, she thought.

The room was sparkling clean, and all she had to do was make up the bed and put hangers and plastic bags from the cleaners in the closet. The Emerald Room had an unusually spacious closet, which made the ocean-view room rather special.

She was bending over the four-poster bed to smooth out the bottom sheet when she heard something that sounded a lot like dripping water. One of the inn's selling points was its en suite baths, and Bill Dekker had worked very hard to bring the plumbing up to par, so she had to hope it was just that a faucet wasn't turned all the way off.

Rushing to check, she confirmed that the shower was indeed leaking, and no amount of tightening the handle stopped the steady *drip, drip, drip*. In the best of circumstances, it was merely one of life's irritating background noises, but today it was a disaster waiting to happen.

Gracie had already left to pick up the newlyweds, and there wasn't time to clean and ready another room. She put in an emergency call to Bill but only got his voice mail.

"Hi, Bill! It's Sam Carter over at the Misty Harbor. Can you please come over at your earliest convenience? We have guests on the way, and the shower in their room is leaking."

The phone rang a moment later, and Sam answered.

"Hi, Sam. It's Bill," said the reassuring voice.

Bill Dekker had done a major portion of the renovations to the inn. If anyone could help with this emergency, it was Bill, Sam hoped. She simply didn't have time to call around and check with other plumbers on the island.

Explaining the problem in as few words as possible, she ended the conversation by saying, "Do you have time to come over now? I'm desperate." She wasn't above pleading with the good-natured handyman.

"Sure, Sam. Don't panic. I can be over in about half an hour. Does that work?"

Sam hated to be pushy with someone who was doing her such a big favor, but she was in a time crunch. "Actually, Bill, Gracie is meeting our guests at the ferry as we speak."

"Then I'll get there as soon as I can," he promised, ending the call before Sam could thank him.

Sam hurriedly finished making the bed, but there wasn't time to admire the new ivory chenille spread. She rushed downstairs to watch for him and stood by the kitchen door, impatiently checking her watch every thirty seconds until she heard Bill drive up.

"It's too bad it's leaking," Bill said, as she let him into the kitchen. "It's probably nothing serious. I may just need to retighten something."

"Bill, thanks so much for coming on such short notice. And I'm so sorry, but would you mind terribly taking off your shoes?" she asked, eyeing the dried muck on his oversized work boots. "I've just mopped and vacuumed, and I don't have time to do it again before the guests get here."

She was so grateful for Bill's congenial nature. He sat on a kitchen chair and very slowly unlaced his dirty boots.

"Up here," she urged, leading the way although Bill knew the layout of the inn as well as she did.

"Do you see the problem?" she asked anxiously.

She'd learned from years of teaching that no one worked their best when they were micromanaged, but this was an emergency. She tried to peek around him to see what he was doing, but his broad shoulders blocked her view. The clanking seemed excessively loud to fix such a small problem, and he kept taking different tools from the thick leather belt he wore over faded overalls.

"Can you fix it?"

"No problem," Bill said in a reassuring tone.

"That should do it, Sam," he said after what seemed like a long time.

"Thank you for taking care of it so quickly. I don't know what I would have done without you." Sam ran her hand through her unusually disheveled shoulder-length blonde hair and followed Bill to the back door.

"What do I owe you?" she asked, as he sat down to lace his boots back up.

"No charge, Sam," he said. "It was my fault for not tightening it better, and I'm always happy to help all of you out." He bent over to lace up the other boot. "So Gracie's picking up your first guests?" he asked with studied nonchalance. Sam didn't miss the slight flush on his cheeks as he posed the question.

"Yes, and I'm expecting her back soon," Sam said, wondering if it was her imagination that Bill was taking a long time to lace up his work boots.

"How soon?" he asked, a little too casually.

"I'm not exactly sure. Would you like to have a glass of lemonade while you wait for her?" Sam didn't really have time to play gracious hostess, but Bill had saved her so much anxiety she didn't want to appear to be pushing him out the door. Besides, she was curious about his interest in Gracie.

He paused. "No, no thank you," he said, finally tying his boot. "I just thought if she was due back soon…" He grinned.

Sam returned his smile. "You just thought you'd say hello to her, right?"

"Sure," he said, breaking into an even bigger grin. "You know I've had a mad crush on her since we were kids and met at the beach," he said, winking at Sam.

"I never would have guessed," Sam teased,

Bill's face flushed. "That obvious?"

"To me. I'm not sure whether Gracie's really noticed. If she has, she hasn't said anything to me."

"Well, please don't tell her I said anything about her, okay?" Bill said.

Sam laughed. "I won't. You saved me today. I won't reveal any of your secrets to my sister. Deal?"

"Deal," he said, smiling back at her. They shook on it, and Sam thanked him again.

As soon as Bill was out the door, Sam grabbed the bucket with cleaning supplies and retraced his steps. Since he'd willingly removed his mud-caked boots, she mostly had to wipe up a trail of sand on the steps.

Fixing a leak wasn't a neat job, and the bathroom needed more than a lick and a promise. Sam got down on her hands and knees and scrubbed until all traces of debris were gone. Why had she ever thought it would be glamorous and exciting to run an inn? In her more skeptical moments, she was afraid Caroline had sold them a bill of goods.

Don't be an old crab, she admonished herself. *I'm just having first-guest nerves.* Before long, the room and bathroom were as perfect as she could get them.

On the way out, she noticed one more thing she needed to do. Last winter she'd found some lovely padded satin hangers on sale at a giveaway price. They were still lying on the dresser, so she put down the pail of supplies and went to hang them on the bar running along one side of the closet.

The space behind the gleaming ivory door was small, but then, most guests would only bring enough clothing for a few days. She stepped into the confined area and arranged the hangers, acting as much by feel as sight because there was no light. The walls were unvarnished wood with the patina of age, so they'd decided not to paint them. Maybe plain old wire hangers would have sufficed, but she loved the feel of the slippery padding. It was one small detail, but Sam believed that such small niceties added up. She stepped back to admire them as best she could in the dim light, backing into the closet wall opposite the rack.

Much to her surprise, the wall behind her back seemed to move. She turned and examined it, running her fingers over the slightly rough surface. No, she hadn't imagined the movement. The paneling shifted slightly under her fingers.

In spite of her time constraint, Sam couldn't contain her curiosity. She disconnected the small lamp on the bedside table and found a plug close enough to allow her to shine it into the closet. Much to her surprise, the wall wasn't one solid sheet of wood. There was a distinct crack down the middle, wide enough for her to slide her finger into it.

"Now if I just don't get splinters...," she muttered, biting her lip in concentration as she got a grip and slowly pushed half of the panel inward.

Sam expected to see nothing but rough beams or possibly a space to store luggage, but she couldn't have been more wrong. The dim light of the lamp revealed an actual room.

"Oh my," she said, forgetting the imminent arrival of Gracie and the guests. "What on earth is this?"

The space was filled with pieces of old furniture and other objects she couldn't identify without stronger light. The ceiling was low and the space tight, but it was considerably bigger than the closet. What in the world had she found? Why hadn't they noticed the dead space between rooms before this?

She cautiously took one step into the hidden room, wary of possible rot in the board floor. It seemed to support her weight, but she didn't want to crash through to the lower level if it gave way.

As much as she strained to see, she couldn't begin to make out the whole contents of the space. Sam could hardly wait to tell her sisters. Was this a treasure trove or just trash they'd have to deal with? There was no way she could tell without actually entering the room with a powerful flashlight.

Before she could continue her visual exploration, Sam heard the unmistakable purr of the station wagon approaching the front entrance through the open window. As hurriedly as possible, she forced the moveable panel back into place and glanced around the room to make sure everything was ready for the guests. Her bucket of cleaning supplies was still sitting in the middle of the rug on the hardwood floor.

She picked it up and ducked down the back steps that would have been the servants' stairs when a wealthy whaling family had owned the house in the 1800s. The steps were narrow and uneven, and she never used them without feeling sympathy for the housemaids who had to run up and down them, working long hours with few breaks and little pay.

Sam only had time to hide the bucket and comb through her hair with her fingers before Gracie was escorting the honeymooners into the foyer.

"What a beautiful staircase," the young woman was saying as she admired the curving steps. The grand staircase was the first thing people noticed when they entered the inn.

"This is my sister, Sam Carter," Gracie said, coming in behind the pair, pulling what looked to be their largest piece of luggage. "Our guests, Mr. and Mrs. O'Hanlon."

"I'm Erin," the new bride said, stepping forward to clasp Sam's hand. "This is my husband Kyle."

"It's so nice to have you," Sam said warmly. She glanced over at Gracie, whose labored breathing revealed the exertion of carrying the luggage. Obviously, they'd need to talk about luggage handling. Maybe, when the inn was filling up regularly, they could hire a high school boy or a pensioner as a combination bellhop and handyman.

Caroline was the designated greeter. It was her job to register guests, take reservations to rent bicycles, and show them to their rooms. But for some reason, she was nowhere in sight, although she certainly knew the honeymooners were expected.

Sam felt too grubby to act as hostess after the plumbing crisis, not to mention the cleanup. She was grateful when Gracie stepped up and did Caroline's job.

"If you'll excuse me," she said, intending to find Caroline. She could hardly wait to tell both her sisters what she'd found.

Sam grabbed two of the bags and started up the stairs, surprised by how heavy the larger one was. Unless she was misjudging the weight, the bride must have packed a full-sized iron and half a dozen other appliances. *We need to have a talk about what guests can use in their rooms,* she thought. *Even though the inn's been rewired, we have to ban some activities, like cooking.* Despite Gracie's thorough list-making, Sam realized there were still so many things they had to consider as innkeepers.

A little breathless at the top of the stairs, she put the luggage in the Emerald Room, resisting the temptation to take one more peek at the hidden space before the guests occupied the room. Of course, there wasn't time, but the prospect of exploring it was enticing.

Sam confirmed that Caroline wasn't on the second floor, and she could think of no immediate reason for her to go into the attic. Sam went back to the main floor and found her missing sister taking pictures of the newlyweds.

"You're our first guests," Caroline said, taking several shots of the grinning couple as they stood with arms entwined. "I think your picture should hang somewhere in the inn. Of course, I'll have a copy made for you as a souvenir of your visit."

As Caroline led the guests to their room, Sam hustled Gracie into the kitchen to share her big news.

"Guess what I—" she started to say, but her sister was still unwinding from her maiden trip to pick up the guests.

"I hope I don't have to drive that monster station wagon in the parade," Gracie said, plopping the chauffeur's hat down on the table. "And this hat is ridiculous. It slips over my eyes, and I can hardly see where I'm going."

"You'll get used to the Packard," Sam said. "I struggled at first when George showed me how to drive it. But he did a nice job, don't you think?"

"Yes, it certainly looks great, but that doesn't make it easy to drive. What were you going to tell me?"

"I found a hidden room!" Sam said. "And it's full of stuff, furniture mostly, but who knows what we'll find."

"Really? We've been over every inch of the inn," Gracie said.

"I know, but when I was putting hangers in the Emerald Room closet, I accidentally pushed against one of the walls, and it moved. I managed to push one panel open, and there it was—an honest-to-goodness hidden room. There wasn't time to explore it, but I can't wait."

"It's hard to believe anything worthwhile is hidden there," Gracie said, getting a drink of water.

"I don't expect to find a Chippendale chair or a set of Shaker boxes," Sam said, "but isn't it exciting to know we have a secret room?"

"What's exciting?" Caroline asked as she walked into the kitchen.

Sam explained what she'd found, and her older sister was even more excited than she was.

"As soon as they go out for dinner, we'll take a look," Caroline said. She sounded more chipper than she had since she'd learned that George would not be coming back for the festival.

"I'm not sure that's a good idea," Gracie said. "What if they come back while we're doing it? They'll think we're snooping in their things."

"I'm afraid Gracie's right," Sam said. "We can't invade our guests' privacy."

"And what if we can't get the panel back the way it is?" Gracie asked. "We don't want curious guests rummaging in there."

"That's a good point," Sam agreed. "I'm not sure how safe the floor is. If a guest fell through, we could be sued and lose the inn."

"We do have liability insurance," Gracie pointed out, "but it wouldn't exactly be great PR if our inaugural guests got hurt."

Caroline pursed her lips but didn't protest. "I guess our guests are the number one priority right now, but as soon as they check out, we have to see what's in there."

Sam wholeheartedly agreed, and Gracie nodded in assent. Whatever the room did or didn't contain, it would be a shared adventure to explore it.

CHAPTER
Five

Gracie sighed when Caroline plunked another bucket of daffodils on the worktable in the kitchen in front of her. "These are the times that try men's souls," Gracie said. She was trying to wire the yellow flowers in a garland without crushing them.

"Benjamin Franklin?" Sam guessed, struggling to cut a length of wire with decrepit pliers. "Wait. Thomas Paine."

"No matter," Caroline declared. "We're women. We can do this."

"Of course we can," Gracie agreed, "but will we have to work all night to get everything ready for the parade?"

"If that's what it takes…" Caroline sounded like a cheerleader for a losing football team.

"I still don't think I should be the one to drive in the parade," Gracie protested for the umpteenth time.

"It can't be me. I'm still not used to the island roads. That's why I was hoping George could drive." Caroline's voice was sad when she mentioned him, but Gracie couldn't think of anything to cheer her up.

"I have to concentrate on fixing breakfast for the guests," Sam said. "Anyway, I still have trouble with the clutch. The motor dies when I forget to use it. Can you imagine how embarrassing it would be to stall in the middle of the parade?"

Gracie could imagine all sorts of things going wrong, not the least of which was rain that would make the cobblestone road through town slippery. She hoped the weather forecaster was accurate in predicting mild temperatures and sunshine.

"I've only driven it once to get the newlyweds," Gracie reminded them unnecessarily. "That hardly makes me an expert."

"You'll do fine," Sam assured her. "Anyway, we'll be in the wagon to give you moral support."

"And driving suggestions," Caroline added.

Gracie groaned, imagining the kind of advice her older sister might offer.

"Max has to ride in the backseat," she said. "I'll have my hands full without any distractions."

"He really likes to stick his head out the window on the passenger side," Caroline said.

"No!" Gracie loved the cocker spaniel, but she was much too worried about driving at the right speed with the correct space between vehicles to have Max bouncing around on the seat beside her.

Caroline shrugged. "All right. I'll ride in back with Max."

Gracie worried when her sister agreed without a more spirited argument. She wondered whether there was more to George's absence than Caroline was telling them. Not for the first time, Gracie thought that she should have been the oldest sister—the responsible one, the one who counseled and looked after the others. Caroline had never fit into that role, but Gracie was hardwired to be concerned about others. She tried not to stick her nose in where her advice wasn't wanted, but friends seemed to gravitate to her when they had problems.

"How does this look?" Sam asked, holding up the chauffeur's hat. "I tried not to cover the gold braid."

Gracie groaned. The cap had been bad enough before. Now it looked like something a demented dictator would wear. "You can't be serious!"

"Too much?" Sam looked over her handiwork and nodded in agreement. "You're right. Less is sometimes more."

"I should arrange daffodils in the urn on the front porch," Gracie said. She needed some air after several hours of intense effort.

"Good idea," Sam said. "We won't have any time to spare tomorrow morning. By the way, do we all have a yellow shirt to wear in the parade? If not, I have an extra."

"Not your bumblebee sweatshirt?" Caroline asked, coming to sharp attention.

"It's cute. Jamie gave it to me for my last birthday."

"Not that your daughter doesn't have good taste," Gracie said, trying to be tactful, "but all those bugs crawling up the arms would make me itch. If it's cool out, I'll wear a tan hoodie. Otherwise, I'll wear a red shirt to match the wagon. Is that coordinated enough?"

"You don't need to be snarky," Caroline said. "I'll wear red too."

"It doesn't matter," Sam said. "It was only a thought. People are supposed to look at the vehicle, not us, and Max is a great scene stealer."

"Then why are we bothering with daffodils on our heads?" Gracie asked.

"The idea is to attract attention for the inn," Caroline pointed out. "We want to look like a fun group."

"But I'm not fun," Gracie pointed out. "No one has ever called me fun."

"I love you anyway," Sam said, walking over to give Gracie a hug. "Do you need help putting daffodils on the front porch?"

"No, thanks. I can manage," she said, gathering flowers from the fridge.

The sun had already set, but Gracie liked the brief time before total darkness when the sky was deep midnight blue with the twinkle of distant stars. Whatever else came of their venture with the inn, she felt blessed to be surrounded by beauty on land, sea, and sky.

Sometimes the three of them fell into their childhood pattern of bickering and making up, but she never questioned the love they shared. The real question was: Could they work together well enough to make a success of the inn? Caroline seemed oblivious to the financial risk they were taking, and Sam seemed to believe that enough hard work could accomplish anything. Gracie wished she could share their optimism, but taking on the inn had involved a tremendous life change for her. Was she up to it? She didn't know.

She had to switch on the porch light to see what she was doing. It gave a golden glow to the freshly painted rails and columns, and she couldn't imagine a more inviting entrance.

Maybe guests would love the historic inn as much as she and her sisters did. She sincerely hoped so, but she also knew the island had more than its share of beautiful hotels and inns to attract visitors. Could Misty Harbor Inn fulfill their mother's dream of a permanent home on the island and still be a financially sound investment?

The hose was coiled out of sight behind some bushes, and she managed to drag it close enough to fill the urn with water. She started arranging daffodils, taking care to place each one in the exact spot she wanted. The bouquet should easily last through tomorrow, the most important day of the weeklong festival.

It was a shame they couldn't open all the rooms for guests this week, but there was still work to be done. At least the honeymooners gave them a chance to practice the routine of running the inn. Already their visit was bringing up issues the sisters would need to address. Sam and Caroline seemed to know exactly what they needed to do, but she was still at loose ends. Aside from driving the Packard, which she dreaded, did they really need her there?

The sky always seemed bigger and the sun and moon brighter on Nantucket, but could it compensate for being away from her home and family all summer?

Gracie put the finishing touches on the display and returned the hose to its place of concealment behind the bushes. She was about to go inside when the newlyweds rode up on the bicycles they'd rented for their stay.

"I'll put the bikes back where they belong," Kyle said, skidding to a stop at the bottom of the steps.

"Fine." Erin let the bike she'd been riding fall to the ground, making Gracie cringe.

They'd purchased renovated used bikes, expecting them to have hard usage. Still, she was surprised because Erin didn't seem like a person who would be careless with property that didn't belong to her. Kyle dismounted and picked up the bike she'd dropped, wheeling both of them around the side of the house.

"Good evening," Gracie said, not wanting to startle Erin.

"Oh, I didn't see you there," she said. "I'm sorry about the bike. I shouldn't have let it drop like that."

"I'm sure it's okay." *Or maybe not*, she thought and wondered why Erin had sounded so angry with Kyle. "Did you have a nice dinner?"

"It was fine," Erin blurted. Her shoulders were clenched.

"I'm sorry. Maybe I can recommend a better place tomorrow." Gracie picked up the empty bucket but hesitated.

"Oh, it wasn't the food," Erin admitted. "Sometimes Kyle is so— so, I don't know. All he thinks about is work. We'd still be going to Hawaii if it weren't for his job."

"I'm sure you're disappointed not to be going there. My husband and I talked about visiting the Hawaiian islands, but we never got around to it. Now it's too late."

"I'm sorry," Erin said. "Are you a widow?"

"Yes. My husband Art passed away several years ago, but I still struggle. Losing someone you love isn't something you get over."

"You must think I'm awfully shallow," Erin said. "I know Kyle's working hard for our future, but you'd think he could forget about his job for a few days. It is our honeymoon, after all."

"I'm sure you'll both have a lovely time," Gracie said. "Nantucket has a way of charming visitors."

"I hope," Erin said without much conviction. "I love what you've done with the daffodils."

"Thanks. Unfortunately we have a lot more to do to get ready for tomorrow. My sisters are hard at work making garlands, hats, and such. At the rate we're going, we'll be at it all night." Gracie opened the door and held it for Erin to go in ahead of her.

"I love working with flowers. I worked part time for a florist when I was going to community college. Are you using daffodils for all the decorations?"

"Yes, my sister managed to buy them yesterday before the vendors were sold out. We don't have enough in our own garden, not that I'd want to pick them anyway."

"Can I help?"

"With the decorations?" It was the last thing Gracie had expected from a newlywed.

"Please? I'd love to!"

"Well, I'm sure we'd be glad to have help." Gracie was afraid Erin was offering to spend her time on this as a way to punish her new husband, but she couldn't think of any courteous way to refuse.

Erin insisted on carrying the empty flower bucket. She followed Gracie to the kitchen where Sam was running cold water over her bleeding thumb.

"I couldn't have picked a worse time to cut my thumb," she complained. "Caroline ran to get me a bandage."

"Is it very deep?" Gracie asked, forgetting about Erin for a moment.

"No, but it'll be a nuisance while I'm trying to finish these garlands."

"Here's the first aid kit," Caroline said, returning to the kitchen.

"Erin would like to help us," Gracie said. "She's worked in a flower shop, so she can probably teach us some tricks."

"I doubt that," the younger woman said, "but I do love being around flowers."

"I think we could do with fewer flowers on the Packard," Sam said, "but Caroline wants it to look like something in the Tournament of Roses Parade."

"It's a big vehicle to decorate," Caroline reminded her while she applied the bandage to Sam's thumb.

"How can I help?" their guest asked.

Gracie thought Erin should tell her husband where she was, but she really couldn't tell the newlywed what to do.

"How are you at making garlands?" Caroline asked, hoping to get her started on a long one to hang on the front porch in the morning.

"Let me see how you're doing it," Erin said.

Gracie could hear the strain in Erin's voice, but soon the four of them were laughing at the comical effect of a hat Caroline was making.

"How are you going to keep it on your head?" Erin asked.

"Willpower," Caroline said. "That and half a dozen hair clips." She modeled it, strutting around the kitchen like a model, the garland balanced on her head.

Gracie kept one eye on the kitchen door, which was closed because they wanted to keep their living and working areas separate from the public areas of the inn. Would Kyle miss his bride and come looking for her? Or was he preoccupied with his job, as Erin seemed to think?

Gracie remembered how hard it was to be young at times. Slights hurt more, and issues of everyday life were magnified. She remembered crying over a burnt cake she'd tried to make for Art's birthday and feeling devastated when he couldn't be home for hers.

Erin's laughter interrupted Gracie's thoughts. Decorating certainly raised Erin's spirits, but maybe she was trying a little too hard to be nonchalant about the disagreement with her husband.

The kitchen door flew inward and startled everyone.

"Has anyone seen my wife?" Kyle looked around and saw her working on the garland.

"I'm helping with the daffodil decorations," Erin said as though it were no big deal.

"I didn't know where you were."

Kyle looked so miserable and out of place in the room full of women that Gracie felt sorry for him. Probably the last thing he wanted to do was to make up with his wife in front of strangers. For a moment, she thought Erin would refuse to go with him, but she dropped what she was doing and said a quick good night.

"They're a cute couple," Caroline said after they left. "Wish he'd waited a little longer to come for her. She makes a neater garland than I do."

"I don't think that's why she's here," Sam said in a practical voice. "Now, what can I do without inflicting further bodily harm on myself?"

"You could take Max outside while we finish up here," Caroline said.

"Sure." Sam whistled for the inn's mascot and retrieved his leash from a peg on the wall.

Gracie was pleased at how fast they finished the decorations. She cleaned up after Sam went outside, thinking as she worked that Caroline hadn't been herself this evening. She had little to say and didn't seem especially interested in the results of all their work. Was she regretting her decision to buy the inn? Her enthusiasm had evaporated since George had told her he wasn't coming for the festival.

They should be celebrating the inn's first guests, but Caroline was preoccupied, Sam was tense, and Gracie was just plain worried. Had too much time passed for them to recapture the joyful relationship they'd had in their youth?

CHAPTER
Six

Caroline stood beside the Packard wagon waiting to go into town for the parade.

"Gracie, Sam!" She was tempted to whistle for them the way she did for Max, but she knew that kind of summons wouldn't sit well with her sisters—especially Gracie. Instead she tapped her foot impatiently and waited for them to appear.

Max was restless inside the wagon, and she had to slip in beside him to adjust his daffodil collar. She hoped he wouldn't destroy it before the parade was over. She didn't want Gracie to be right, even though she knew she was being petty to think that way.

In fact, since George had bailed, the festival didn't seem like fun anymore. She was struggling to hide her disappointment, but her sisters probably saw through her forced enthusiasm. It was hard to fool the two people who knew her best.

"We're ready," Sam said, coming out with Gracie right behind her.

They'd opted for red tops, and Caroline had to give her younger sister credit for wearing a faded T-shirt, even though it wasn't very flattering. Gracie was wearing an oversized sweatshirt with the cuffs folded over. By the time the parade was over, she was going to be overheated.

Caroline unzipped her thin red nylon windbreaker, already a little warm. She was wearing a red tank top under it in case it got really warm during the parade. The sisters of Misty Harbor Inn would make a colorful team, and anything that drew attention to their new enterprise was good.

"You don't really expect poor Max to keep that on all day, do you?" Gracie asked as she walked around the front of the vehicle to get in on the driver's side.

"As a matter of fact, I do," Caroline said. She ruffled Max's floppy ears. "You'll keep it on won't you, my good boy?"

Sam smiled as she got in beside Gracie. "It's really not practical, Caroline, but maybe he'll at least make it through the parade."

Gracie took a sip out of the water bottle she'd brought with her and frowned at the hat Caroline had brought to the car. "You insisted I drive the car, but I'm not going to be able to see with this thing on my head. What if it slips over my eyes at a crucial time?"

"Let me anchor it for you," Caroline said, leaning over the front seat with some hair clips in hand. "It's the crowning touch. Please at least give it a try."

"Ouch!" Gracie yelped. "You pulled my hair."

"Sorry, but you don't want it to fall over your eyes. Hold still."

Caroline was afraid Gracie might be right, but her sister was so cute in the hat, it was worth a try.

The banner was her biggest worry. She wasn't even sure the parade committee would let them keep it on the vehicle. And she didn't have confidence in the way she'd attached it. As long as there wasn't any wind, the tape should hold it in place on either side, but this was Nantucket. The odds were against absolute calm.

"You did a good job on the banners," Sam said, turning around to compliment Caroline. "I only noticed one tiny smear. I doubt the people watching the parade will see it."

"Thanks, I just hope it stays on." Caroline rolled down a backseat window so Max could ride with his head sticking out. She wrapped his leash around her hand, knowing from experience she had to hold on to the cocker spaniel. When he rode in the car, he turned into Wonder Dog, able to leap fire hydrants at a single bound.

"Whew," Gracie said as she rolled down her window, "it's a little windy out today."

Caroline stuck her head out beside Max's, checking on the banner.

"Don't worry, I think it'll hold," Sam said reassuringly.

"I think we're good to go," Caroline said, impatient for Gracie to start the motor and get moving.

"I should've worn driving gloves," Gracie said, wringing her hands instead of starting up.

"You did fine picking up the newlyweds," Sam said.

"Yes, but I didn't have thousands of people watching."

"Just a little stage fright," Caroline assured her. "Once we get moving, you'll get into the groove."

"Into the groove? I can't believe I thought this car was a good idea. Of course, at the time I didn't plan to be the one always driving it." Gracie started the vehicle and let it idle for a few moments. "Is the motor supposed to sound like that?"

"It always does until it warms up a little," Sam assured her. "Remember, this car is older than we are."

"For goodness' sake, let's hit the road," said Caroline. "I can't imagine anything more embarrassing than arriving too late to be in the parade. That's not what you're trying to do, are you? I remember when you didn't want to ride on the Girl Scout float for the Fourth of July parade. You poked around until Mom practically dragged you out of your room."

"I was a Brownie, not a Girl Scout, and I was afraid of falling off that silly cat."

"It was an endangered species of tiger, if I remember right," Sam said. "You're not going to fall out of the Packard."

"Okay, I'm putting it in gear," Gracie said.

Caroline winced at the slight grinding noise, but at least they were moving forward. She was tempted to take over driving herself, but she wasn't sure about shifting gears during the parade. Today wasn't the time to practice, but it definitely was on her to-do list. She settled back to enjoy the ride into town.

The hum of the motor and the smoothness of the ride lulled her into a catnap, but she awoke with a start, thankful the leash was still wrapped around her hand.

The aging car swerved sharply, and Max gave a startled yelp. Gracie still had a grip on the steering wheel, but she was partly off the road—as luck would have it—on a firm shoulder.

"What on earth happened?" Caroline asked.

Gracie stopped the car and slumped back on the upholstered seat.

"I tried to drive around a branch in the road. I think we're okay. I'm not used to the steering this thing yet."

She got out and circled the car and then nodded her head and resumed her place behind the wheel. But they couldn't proceed until

Carolyn got out to make sure her lovely banners weren't going to soar away in the breeze.

"The daffodils are still in place, so at least they survived. And my banners look like they'll make it to the parade."

"Banners probably aren't allowed in the parade," Sam said. "They may make us take them off."

Caroline appreciated the sympathetic look Gracie gave her in the rearview mirror and was gratified when Sam reached over the seat and squeezed her arm.

Sighing, Caroline had to admit her sister could be right. She'd lost her copy of the parade rules, but there may have been a prohibition against advertising banners.

"Hopefully nothing else will go wrong," Gracie said as she carefully maneuvered the Packard toward the cobbled pavement of Main Street.

When they reached the starting point, a committee member did insist on removing the banners as Sam had predicted. In spite of not being able to display them, Caroline enjoyed being part of the bustling activity of lining up for the parade. The wind was gentle in the shelter of the venerable buildings lining Main Street. The brick facade of an art gallery featured window boxes with daffodils nodding in the breeze. Children were riding bicycles festooned with the colorful yellow flowers along the tree-lined sidewalks. Younger boys and girls were running along the walks, trailing yellow balloons behind them.

Caroline admired the way Gracie maneuvered the Packard into its designated spot between a Cadillac convertible and a Ford Model A. The classic station wagon looked positively jaunty with garlands of daffodils wrapped around the bumpers.

"Look at that truck," Sam said, pointing to a buttery yellow vehicle with daffodils spilling out of the bed and American flags affixed to the antennas.

"I'm too busy looking at all these children on bikes, hoping one doesn't dart in front of me," Gracie said.

"Someone should shoo them away from the street," Caroline said, trying to keep Max from bounding out the window. She settled him down on her lap, but he was much too excited to stay there.

"But it's fun to see them getting into the spirit of the parade," Sam said.

Caroline detected a note of wistfulness in her younger sister's voice and wondered whether she still missed teaching. But this wasn't the time to worry whether her sister had regrets about retiring from the classroom and coming to the inn.

Gazing out the window, Caroline glimpsed a couple about her age strolling hand-in-hand, weaving effortlessly through the crowded sidewalks. Her heart gave a little lurch. Had George left yet to deliver the yacht? And would he call her before he did? Their last conversation had ended abruptly, and there were things she wanted to say to him.

"Hey, are you okay?" Sam called to Caroline from the front seat after a long pause in their conversation.

"I'm fine," Caroline said, forcing herself to sound cheerful. "Look, the parade's starting up ahead of us. All right, Gracie. Be ready to follow the old truck. Be sure to wave to the crowd, Sam. Make it look like we're having the time of our lives."

She tightened her hold on Max's leash as he tried to climb over the back of Sam's seat to get to his favorite perch in front.

Gracie carefully kept her place in the line of cars for several blocks, even though she had to brake frequently to keep from overtaking the vehicle in front of her. Caroline waved on one side and Sam the other, enjoying the response from the crowd lining the parade route.

They were perhaps halfway through the parade when Caroline wrinkled her nose, getting a whiff of something unpleasant. She looked around on all sides to find the origin, but there was nothing on the street to explain the bad odor.

"Do you smell that?" she asked her sisters.

Both Gracie and Sam sniffed and agreed.

"It must be the exhaust from the Model A in front of us," Gracie said.

"No it's not," Caroline cried out. "It's us!"

"The engine's smoking!" Sam shouted.

Suddenly, the car lurched to a complete halt in the middle of the street. Gracie pumped the accelerator and turned the key frantically.

"What happened?" Caroline asked.

"I must have stalled the engine. I can't get the car started again!"

"But that wouldn't make the car smoke!" Caroline shot back. The three sisters scrambled out of the smoking car. In a mad rush, they left Max on the backseat, wagging his tail. Black smoke wafted out from under the hood as they hurriedly made their way to the sidewalk.

"Oh dear!" Caroline moaned, "This day is not turning out well at all."

The slow-moving line of cars behind them came to a standstill as smoke wafted lazily from the hood. Caroline rarely cried, but she might make an exception for this.

"What are we going to do?" she asked in desperation.

Several drivers left their vehicles and rushed to their aid, and a few men among the spectators joined in the effort to push the old Packard to the side so the parade could continue.

"Put it in neutral," one of the helpers yelled.

Gracie stood paralyzed by the breakdown, but Sam quickly slipped behind the wheel and complied.

Caroline spied Cubby Brewster, one of the parade organizers and a member of Harvest Chapel, her church. He was red-faced under his bright orange hair, which was only slightly speckled with gray, but he looked more harassed than angry at their mishap.

"Ladies," he called out, "we'll move your car to the side alley next to the candy shop to get it out of the way."

"Good idea, thank you," Gracie started to say, but Caroline's panicked shout drowned her out.

"Max, come back here!" she cried out.

He'd scooted over the back of the front seat and made his escape before Sam could close the door on the driver's side. The open car door had proved too tempting to the daffodil-bedecked dog.

"I'll help you catch him," volunteered Shirley Addison, brandishing a flower-festooned umbrella even though the skies were clear.

"Oh, thank you!" Caroline said to the inn's octogenarian neighbor who'd been watching the parade from the sidewalk. Caroline was somewhat surprised at Shirley's offer, considering how many times Max had gotten into her flower gardens and yard.

"Max!" Caroline ran after him, followed by her sisters and Shirley, who moved with surprising speed and agility—all of them shouting the dog's name.

Caroline watched in horror as he snatched a hot dog out of the hand of a man bending over to adjust the bonnet of a child in a stroller.

"Hey, that dog took my hot dog!" the man bellowed while the woman beside him snatched the young child from the stroller.

"He won't hurt anyone," Caroline called out, but the couple ducked into a doorway, shielding their toddler with their bodies as though Max were a rabid pit bull.

"We'll take care of the Packard," Cubby called after them.

Out of the corner of her eye, Caroline saw a crowd of able-bodied men of all ages pushing the stalled vehicle toward the alley. There was nothing she could do to help them, so she turned her full attention to her runaway pet.

With Sam, Gracie, and Shirley following close behind, Caroline weaved her way around parade-goers lining the streets.

"Did you see a dog wearing a garland of daffodils trailing his leash behind him?" she asked a cluster of preteen boys when she lost sight of Max.

"I did," a gangly boy with a mop of pale yellow hair said.

"He took my cookie," a younger girl beside him wailed.

"I'll get you another one, Lindsay," Shirley offered, sounding only a little out of breath. She headed toward a vendor with the girl's hand in hers. "I've had enough chasing about," she called out to Caroline.

Caroline thanked her agile neighbor, hoping Max wasn't leaving a trail of cookie-less children in his wake. The boys shifted their attention from the stalled parade to the runaway, following her as she called his name.

"Which way could he have gone?" Caroline asked a few minutes later when she and Sam slowed to catch their breath.

"Ms. Marris, I think we saw your dog," one of two teenage boys said.

She recognized them from church and stopped to find out what they knew. They were wheeling bikes down the crowded sidewalk, and she enlisted them to search the side streets and alleys for the runaway cocker spaniel.

"Do you think you can catch up with Tommy?" Caroline asked, still trying to catch her breath from all the chasing she and Sam were doing. Gracie had taken off in another direction.

"Sure thing!" Ben said as both boys leapt onto their bicycles and started pedaling in the direction Tommy had indicated.

Caroline and Sam followed as fast as they could.

"Hurry up," Caroline urged Sam, "I can still see them."

"I'm hurrying, I'm hurrying," Sam said.

Caroline rounded a corner with her sister and stopped short. She could see a tail thumping, but that's all she could see of Max. He was surrounded by children, and Tommy and Ben were making their way through the small crowd. Before she and Sam could get to the center of the group, Tommy came toward them holding Max's leash with Ben trailing behind him.

"Max!" Caroline cried. "What have you gotten yourself into?"

The dog was covered from tail to front paws in a sugary web of pink cotton candy. His little pink tongue was busy trying to lick the festival treat off the disheveled daffodil wreath now hanging askew from his furry neck.

"Did he steal more treats from someone else?" Caroline asked, feeling the worry lines etch ever deeper into her forehead.

"Nah," Ben said.

"Those kids offered him some of their cotton candy," Tommy said. He laughed. "You should see the kids!"

"Oh dear, we'd better go apologize to their parents," Sam said.

"We took care of it for you," Tommy said. "They're going to the picnic when the parade's over. They'll probably get cleaned up throwing water balloons."

"That's what we did at their age," Ben added.

"Well, that will take care of their stickiness," Caroline said, wondering how on earth she would get a candy-covered canine home with no car.

Max was going through contortions trying to lick his sticky coat.

"You boys deserve a reward," Caroline said, glad she'd tucked a few dollars for refreshments into the pocket of her jeans.

Both teenagers laughed and turned down her offer.

"It's the most fun we've had today," Ben said.

"It was awesome!" Tommy said. "Not every day you see a cotton-candy-coated dog."

"I can't thank you enough," she said as they got on their bikes.

"Hey, thank you," Sam chimed in.

Just then Gracie caught up with them, her face flushed and her sunglasses on the tip of her nose.

"You found him!" she said. "I was checking doorways and places he could hide."

"Thanks to Ben and Tommy," Caroline said as the boys rode away with grins on their faces. "We need to get the car taken care of. It'll have to be towed to a garage, but everything will be closed for the parade. I don't know where we'll find a mechanic today—or a ride home."

Shirley rejoined them after taking care of the unhappy child, and Cubby caught up with them.

"Thank you so much for helping with the car," Caroline said to Cubby. "I know you have a lot to do just managing the parade."

"Actually," he said, "once it gets started I'm free to enjoy the festivities unless something goes wrong. Too bad about the Packard. She's a beauty, and certainly not the first vehicle to break down in the parade, although I haven't heard of any others today. I'm just glad I was here to help."

"So are we!" Caroline said emphatically.

"We haven't had that much excitement in the parade since Bill Weaver's Mustang convertible ran into Homer Hooper's back bumper a few years back. Didn't do much damage except for scattering daffodils everywhere, but I thought old Homer and Bill were going to resort to fisticuffs. Antique-car owners treat their vehicles like babies."

Cubby mopped his sweaty brow with a monogrammed hand-kerchief just at the thought of it, which made Caroline very glad she and her sisters hadn't caused that kind of trouble for Cubby.

"We still have one small problem—or maybe not so small," Sam said. "Where can we find a tow truck and a garage that's open?"

"We always have a tow standing by for situations like this," Cubby said. "Harv Gainer's on call today. I already called him on my cell phone. He'll meet you by the Packard, and I'm sure he'll see you get a ride home." He looked down at Max. "Maybe you can wrap your dog in something. Wouldn't want to get that pink stuff all over anyone's vehicle."

"Well, thanks again to both of you," Caroline said, including Shirley who'd backed away to avoid Max's sticky coat.

"Let's get this car towed," Sam said, "and this dog home to a bath!"

"You know," Caroline said, linking arms with her sisters while retaining a firm grip on Max's leash, "this is one of the best things about life on the island. The people."

"The people from Harvest Chapel sure helped us out today," Sam said. "I don't know what we'd have done without them."

"Look at all the fun we can have here in just one day," Caroline said playfully. "Chauffeuring, breaking down, searching for Max..."

"You really should consider moving here, Gracie," Sam said. "Things are never boring, and we've met a lot of good people."

Gracie didn't say yes, but she didn't say no either—which for the moment made Caroline happy. She needed both of her sisters in her life, especially if George had given up on her.

CHAPTER
Seven

"Can't you give us a hint about what's wrong?" Sam asked the tow truck driver after he'd hauled the Packard to a garage.

"You'll have to ask the mechanic on Monday," the burly young man said in a voice suggesting he had heard that question too often.

"How often do you tow a car smoking like a volcano?" Caroline asked, causing Sam to smile at her sister's dramatics. The smoke had not been nearly that bad.

"Sorry, ladies, I gotta get back to my post in case any other cars break down in the parade. I'm really sorry I don't have enough time to take you home. Maybe you can call a friend?"

"Good idea, Harv. Thanks for your help," Gracie said as he got back into the tow truck.

"What do you want to do, watch the rest of the parade or start walking home?" Sam asked.

"Walk home," Gracie said.

"Watch the parade," Caroline said simultaneously.

Sam wondered how often she would be the deciding vote when her flamboyant older sister disagreed with the more conservative Gracie.

"We've probably missed most of it," Sam pointed out. "Why don't we wander over to the finish line since it's on our way home?"

"I wish I'd worn my walking shoes," Gracie said, bending to tighten the laces on what appeared to be perfectly sturdy footwear.

"You did a good job driving," Sam complimented her.

"Until the wagon started blowing out black smoke," Gracie added unhappily. "I feel bad I stalled the engine."

"Don't worry," Sam assured her. "I was sitting right beside you. You did the best you could when we saw the smoke. I would have panicked too."

"Let's get started," Caroline said. "If the parade is over, I'd like to get back in time to call George before he sets sail—if he hasn't already." Again, she chastised herself for having left her cell phone at home.

Sam led the way back to the parade route, worried about the cost of repairing the Packard. She loved the idea of using it to pick up guests, but was it going to be a money pit? She decided not to mention her worries to either sister. Gracie would go into panic mode, and Caroline would be dismissive.

"Look at that truck," she said pointing out a flower-covered replica of a boat in the bed of the truck.

Sam spotted a few other vehicles owned by people she knew, but her sisters didn't seem interested in her commentaries. Caroline had a faraway look that was very unlike her, and Gracie kept stopping to retie her shoes.

"Go ahead without me if you like," she said, sitting down on the nearest curb to pull off one shoe. "It feels like I have a stone, but I can't find it."

"Let me look," Caroline said impatiently, taking the shoe and running her finger over the inside. "There's nothing in it. Maybe it's your foot."

"It can't be, because my foot doesn't hurt when my shoe is off." Gracie retrieved her footwear and thrust her finger into the toe. "There, I knew it!"

She extracted a pebble the size of a grain of rice.

"You're like the Princess and the Pea," Caroline complained. "If that stone were any smaller, you'd need a magnifying glass."

Sam was surprised by Caroline's cross words. It was totally unlike her to have down moods. *Is there something she's not telling us about George's absence?* Sam wondered.

"Sorry to hold you up," Gracie said, not sounding the least bit contrite. "If you want to hurry ahead of me—"

"Of course not," Sam said before Caroline could agree to leave Gracie behind. "It's a beautiful day for a walk. Let's make the best of it."

They slowly followed the parade route, enjoying the really old cars the most. Sam loved one that looked like a topless buggy with a motor, but she didn't know enough about antique vehicles to know what it was. The owners were dressed in costumes from the early 1900s and looked like they were having the time of their lives.

"That Buick isn't very old," Gracie said as they watched a long green convertible. "I remember our neighbors having one just like it when I was in grade school."

"They haven't made cars that big and cumbersome for at least fifty years," Sam said. "It must have been old when they had it."

"Have you seen enough of the parade?" Caroline asked. "I can go on alone if you want to stay."

"I'm ready to go back to the inn," Gracie said.

Sam couldn't help but notice that she didn't say "go home." Would Gracie ever commit to living in the inn year-round? Much as she loved her children and granddaughter, maybe it was time for her to move on. It wasn't as if they weren't welcome to visit anytime.

Sam spotted two familiar faces as they were passing a café on the other side of the street with tables outside to watch the parade and enjoy ice cream treats. Erin was sitting with her arms crossed and what looked like a scowl on her face. Kyle was watching the parade with a blank stare, his body turned away from her. They definitely weren't enjoying themselves.

"Don't look now, but our honeymooners are sitting across the street," she said.

Of course, both her sisters looked anyway, but the pair seemed indifferent to everything around them.

"Oh dear, they don't look very happy," Gracie said. "I know they had a quarrel Friday evening, but they should have made up by now."

"What were they arguing about?" Sam asked, feeling a bit guilty about her curiosity. They were, after all, the inn's first guests, and she shouldn't pry into their business. She did want them to have a wonderful visit, though. It would be a shame if they left with bad memories of the island and their honeymoon.

"I guess he's too wrapped up in his work and not attentive enough," Gracie said.

"Then she *should* be put out," Caroline chimed in. "If he's ignoring her on the honeymoon, what will their marriage be like in the future?"

"It's none of our business," Sam said more sharply than she'd intended.

"This should be the happiest time of their lives." Gracie said.

Sam sighed, sadness almost overwhelming her. Her marriage had lasted a very short time, and she rarely agonized over it anymore. But she hated to see a young couple in trouble already.

"Not all marriages are meant to be," she reminded her sisters. "I married someone I really didn't know. You know how controlling he was after the wedding. I never would have married him if I'd known his true personality."

"He fooled me," Gracie said in a consoling tone. "I thought he was a sweet man, so considerate and kind. There was no way you could have known he had a mean side."

"It didn't take me long to realize he would only get worse," Sam said. "I hated the idea of divorce, but there was nothing else I could do."

"You couldn't let Jamie grow up under those circumstances," Caroline said, apparently listening in spite of her distracted air.

"Well, I hope Erin will fare better than I did," Sam said. "I'd hate to think her husband is as self-centered as mine was."

"He seems like a nice young man," Gracie said. "I wish there was some way I could help them."

"They'll have to figure things out for themselves," Caroline said, picking up the pace.

"True," Sam said, although she wondered whether early counseling might be helpful to the newlyweds. Her husband had vehemently refused to "involve strangers" in their marriage, a stance he'd maintained until their divorce was final.

Sam loved to walk on the island, but Caroline was moving so fast it became an effort to keep up. They followed deserted roads because most of the people on the island were in town enjoying festival events. It was a good opportunity to enjoy the ocean breeze and bask in the spring sun.

"Slow down and enjoy the day!" Sam called out to Caroline's back.

She was just a bit embarrassed because her sister was nine years older and could still set a faster pace. In fact, she seemed driven to get to the inn as quickly as possible.

"A nice, brisk walk is good for you," Caroline said over her shoulder.

"So is a pleasant, relaxed stroll." Sam wasn't sure what was up with her sister, but she wasn't her normal self.

"I have another stone in my shoe," Gracie said, dropping behind.

"You need new shoes," Caroline said impatiently. "Those old things must have sprung a leak."

"I didn't expect to be walking home," Gracie said. "Go ahead without me. It's not as if I don't know the way."

"Yes, go ahead, Caroline," Sam said. "I'll stay behind with Gracie and enjoy the walk."

"Very well."

Sam didn't know whether she was annoyed or relieved. Usually Caroline wore her emotions on her face, but she certainly wasn't herself today. Or maybe she didn't know her older sister as well as she thought. They'd worked hard together to get the inn ready for guests, but Caroline had lived alone in England for a long time. Maybe there were still things to be learned about the eldest of the Marris sisters.

Caroline wasn't proud of herself for being so abrupt with her sisters, but her uneasiness about George was growing. Everything in their relationship changed when he'd proposed to her. She had thought he'd still come for the festival, but now that she thought about it, he hadn't sounded particularly enthusiastic.

Did he think she only wanted him on Nantucket because she needed help? Was he nursing hurt feelings?

It wasn't as if the idea of marriage to him had never entered her mind. It was just that she didn't feel quite ready. She had been certain he would understand. He encouraged her creative side and always seemed to enjoy her adventurous nature. Surely he understood what a huge step marriage would be after living so long as a single woman.

Or did he? Was it a male ego thing? She'd never thought of George as egotistical or self-centered. He was the soul of kindness and consideration.

Maybe he thought she was taking him for granted and wanted more from her. She was torturing herself with doubts about their relationship, and her only option was to speak to him again before he left. How long would it take to get the yacht ready for its maiden voyage? He would have lay in supplies and fuel and take care of all kinds of little details.

The more she thought about it, the more important it seemed to talk to him before he left. She was nourishing a tiny hope: Perhaps he wanted her to come along with him but was too proud to admit it.

Of course, she would feel bad leaving her sisters when the inn was about to open, but now that Gracie was here, the two of them could certainly cope.

What would be the quickest way to get to Annapolis? She could take the ferry to the mainland—it ran frequently in the season. Then if she rented a car, she surely could get there without holding up the departure for more than a day, if that.

Her calves were aching from the fast pace, but she kept going, thinking of the things she'd need to pack. Casual clothes would

serve, but maybe she'd throw in her sapphire blue evening gown—
George's favorite—just in case they had time for an evening in
Cannes.

She should've brought her cell phone with her, but she hadn't
steeled her nerve to call until they got to town. She didn't let herself
think of the possibility that George had already left—or that he really
didn't want her to come with him.

By the time she half-ran, half-stumbled into the inn, she was
much too breathless to talk. She hurriedly splashed cold water on
her face in the family bathroom and gulped down several paper
cups of water. When she was more composed, she went into
her bedroom, closed the door, and punched in George's work
number on the phone.

"Hello, Caroline." He sounded far away and distracted.

"I hope I didn't catch you at a bad time," she said.

"I'm in the middle of checking off items on my inventory and
getting everything stowed aboard."

"I know it's a lot of work to get ready for a delivery." Now that
she had him on the line, she wasn't sure how to proceed. "I'm sorry
you weren't here for the parade. It was something of a disaster. The
Packard broke down, and black smoke poured out of it."

"What?" he asked. "I checked everything nine ways to Sunday
before I left. I can't imagine it's anything too serious." He sighed.
"Caroline…"

"George, please wait. I wanted to talk to you before you leave.
When I turned down your proposal, I only meant it wasn't a good
time."

"Look, Caroline, we can talk when I get back. I have a million
things to do."

"When are you leaving? I was thinking there's really no reason why I can't come with you. You'd be surprised how quickly I can get there."

"Not this trip. I have to concentrate on getting the yacht to the new owner. This sale can make the season for me."

"When are you leaving?"

"Soon, very soon."

It wasn't a very nautical answer. Caroline's heart sank. There was a time when he would have postponed the trip for her. Was she being unreasonable in wanting to be with her best friend in the world? Or was her longtime friendship in serious trouble?

"You know I could be helpful. I'd even do the cooking so you and your crew could focus on the boat. I'm sure that big yacht has a spare room."

"Thank you for offering, but this isn't a pleasure cruise. You wouldn't enjoy it."

Does he mean he wouldn't enjoy having me there? she wondered, terribly afraid that was exactly what he meant.

"If you're sure…"

"I'll get in touch when I get back."

"Well, have a nice trip," she said, trying to sound upbeat.

"Thanks."

The phone went dead in her ear. She flinched. *George was never too busy to talk to me before I turned down his proposal,* she thought. *What if he's shutting me out of his life?* It felt so unfair. She'd known lots of couples who enjoyed each other's company without marriage vows—well, one or two anyway. It wasn't as if she didn't want to be George's wife sometime in the future. When had they stopped communicating? When did he become indifferent to what she was feeling?

She heard her sisters coming in through the kitchen door. Part of her wanted their sympathy, but she was too proud to break down in front of them.

Was being an innkeeper enough if George wasn't in her life anymore? She didn't want to think about it. The prospect of losing his friendship—and love—was too devastating to dwell on.

CHAPTER
Eight

"Oh, I didn't know anyone was in here," Gracie said, startled by the sight of Erin in the inn's library.

The young woman was curled up in one of the room's twin wing-backed chairs with a book lying unread on her lap. The library was in gloom most of the day, but early in the day the darkness of the wood pancling was offset by light spilling in from the windows between the chairs. It was a comfy, inviting room, but Gracie hadn't expected to find their young guest there alone.

"Kyle went off to play golf with some potential client his boss wanted him to meet," Erin explained, smoothing the skirt of a pretty yellow and orange print dress. "I don't play, so I thought I'd curl up with a good book."

"Did you manage to find one that interests you?" Gracie asked, a bit sad to see the honeymooners engaging in separate activities.

She sighed. "I've started rereading *Jane Eyre*."

Gracie suppressed a grin. "I'm not sure that's the best honeymoon reading," she said lightly.

The new wife laughed, but it sounded forced to Gracie.

"Probably not," Erin agreed, setting the volume aside. "It's so nice out I was thinking of taking a bike ride, but I don't especially want to go alone."

"Well, I have an idea," Gracie said, hoping she wasn't overstepping her role of innkeeper with the offer she was about to make. "Do you like to build sand castles? I haven't built a sand castle in years. Would you like to ride bikes—rental is on the inn—to the beach and build a sand castle with me?"

She remembered how much Erin had enjoyed helping with decorations for the parade. Even if she had joined in the activity to annoy her husband, she did seem to like creative activities.

"It might be fun if you'd like to try it," Gracie said.

She could tell Erin was seriously mulling the invitation and hoped she'd accept. The day was too beautiful for the young woman to be inside reading a gloomy book about Jane Eyre's problems with the mysterious Mr. Rochester.

"Yes, that sounds like fun. Thank you!" Erin said.

"Great! Let me get my sunscreen and hat, and I'll pack a light picnic lunch for us. Do you like peanut butter and jelly?" Gracie asked.

"One of my favorites," Erin said. "I'll run up and change my clothes. Biking in a dress might not be the best plan."

Gracie looked around for her sisters to tell them where she was going, but both seemed to have disappeared. She knew how badly Sam wanted another look in the secret room and hoped she hadn't opened it again when she went up to clean the honeymooners' room. If she had, it was too late to warn her. Erin had sprinted up the stairs to change into an outfit for biking.

Gracie went to the kitchen and packed lunches for both of them, putting the food in lightweight nylon bags that would be easy to carry on the bikes. She was looking forward to a picnic of sandwiches, chips, and bottled water. There were probably all kinds of jobs she could be doing around the inn, but neither Sam nor Caroline had accepted her offers of help. It was nice to have something to do, and she thought entertaining a guest was a good use of her time.

When the lunches were made, she hurried to her room in the family area of the first floor. Her jeans and flowered tunic were fine for biking. She located an old red baseball cap she used to wear to her children's soccer games for sun protection. As an extra measure, she slathered on sunscreen. Even though the day was pleasantly cool, she knew the combination of wind and sun could turn her into a lobster.

Several minutes later, Gracie stood waiting for Erin by the bikes. She checked her watch several times, hoping she hadn't changed her mind about going.

"Sorry, it took me so long," Erin called out, sprinting toward Gracie with a small nylon backpack slung over her arm. "I never can figure out what I need to take on a trip, even a short bike ride. And I had to leave a note for Kyle. Wouldn't want him to think I went missing."

Gracie readily believed Erin was an over-packer. It explained the amount of luggage the honeymooners had brought on their trip.

"It took me a little time to get ready too," Gracie assured her. "I thought we'd ride out to Dionis Beach. It's only a few miles from here, and it won't be an especially hard route. I like it because it's sheltered by dunes. When it's warmer, the beach has nice calm waters for swimming." If she decided to make a permanent move to the island, it would be a great place to take her grandchildren.

Soon they were pedaling toward their destination under the bright late morning sun. Gracie had always liked biking, although her calves told her she hadn't done enough lately. She tried to stay active and fit, but apparently she hadn't worked out enough in recent months. She was going to be stiff after this excursion, but Erin's happy attitude made it worthwhile. She wondered what she would do to keep in shape if she lived on Nantucket year-round. Certainly, she would miss the friends who went to exercise classes with her.

Gracie spotted the boulder marked "Dionis" and called out for Erin to turn. As she headed toward the beach, she was exhilarated in a way she hadn't been in a long time. She still had doubts about running the inn, but she shared her sisters' love for the wonderful outdoor life on the island. The long, sandy beaches and great expanses of ocean were a vacationer's paradise, and the idea of enjoying them in all seasons had a magnetic appeal.

After parking their bikes, Gracie led Erin through the dune grass and down a path marked by wooden fencing. The shoreline ahead was strewn with seaweed, seashells, and the debris of a long winter. It was a beachcomber's dream come true, especially before tourists flocked to the seaside in search of souvenirs.

"Wow, I love it," Erin said. "Do you think the water's too cold for wading?"

"Probably, but it never hurts to stick your big toe in to test the water." Gracie was tempted to test the temperature herself even though it was probably shockingly cold.

"The surf here isn't very high," she told the younger woman. "And there are always lifeguards on duty during the season. It's a good beach for children."

Erin pointed down the beach, and Gracie turned to look. A few young mothers were chasing toddlers down the beach while white seagulls screeched overhead, seemingly wanting in on the merriment.

"They seem to be having a great time," Erin said, staring at the colorful group.

Gracie thought she detected a note of wistfulness in the young woman's voice. *Maybe a trip to the beach won't be enough to raise her spirits.*

"This looks like a good place to build our sand castle," Gracie said after they tramped a few hundred yards down the sandy beach. "We need a spot near the water but not so close that waves will ruin our work. Even a gentle swell can topple sand art."

Using a small bucket she'd brought along, Gracie carried water from the ocean while Erin started to dig below the surface sand to start forming and stacking sand patties. When Gracie sprinkled her water over the dry sand, it turned a dark color, perfect for building.

"I thought this would be a good way to make sturdy towers," Erin explained as Gracie sat on the sand to see what she was doing.

"They look like thick pancakes," Gracie said, starting to make patties of her own.

"Put the larger ones on the bottom and agitate them from side to side so the sand settles," Erin said. "Then we can seal them by gently pouring more water over them."

"You certainly have good ideas on how to do this," Gracie said, surprised at the organization Erin was putting into the project. She'd seen sand art at other beaches and was always astonished at what could be done with nothing but beach sand and water.

"I really do like craft projects," Erin said. "I like to imagine all kinds of fun things to do when I have children—if I have children."

Gracie was concerned by the catch in Erin's voice. One minute she seemed perfectly happy, and the next she sounded vaguely discontented.

"Is everything all right?" she asked, wondering whether she should pat the young woman on the shoulder with her sand-caked hands.

"Yes, I'm fine," Erin said with a slight sniff. "I'm sorry to let my worries intrude on this lovely outing. This was such a fun idea and here I am, feeling all weepy—probably over nothing."

"Do you want to talk about it?" Gracie asked, feeling somewhat awkward. She didn't want to pry, but her heart went out to Erin. This was her honeymoon, and it should be a joyous time.

"Well…we need to work fast so the sand stays wet," Erin hedged.

"Yes, you're right. I'm thinking of a castle King Arthur would've lived in."

"If there was a real king named Arthur," Erin said. "I was thinking of a fairy tale castle with lots of turrets and towers."

"Sounds perfect," Gracie said.

"I'm pretty good at working and talking at the same time," she said, slapping at the sand with far more force than necessary

Gracie silently debated whether to ask more questions but decided to wait until Erin wanted to tell her what was bothering her.

"Tell you what, you work on the towers while I start molding the wet sand into brick shapes and laying them on top of each other to make the connecting walls," Gracie said.

Gracie was gratified to see Erin look less petulant. She was childlike in many ways, but it was still sad to see her unhappy on her honeymoon.

"Good idea," Erin said, expertly shaping more sand pancakes.

They worked in companionable silence for a few more minutes until Erin exhaled deeply and looked at Gracie, who stopped what she was doing to give the young woman her full attention.

"I always dreamed of getting married. I always dreamed of having a husband all to myself and raising a big family together," Erin said in a pouty voice. "I want to start right away, but Kyle insists we should wait several years. He wants to be more secure in his career, so we can move into our dream home before we start having children. He has big plans for us—like traveling around the world—but I know it's not going to happen. His job always seems to come first, even before our honeymoon in Hawaii."

Gracie worried because Erin seemed to have unrealistic expectations. But it was disturbing that Kyle couldn't leave work behind on their honeymoon. She sensed the young bride needed to talk more than she needed advice.

Erin trickled water on a perfectly formed sand tower and continued in a hushed voice, although they still had that section of beach to themselves.

"I wish we would've talked more about what we want from life before we got married," she said. "I want Kyle to be successful, but sometimes he acts like his job is the only thing that's important. He comes from a big family—he's one of five siblings—and I assumed he'd want to have a big family too. But all he thinks and talks about is his stupid job!"

Gracie was distressed by the anger and disappointment on Erin's face, but she continued to make sand bricks, giving the younger woman time to finish what she was saying.

"I don't want you to think I don't love my husband," Erin said in a halting voice while she continued to add towers to the castle walls.

"I don't think that at all," Gracie assured her. "Love shines in both your faces."

"Do you really think so?" Erin asked, digging her fingers into wet sand as she stopped working on the castle.

"Absolutely. In some ways, you remind me of my husband and me when were first in love. It's a special time in anyone's life. There will be plenty of time later to work out your differences. That's part of the dynamics of marriage: two very different people compromising and supporting each other."

"You've given me something to think about," Erin said, although she didn't sound convinced. "Thanks for listening and not judging." She sat beside the partially completed castle with her hands motionless on her lap.

"I like the way you make towers," Gracie said when the silence between them started to get awkward.

Erin looked at what she'd done and started to make windows and wall designs with her fingernails.

"Would you like a plastic knife from one of our lunch sacks to do that?" Gracie asked. "Your manicure will be ruined."

Erin laughed and seemed to put aside her melancholy mood. "I guess my fingernails aren't the best tools for making turrets, are they? I got my first French manicure for my wedding."

Gracie handed her a black plastic knife. "Your nails look lovely— when they aren't covered with sand, that is. Are you hungry yet?"

"Not yet, thanks. Let's finish our castle and dig a moat to protect it from invaders," Erin said.

"Who would invade a fairy tale castle?" Gracie teased.

"Breaking waves and dogs catching Frisbees." Erin grinned, gesturing at a young couple frolicking farther down the beach with a russet-colored golden retriever.

"Right!" Gracie agreed.

Erin stared at the couple with the dog for a minute more and then turned to Gracie. "It was actually love at first sight for Kyle and me. We met at a newly formed adult fellowship group at church. We didn't really know each other very long before we got engaged and married. Now I'm afraid maybe we rushed into something he wasn't—we weren't—ready for." Erin looked miserable and added, "Sometimes I feel like I don't even know him."

Gracie thought it was time for her to gently weigh in. "Has he come right out and said he doesn't want children?" she asked.

"Well, no, not in those exact words," Erin said. "He just wants to put it off until he's made a success of his job. I can understand being financially secure, but I just can't shake the feeling we were in such a rush to get married that we may have both made a mistake."

Looking at Erin, her eyes brimming with tears, made Gracie's heart ache, but she also thought she knew what the young wife needed to hear. Taking a deep breath, Gracie put down the sand brick she'd been patting.

"My late husband and I rushed into marriage too," Gracie began slowly, gratified to see how carefully Erin was listening. "We wanted to get married before he got shipped off to Vietnam. We were young and in love—just like you and Kyle," she added.

Erin reddened. "I'm embarrassed. I shouldn't complain so much about Kyle's job, but it hurt when he went off to play golf with a potential client and left me alone," she said. "I can't imagine how hard it would be to have him go off to a war where he might not come home at all."

"Everyone's situation is different, dear," Gracie said. "We were in a hurry to have a baby, and our first child was born while my husband was still overseas. I worried every day he wouldn't come home and prayed constantly for his safe return. It was a very difficult time for both of us, but we weathered it."

"You had to be brave," Erin said admiringly. "I'm not going through anything like that."

"We all struggle with different issues, big and small," Gracie said. "Making a marriage work is hard. Communication is often the key, but sometimes you find yourself at a loss for words."

Erin smiled again. "Usually I have the opposite problem. I don't know when to quit talking," she said ruefully.

"Talking is good," Gracie said. "So is listening."

"Well, you're an awfully good listener," Erin told her. "Thank you so much for letting me agonize over my concerns and for giving me some good advice. Maybe you should hang out a counselor's shingle."

Gracie laughed, imagining what her sisters would think about using the inn as a counseling center, but she was pleased she could help Erin.

"Spending some time together as a newly married couple is something my husband and I missed out on. Things worked out that way for us, but you have an opportunity to do things with Kyle before you become parents."

"If we become parents," Erin said.

"It's possible that having grown up with that many siblings, Kyle saw his parents struggling financially," Gracie added. "It's not a bad thing to want to be established in a good job before starting a family."

Erin nodded slowly. "You know, we never spent much time talking about our childhoods. I bet you're right."

"Well, now you and Kyle have a lifetime together to talk about things," Gracie said. She reached out and hugged Erin as she would one of her children or grandchildren when they were in distress.

"Oh, I hope I didn't get too much sand on you!" Erin apologized after she returned the hug.

She tried to brush away the sand but mostly succeeded in stirring up more.

"I think we're both covered in sand already," Gracie said, "and I'm glad I could help. Now, let's build the moat and eat lunch."

"Sounds like a great idea," Erin agreed, scooping out big handfuls of sand around the multitowered sand castle while Gracie fetched more water from the shoreline to pour into the moat.

When they were finished, they admired their handiwork.

"Let me take a picture with my cell phone to show Kyle," Erin said, going to retrieve it from her bag. "Oh, he sent me a text saying he misses me. Maybe I'll take up golf or teach him how to make a sand castle while we're here."

"Good idea!" Gracie said, handing Erin a slightly smashed peanut butter and jelly sandwich. It tasted wonderful because she was sharing it with a happier Erin.

Gracie led the way back to the inn, pedaling slowly as her legs rebelled. The time with Erin was more than enough compensation for a few aches and pains. She still wasn't sure what her role was at the inn, but it was gratifying to make a new friend and perhaps help her just a little.

CHAPTER
Nine

Sam felt most at home when she was in the inn's large, comfortable kitchen. It had been renovated along with the rest of the inn in the 1950s, with piecemeal changes in later years, but despite what the sales flyer had told them about the inn's "modern kitchen," the kitchen had needed a lot of updating.

It had taken a year of hard work—with help from many local craftsmen—but the inn's kitchen now reflected the charm of the original mid-nineteenth-century room. They'd found a beautiful wood floor under the linoleum, and the sisters had stripped and refinished it to a sparkling sheen. The brick fireplace was stripped of layers of paint, and the old cupboards had been painted a cheery, fresh cream color.

They hadn't scrimped on appliances, installing a commercial-grade fridge and a modern stove and dishwasher. For the present, the inn would only provide breakfast and box lunches, but if they decided to offer a dinner service, the facilities were more than adequate.

Before Sam could begin Tuesday's breakfast for the honeymooners, who were still their only guests, Gracie joined her in the kitchen.

"Anything I can do to help?" she asked.

"You can answer the phone," Sam said. "We couldn't have attracted more attention in the parade if we'd shot off fireworks. Locals have been calling to see if we're open for business. I suspect some are just checking out the competition, but word of mouth is a great way to start getting guests."

"Maybe inns that are overbooked will send some business our way," Gracie suggested.

"It's not impossible. Most of the owners I've met are pretty congenial. In a good season there's more than enough guests for everyone—I hope."

"What should I tell people who call?" Gracie asked.

"That the newspaper article was correct. We're officially opening May first."

"That sounds simple enough. What do I do while I'm waiting for the phone to ring?"

"Don't worry, there are plenty of jobs," Sam assured her.

"Something smells good. How long have you been up?"

"Since around six. I wanted to make cranberry bread for today's breakfast. I put together an egg, cheese, and mushroom casserole last night—it has to be done ahead of time so the bread will absorb the egg mix. It's hard to guess when the newlyweds will come down for breakfast."

"I thought you were only going to serve from seven to nine," Gracie said.

"Yes, but when we only have two guests, I can be flexible. Can I fix something for you?"

"I'll just get myself a bowl of cereal," Gracie said, going to the cupboard and looking over an assortment of individual servings.

Before she could make a choice, the landline they used for inn business rang. Gracie reached for the phone, picking it up before the second ring. "Misty Harbor Inn."

Gracie listened to the caller for what seemed like a long time, then muffled the phone and turned to Sam.

"A woman wants to book two rooms Labor Day weekend. She's hosting a family reunion and doesn't have room for everyone."

"Sounds good," Sam said. "You don't need to check with me. Just look at the reservation book. It's pretty empty right now."

"I just thought…" Gracie went back to the caller and carried the phone to the foyer.

"I know I've been gone for a month," Gracie said when she returned to the kitchen, "but I'm a little confused about who's doing what. I'm beginning to feel in the way."

Sam took two beautiful loaves from the oven and set them on racks to cool.

"I guess we have been stumbling over each other a bit," Sam admitted. "Why don't we have a strategy meeting this afternoon, say at two o'clock? Sometimes I expect to do something, and Caroline has already done it. Or she leaves a job undone, and I have to hustle to do it at the last minute."

"Yes, a meeting is a good idea," Gracie said. "Because if you don't really need me here, I have lots to do at home."

"Don't think that!" Sam said. "This is the calm before the storm. When all our rooms are full, Caroline and I talked about bringing someone in part time to help with the housekeeping. We think it will be more than we can handle alone."

"I didn't know you'd made that decision," Gracie said, sounding unhappy about being left out of the loop.

"We'll go over our whole operation this afternoon. Why don't you find Caroline and tell her?" Sam suggested.

"Yes, I'll do that," Gracie said, losing her appetite for cereal. "She's been sort of distracted lately. I don't want her walking into town or something when we really need to firm up our plans."

"She hasn't been herself," Sam agreed. "I wonder what's going on with George. She's taken him for granted so many years. Maybe this is her wakeup call."

"Maybe she just misses him," Gracie speculated, interrupted by the ringing of the phone, which she hurried to answer.

Sam tuned out the conversation as she checked her watch. The newlyweds had promised to give her an hour's notice when they wanted breakfast. Meanwhile, she couldn't get on with the day's work until she heard from them. She made a mental note to stick with the 7:00 AM to 9:00 AM schedule in the future. It was good they had one pair of guests ahead of the official opening. They needed a chance to work out the kinks before they had a full house—which she fervently hoped they would have in the near future.

"It was a woman who wants to come look at our accommodations," Gracie reported. "I told her any time later this afternoon would be fine."

"Does she want to stay here?"

"No, she has a great aunt who would like a quiet retreat for a month or so. I guess she's writing a book? Anyway, she wants to see if our facilities are 'acceptable.' Her word, not mine."

"A great aunt sounds elderly," Sam mused. "We're really not set up for assisted living care. Well, it can't hurt to let her check us out. Caroline's good at giving a tour of the inn. I wonder where she is."

"I know she's not in her room," Gracie said. "The door was standing open."

The phone rang again, and this time Sam picked it up herself.

"Yes, that will be fine," she said after listening for a moment.

Sam hurried to the fridge and took out the breakfast casserole, setting it on the stove until the oven warmed up.

"Our guests will be ready for breakfast," she told her sister. "I've set their places in the dining room, but you can make coffee if you like. I plan to serve from the sideboard."

"Do you want me to be the waitress?"

"No, it wouldn't be a good use of time for both of us to work breakfast. If you can make the coffee and then go find Caroline, that would be helpful. I don't understand why she's gone missing again when we have guests. I was hoping she could make up their bed while they have breakfast."

"I can do that," Gracie offered.

"Well, check with Caroline first. Maybe she's already planning to do it."

Sam didn't miss the dejected slump of Gracie's shoulders as she left the kitchen. *We really do need to assign specific tasks*, she thought. *The last thing we need is for Gracie to go home because she doesn't have enough to do or feels unneeded.*

Sam gave the dining room a last-minute check. She'd taken the extenders out of the banquet-size table to make it more inviting for two people. Caroline had brought a lovely set of china from England, which Sam had chosen to use for their first guests. The only drawback was that the plates and cups had a silver rim, so they couldn't go in the dishwasher. *But then*, Sam thought, *how long could it take to wash a few dishes?*

The table service had originally belonged to their maternal grandmother. It was silver plate and showed some wear, but they'd polished it as best they could. For now, it was much classier than modern stainless steel. The ivory linen tablecloth was a family heirloom too, one Sam planned to remove when children stayed at the inn.

She had no sooner taken the breakfast casserole out of the oven than she heard the newlyweds coming down the stairs. They were laughing, and it was good to hear them having fun. It wouldn't be a very good start to their new business if the first guests were miserable.

After serving individual fruit cups, Sam put the casserole and the freshly baked cranberry bread on the sideboard and invited the young couple to help themselves.

"Looks luscious," Erin said, taking a small serving.

"This place is really cool," her husband said, waiting to spoon a portion onto his plate. "How old is it?"

"It was built in the mid-1800s by a man who had made his fortune in the whaling industry," Sam said.

"Just like Moby Dick," said Erin as she took her place at the table but waited for her husband before she began eating.

"I don't think the original owner was done in by a white whale," Sam said in a good-natured voice, "but there is some intrigue associated with the house."

"Tell us," Erin urged as her husband heaped his plate with casserole and cranberry bread.

"When he was older," Sam narrated, "he married a much younger woman. By all accounts, it wasn't a happy marriage. He died in the late 1870s and his wife, Hannah, vanished only a couple of years later. She was never seen again."

"A real mystery," Kyle said, taking his place at the table. "Maybe her bones are spirited away somewhere in the house."

"Really, Kyle," his wife said with a shudder. "That's not a very pleasant thought. Anyway, certainly someone would have discovered them after all this time."

Sam returned to the kitchen, but she couldn't get Erin's comment out of her mind. There'd been a lot of changes and renovations in the house's long history, but it was full of nooks and crannies—potential hiding places. She thought of the room she'd just discovered. No one had suspected it was there, and she could hardly wait to explore it. Would she dare have another look when the newlyweds were out? No, she'd promised her sisters to wait until the guests checked out. It would look really bad if Erin and Kyle came back unexpectedly, and, of course, the hidden room would be a magnet for the young couple if they knew it was there.

She hadn't had time for breakfast, so Sam sat on a stool by the worktable and sampled her cranberry bread.

"*Mmm*, delicious," she said, loving the distinctive taste and texture of the cranberries. She'd frozen several large bags of them during the last season, and she had lots of ideas to use them. In her few idle moments, she thought of making cranberry items to sell. She wouldn't have time to bake on a large scale, but perhaps guests would like to take some loaves or cookies home as gifts or just to eat themselves. She'd have to give it more thought.

The young couple had seemed genuinely interested in the history of the house, which gave her another idea. As a retired teacher, she didn't think people should ever stop learning. Maybe they could put together something about the house. She could envision attracting guests and others who might be interested.

She helped herself to a second slice of cranberry bread while her mind was churning with ideas. Rather than offer it as a history class, maybe they could host occasional tea parties with a program about the house. It could even be a way of selling her baked goods, if she had time to come up with a workable plan.

"I hear we're having a meeting," Caroline said, poking her head into the kitchen. "Do I need to be there?"

"Absolutely," Sam said. "We have to get better organized. Gracie doesn't know what to do with herself, and I have more work than I can handle."

She didn't mention Caroline's frequent disappearances, but all three of them had to work together if the inn was going to succeed.

"Oh, by the way, we have a woman coming later this afternoon," Sam said. "She has a great aunt who might like to stay for a month. Would you mind giving her a tour of the house?"

"I guess," Caroline said with a noticeable lack of enthusiasm.

"Is everything okay?"

"Sure, fine. I'll see you at the meeting," Caroline said.

It wasn't like her to go off on her own without volunteering to help in some way. After the newlyweds left, Sam cleared the dining room, but she couldn't stop thinking about Caroline. She wondered what was wrong with her sister and whether it would affect the smooth running of the inn.

The morning went quickly. Sam was the first one in the library at the appointed time for the meeting. Gracie joined her almost immediately.

"We should have regular meetings, maybe once a week," Gracie said. "Once the inn has more guests, we're going to get a lot busier. That means we have to be more organized about who's responsible for what."

Sam doubted she could be much busier than she had been getting ready to open, but assigning duties and weekly meetings was still a good idea.

"Have you seen Caroline?" she asked when the third Marris sister failed to appear after a ten-minute wait.

"Not since I told her about the meeting this morning," Gracie said with a frown. "She did agree to come."

"Come where?" Caroline asked, breezing in and flopping down on one of the two wing chairs.

The library was the perfect place for a serious meeting. Sam thought it had the ambience of a men's club with its dark cherry bookcases. The shelves had been empty when they bought the inn, but they'd added some titles. Sam was looking forward to shopping used book stores and fleamarkets when she had time, but that wouldn't be any time soon, especially if Caroline kept disappearing.

"You're late," Gracie pointed out. "We really need to go over some things."

"Specifically, who will do what," Sam said.

Caroline looked grieved. "You're upset because I haven't been doing my share," she said. "And rightly so. I'm really sorry about that, but I just haven't been up to it."

"Are you ill?" Gracie asked with concern.

"No, I'm fine."

"You're upset because George didn't come," Sam suggested, wanting to get to the heart of the matter.

"That and other things," Caroline admitted. "But nothing to do with you two or the inn. I'm sorry to be a slacker. When I have a lot on my mind, I like to take long walks, especially when the weather is so nice for this time of year. Helps me clear my head. I'll try to pull my weight from now on."

"I'd like to know exactly what I should be doing," Gracie said. "And please don't tell me I'm the chauffeur."

"Speaking of which, have you heard from the garage?" Caroline asked, easily distracted from their reason for being there.

Sam let out a slow breath. "Yes," she said. "The oil cap wasn't replaced properly after the oil was checked. Which, I'm embarrassed to say, was my fault. I checked it after Gracie brought Kyle and Erin here, to make sure the Packard wasn't losing oil or anything, and then I forgot to put it back on."

"That's it?" Gracie asked. "I was afraid I'd ruined our beautiful old car."

Sam nodded. "The smoke was caused by oil splashing on the engine."

"I think I just panicked, and then I let the clutch out too quickly and flooded the carburetor when I tried to restart it."

"Well, it's nothing serious at all. We can pick it up anytime."

"I'm so glad," Gracie said. "I can go pick it up. Now on to other concerns. Who will be doing what?"

"I guess I'm supposed to be in charge of reservations," Caroline conceded. "I have high hopes for our Web page now that the final version is live."

"And you know I love working in the garden," Gracie said.

"Breakfast is my responsibility," Sam said. "Unless we have a full house and lots of special requests, I won't need any help."

"But that still leaves a lot of jobs up for grabs," Gracie pointed out. "Until business warrants a housekeeper, we'll have to do the cleaning ourselves."

"The fair way would be to take turns cleaning guest rooms," Sam said.

"And we thought owning an inn would be glamorous," Caroline said, her wry humor making her sound more like her old self.

"*You* did," Sam reminded her.

"We need some kind of schedule," Gracie said. "We can't decide who does what on a daily basis."

"You're right," Caroline said with a sigh. "But I'm fresh out of good ideas right now."

"I have a thought," Sam said, remembering how Gracie liked to organize. When her kids were young, she kept a regular flow chart of their school activities, sports, and appointments. "If you're willing, Gracie, you can create some kind of database or spreadsheet on the computer, so we can keep on top of everything."

"I could set it so I can print out a schedule every day. That way we'll divide the harder, less pleasant jobs, so no one has to do more than her share. Maybe I can include a box to check when each job is done. That way the same job wouldn't get done twice." Gracie sounded happier than she had since she arrived. "Sound fair to everyone?"

"Sounds great," Sam said. "What do you think, Caroline?"

"Yes, I guess that would be fair. I'm sorry if I haven't been doing my share the last few days. I'll try to stay on top of things. If that's all, I have a few things to do before that woman comes for her tour."

"Wait a minute," Sam said. "Gracie suggested we have regular meetings once a week to talk over any problems we may be having."

"I'm not so sure about that," Caroline said. "We can talk about any glitches as they come up. I don't think we need to be overly organized."

"There's nothing wrong with setting aside a time to discuss running the inn," Gracie said.

"I don't think…," Caroline began.

"Let's leave it for now," Sam interrupted. "We all have a lot to learn about running an inn. For now, we can take it one day at a time."

"I'd much rather have a master plan." Gracie didn't sound happy, but Sam reminded her of the job she was going to do on the computer.

Caroline shrugged indifferently. She presented a more serious problem, in Sam's opinion. Her energy and enthusiasm had carried them through a long year of renovations and preparations. What would happen if she lost interest now?

CHAPTER
Ten

Caroline couldn't get their meeting out of her mind as she folded her personal laundry. She knew she hadn't been pulling her weight the last few days. When George told her he wasn't coming for the parade, it had knocked the wind out of her sails, leaving her uncharacteristically listless.

That's no excuse, she told herself sharply, feeling a bit guilty for putting so much responsibility on Sam.

She had disappeared, taking long walks on the beach as she tried to come to terms with her disappointment. Ever since they'd met in the exotic city of Istanbul, where she had been on assignment for a travel magazine, she and George had shared a special bond. It was a meeting of minds and spirits that flourished without the formality of matrimony.

Now, she feared that without matrimony, she might lose his friendship altogether. She wondered, too, if she was dooming their relationship by tying herself to the inn. For the first time since falling in love with the derelict inn, she doubted the wisdom of the enterprise.

Would Sam be better off if she went back to teaching? Was Gracie as reluctant to live there year-round as she sounded? Was the inn going to impact all three lives in a negative way? *If it does*, she thought, *it will be my fault*.

If the inn failed, they would be financially bankrupt. If it succeeded, their lives would be forever altered. Losing George was a high price to pay, but part of her still wanted to live her mother's dream of staying on the island permanently.

"Do you need help?" Sam asked, coming into the utility room. Caroline realized that she'd stopped folding and been staring blankly at the clothes in her basket.

Caroline looked up. "Oh, no thanks. I'm the one who should be helping you."

"It will be a big boost if you can book a monthlong stay for the woman's great aunt. You won't forget about showing her the inn, will you?"

Ordinarily Caroline would have been miffed at Sam's reminder, but her behavior the last few days warranted it. She smiled.

"I'll hover around the foyer until she shows up. I don't remember her name."

"Sophie Davis. Maybe I didn't mention it. It would be great to have a long stay booked. Find out a little about the aunt, though."

"Like what?"

"Whether she's healthy enough to live independently. Will the stairway be a problem, since all the guest rooms are on the second floor? You know, be subtle but find out what you can about her. Make sure the niece knows we're not full-service on meals. I wouldn't mind delivering breakfast to her room, but she's on her own the rest of the day."

Gracie was the big worrier, not Sam, so when Sam worried, Caroline paid close attention to her concerns.

"I'll find out all I can," she promised.

"Good." Sam turned to leave, but Caroline had something to say.

"Sam, I'm sorry for not helping more the last few days. I just needed a little time to myself."

"We'll all have plenty to do when the inn is full of guests," Sam said. "I've been lax about delegating work to Gracie. I'm afraid she feels unneeded. I think her flow charts will help divide the jobs in a fair way."

"You know lists aren't my style," Caroline said, "but I'll try to cooperate."

"Good. I did have a thought to run past you. The newlyweds were really interested in the history of the inn. What would you think of offering short programs to guests and anyone else who's history-minded? We could make it fun by giving a presentation as part of a tea party. Maybe we could persuade one of the gift stores to sell tickets."

"Sounds good to me," Caroline said, perking up a little.

"I also thought I might develop some cranberry items to sell, bread, maybe cookies. A tea party/history talk would be the perfect opportunity to launch a little side business."

"Are you sure you have time? A little extra revenue would be nice, but I don't want you to overdo," Caroline said, really looking at her sister for the first time in days.

Sam was the mirror image of their mother with sleek, shoulder-length hair and lively blue eyes, but lately there were shadows under her eyes. She seemed thinner and more stressed than usual. No doubt she was working too hard, but Caroline also suspected she was missing her twenty-six-year old daughter.

"What do you hear from Jamie?" Caroline asked. "Will she be coming to the island any time soon?"

"I'd like her to. She needs a change of scenery. I hate the shabby apartment she has in Brooklyn. She says it's full of thrift-shop treasures, but I think she's living with rubbish. Of course, I'd never put it that bluntly."

"I hope she'll be able to visit soon," Caroline said, and then changed the subject. "I'll be sure to meet—what's her name again?"

"Sophie Davis. Do you want me to write it down?"

"No, I'm usually good with names. Lately I've just been—distracted."

Caroline read the sympathy on Sam's face, but she didn't want to talk about George.

"Well, I'll be waiting to hear how the tour of the inn goes," Sam said.

When it was nearly time for Sophie to arrive, Caroline sat studying the guest register and doing mental arithmetic. She counted the days until Nantucket's season wound down, usually after Labor Day weekend, and multiplied the total by the amount they were charging for rooms. When the sums got too large to do in her head, she brought up the calculator on her cell phone. If they were 100 percent full every weekend and had 75 percent occupancy on weekdays, they had a chance of ending the season in the black.

Of course, they'd done the calculations before, but seeing it again in black and white helped her focus on the importance of presenting the inn in a good light.

The front door was unlocked during the day, but there was a small bell on the podium for guests to ring when they came in. When it sounded, Caroline hurried to meet the visitor.

"Hello, it's nice to see you," Caroline said, greeting a rather tall, stately woman in her midthirties with ash blonde hair piled on her head. "I'm Caroline Marris, one of the owners."

"Sophie Davis," she said, extending a beautifully manicured hand.

Caroline had sophisticated friends, but this woman radiated class with her cultured voice, high fashion mauve pantsuit, and perfectly coordinated print blouse. Her toeless shoes belonged on a runway, and her makeup was both subtle and exquisite. The people Caroline saw on the island tended to dress quite casually. This woman was nothing short of elegant.

"I understand your aunt might be interested in staying at Misty Harbor Inn," Caroline said. She'd interviewed too many people in her job to be intimidated by anyone, but Sophie Davis certainly impressed her.

"My great aunt, actually. I'm here on her behalf. She's a retired actress who lives in London, but she does like a change of scenery from time to time. My husband and I would like her to stay with us, but I'm afraid she's too reclusive. We do quite a bit of entertaining during the season, especially my husband's business acquaintances, so she asked me to find quiet lodgings away from town. She tells me she wants to write her memoirs."

"How fascinating," Caroline said. "Let me show you our inn. It's been totally renovated over the last year. We have one couple staying this week, but our official opening date is May first."

She led the way to the parlor, stepping aside so Mrs. Davis could get the full effect of the period furnishings.

"What a lovely piano," the visitor said. "So ornate. Quite old, if I'm not mistaken. Aunt Lorraine will appreciate it, even though I doubt she plays anymore. She has some arthritis in her hands. Are those your relatives in the portraits?"

The paintings of Jedediah and Hettie Montague gave a certain ambience to the nineteenth-century room, but Caroline was glad the grim couple weren't her ancestors.

"No, they're early residents of the house. We kept them because they were in the house when we bought it," she explained.

"My aunt appreciates antiques. She'll love your parlor," Mrs. Davis said as she followed Caroline to the library. "Although I suspect she may keep to her room quite a bit."

Caroline concluded the tour of the ground floor rooms available to guests with a peek into the dining room

"The only meal we serve is breakfast," she said. "I hope that won't be a problem."

"I very much doubt my aunt would join other guests for breakfast. Would it be acceptable for her to have it in her room?"

"That wouldn't be a problem, just so long as she understands we're not a full-service restaurant. We don't mind takeout meals from town, but we can't allow cooking in the room. The fire marshal would be very unhappy."

Caroline's curiosity about the great aunt was growing, and she found herself hoping the inn was up to her standards.

"Perhaps I can see the accommodations now?" Mrs. Davis suggested. "I should tell you, my aunt travels with an assistant. She would need an additional room for him, preferably within hearing distance in case my aunt needs anything in the night."

"We do have one suite with two bedrooms," Caroline said, leading the way up the spiral staircase—the inn's pride and joy. "Is your great aunt able to climb stairs?"

"Yes, with help from Albert, her 'manservant,' as she calls him. You needn't worry about caring for her beyond cleaning her room and delivering a suitable breakfast."

"I lived in England for many years," Caroline said, "so I'm familiar with a traditional English breakfast."

"Splendid! I don't know my great aunt well enough to know what she might require, but I'm sure she'll appreciate your familiarity with all things English. She likes to bring a bit of home with her when she travels abroad."

Although all guests were welcome, Caroline was especially pleased at the prospect of an English visitor. She opened the door of the suite and motioned for Sophie Davis to go ahead of her into the sitting room.

"This is pleasant," she said.

Although both bedrooms had separate entrances, they were joined by a small sitting room with white wicker furnishings and chintz curtains.

"I see this window overlooks the garden. And the large window lets in so much light. That's a definite plus," the visitor said.

"Only spring flowers are in bloom now, but it will be a riot of color later in the season. One of my sisters has planted sunflowers, her personal favorite, but we'll also have hollyhocks, morning glories, marigolds, roses, and possibly some tomato plants among other things."

"Your gardener must be kept very busy." Mrs. Davis stared down through the window. "The garden would be a nice private place to take the sun, not that my aunt ever ventures outside without one of her big hats. She's always been very careful with her complexion. Even now."

Caroline wasn't sure what she meant by "even now," but she was getting more and more curious about the potential guest.

"Is she a widow?"

"Oh my, no! Lorraine Clayworth was a star of stage and screen in her day. She never had the time or inclination to marry."

The name was vaguely familiar, but Caroline was sure the actress's stardom had come before she became a movie fan.

"Was she on television?"

"Please." Sophie leaned in conspiratorially. "Whatever you do, don't ever mention TV in her presence if she becomes your guest. She was featured on one series, and it was an utter disaster. She blamed it for ruining her career back in the 1950s when many shows were shot live. May I see the bedrooms?"

"Of course." Caroline opened the door to the larger bedroom, one she was especially proud of. The walls were a heavenly blue with white woodwork. The bedspread and curtains had been an extravagant purchase, a shiny striped fabric that brought out the exquisite blues of the walls and rug. At first Sam had thought there was too much blue, but she'd had to admit the finished décor was exquisite.

"Each room has its own bath," Caroline said, leading the way to the second bedroom. "We had envisioned this as a children's room when families visit. The décor is a bit more utilitarian."

The gray and green striped wallpaper was actually washable, and the carpet was a sturdy synthetic blend. It was set off by a matching comforter in a sturdy fabric. They'd chosen pale green blinds and light gray paint for the doors and trim.

"This would be satisfactory for Albert," Mrs. Davis said more to herself than Caroline.

The tour had gone well, at least in Caroline's opinion. She led Mrs. Davis back downstairs as they discussed the inn's rates.

"I'll have to confer with her, of course," she said, "but you've done a very nice job in restoring the inn."

She thanked Caroline for her time and left—not exactly the outcome the sisters had hoped for.

Gracie was eager to hear how her sister's tour of the inn had gone. After spending several hours on the computer trying to come up with the best way to organize a list of jobs, she went to the kitchen and poured a glass of iced tea. She didn't have long to wait before Caroline joined her.

"How did it go?" she asked.

"Okay, I guess. The niece was complimentary and seemed to like everything she saw. She has to discuss it with her great aunt—and I suspect she'll visit other places before she makes a decision."

Caroline sounded discouraged, so Gracie didn't press her for details.

"What do you think of Sam's idea about tea parties with talks about the history of the inn?" she asked.

Caroline shrugged. "I'd probably pick more exotic subjects like the ruins of Troy or the Silk Road to China, but that's just me."

"You made your living visiting places like that," Gracie pointed out. "But I think the people who visit Nantucket would rather hear about the history of the island and of our inn in particular."

"You're probably right," Caroline said, sounding a bit weary.

"I do wonder whether people will pay to hear a presentation."

"We could offer it free to our guests but charge a nominal fee for others," Caroline suggested.

"Do you think the tea party idea will be too much to handle?" Gracie asked. "It will mean extra work. Now that I'm working on the flow chart, I can see how much it takes to run an inn. There may not be time for extra activities."

"We'll have to see after we work out the details. Maybe Sam shouldn't try to sell her baked goods. There's only so much time in the day," Caroline said.

"What shouldn't Sam do?" their sister said coming into the kitchen. "My ears were burning from the library."

"We're not sure you should try to bake things to sell," Gracie said. "In fact, the tea party and history talks may be too much to handle right now."

"We need to do something out of the ordinary to attract attention to the inn," Sam said. "You love history, Gracie. You're always reading biographies and such. Maybe you could help write a talk, and Caroline could deliver it. Let me worry about the tea party."

"I wouldn't mind that, if I had help researching," Caroline said, perking up a bit.

"It might be fun," Gracie conceded. "I'd probably want to focus on the people who lived in the house. That's what history is, the story of people and what they did in their lifetimes."

"Maybe we can find out more about Hannah, the young woman who disappeared from the island," Sam suggested.

Caroline shuddered. "I hate thinking something terrible happened to her."

"Maybe we won't be able to find out," Gracie said. "It was a long time ago."

"True," Caroline said, "but you'd be surprised what you can find when you know how to research."

"It would be fun to see if we can trace her," Gracie conceded.

"We can do it in our spare time," Sam said. "After all, no one can work all the time."

"I can see the advertising posters now," Caroline said, sounding more like her old self than she had since George had let her down. "'The Case of the Missing Widow.'"

"That's a bit melodramatic," Gracie said, wrinkling her nose. "We don't want to suggest that Jack the Ripper stalked Nantucket."

"People don't disappear into thin air," Sam said. "She must be buried somewhere."

"It's a big ocean out there," Caroline suggested in a teasing voice.

"If we're going to do this, we want to stick with historical facts," Gracie insisted.

"Does that mean you're on board with the idea?" Caroline challenged.

"Yes, but only if we're as accurate as possible. No lurid suggestions, nothing that can't be proved," Gracie insisted, knowing her older sister had a flair for the dramatic.

"Agreed," Sam said. "I'm really excited about the idea. Jamie's a history buff. I think I'll call her tonight and ask if she has any suggestions about how to go about this."

"Now that we own the inn, I think we should know more about it," Caroline said. "You said the honeymooners were interested in the history of the building. I suspect a lot of our visitors will have questions about the past."

"We need to be prepared to answer them," Gracie agreed.

She wondered what they would discover when they delved into the secrets of Misty Harbor Inn. If the walls could talk, what would they say about the private lives of the people who had lived—and possibly died—in the house before it had become an inn?

"We still have the secret room to investigate," Sam reminded them. "I can't wait for the honeymooners to leave so I can see what's hidden behind the closet."

Gracie wasn't at all sure she wanted to poke around in a sealed space behind the wall, but the contents might throw some light on the original owners. She felt a shiver of excitement—and perhaps dread—when she thought of unearthing long-hidden secrets. She hoped they wouldn't find anything to make them uncomfortable living in the inn.

CHAPTER
Eleven

*T*uesday was their official opening day, but it came and went without additional guests checking into the inn. Sam knew she had to be patient, but after a year of hard work, it was unsettling to see rooms sitting empty. Still, she was grateful for the opportunity to spend a few days making sure every detail of the inn was ready.

May wasn't a big month for visitors in Nantucket, at least not until Memorial Day weekend, but as newcomers on the roster of island accommodations, they needed to attract guests as soon as possible.

Sam decided to raise her spirits by phoning her daughter Jamie. Neither of them were early-to-bed types, so she didn't hesitate to call after her sisters had retired for the night.

"Mom, good to hear from you!" Jamie said when she picked up the phone. "How are things going at the inn?"

"Still a little slow," Sam said, giving her daughter an update on what had been going on, including the idea of a tea party with a presentation on the inn's history.

"I love the idea of offering guests something extra, especially something about history," Jamie said. "That old house shouts out for someone to investigate its past."

"You're the historian in the family. How's your thesis coming?" Sam asked.

Jamie was doing advanced work in American history, and Sam couldn't be prouder of her bright, attractive daughter. In order to meet expenses, she worked as a tour guide at a Brooklyn museum and also part-time as a docent and gift shop cashier at the Metropolitan Museum of Art. It was a busy schedule, and Sam understood why she couldn't come to the island more often.

"The thesis is good, although I could use some time away from my jobs to polish it. I've even talked to my bosses about taking some leaves of absence."

"You could get work done here, and I'd love to have you," Sam said, cheered by the possibility of seeing her daughter. "Maybe you could give us some help tracking down the first family who lived here."

"What have you done so far?" Jamie asked, sounding excited.

"Not much, but I discovered a hidden room behind one of the second floor closets."

"Really?" Jamie gushed. "What's in it?"

"I'm not sure. There's some furniture and lots of odds and ends, but I haven't been inside since I found it. Honeymooners have the room for a few more days. Your aunts insist we can't explore it until they check out."

"I would expect Aunt Gracie to say that, but I'm surprised Caroline can stand to wait."

"She hasn't been herself the past few days. George didn't come for the daffodil parade."

"That's too bad," Jamie said. "But about the room, I don't see any harm in taking another peek when your guests are out of the room."

"If only I dared!" Sam didn't want to admit how much the secret room tempted her, but Jamie was the one person who could understand. "I dream about it at night!"

"It's your inn," Jamie said in persuasive voice. "You have to go in the room every day to clean. What could it hurt to take a look with a flashlight? If no one discovered it during the renovations, there's no way the guests could suspect there's a secret place behind a closet wall."

"You might be right," Sam said, wondering if she had enough nerve to do a little exploring on her own. "When do you think you can come to the island?"

"Soon! We're busy with end-of-the-year grade school tours at the museum, but my boss is training a few new guides. As soon as they're ready to handle groups, I can get time off with a clear conscience. When should I come?"

"It can't *be* too soon," Sam said. "I'd love to have you here."

"I won't be taking up a room you need for guests?" Jamie quizzed.

"No, you can share my room downstairs. Come and stay as long as you can."

"Then I'll be there soon. Love you, Mom."

"Love you too," Sam said, her mood buoyed by the conversation.

The next morning she thought the honeymooners would never come down for breakfast. She'd learned to make entrees that wouldn't spoil if they weren't served immediately, but this was stretching it. As soon as the first guests left, she would only offer breakfast from seven to nine. Perhaps she could leave banana and cranberry breads and coffee on the sideboard for those who insisted on sleeping later.

"We're going to ride bikes all the way around the island," Erin told her when they made their appearance.

"If you don't get pooped out," her husband teased.

"Anything you can do, I can do too," Erin said with mock indignation.

Sam was pleased by their high spirits. Gracie was still a little worried about them, so it would be nice to tell her they were enjoying themselves. But what really struck her was that they'd be gone for most of the day. A complete circuit of the island was a long trip by bike, so it was unlikely they'd be back before late afternoon.

Should I or shouldn't I? she wondered after they left with picnic lunches and backpacks loaded with things they might need.

Caroline helped her make the decision when she announced that she was going out for a walk into town. "I'll probably do some shopping while I'm there," she said. "Is there anything you need at the market?"

"Let me make a quick list," Sam said, hopeful she would be alone in the inn this morning.

After Caroline left, Gracie came into the kitchen and took a bottle of water from the fridge.

"It's so nice out, I thought I'd walk over and get the Packard from the shop, and then I'm going to work in the garden. Let me know if you need me for anything."

"I won't," Sam said firmly. "I'm going to clean the honeymooners' room and do some odd jobs, nothing you need to help me with."

"Well, I'm itching to start digging in the dirt," Gracie said. "Spring is my favorite time of year. I'm just sorry I can't keep up my garden at home. I'm sure Brandon will mow the lawn and check the house, but my poor garden will be neglected."

"Think of the garden here as yours," Sam said. "You're the only one in the family with a green thumb. Remember that time when you cut off a lilac branch you thought was dead?"

Gracie smiled at the memory. "Yes, I used it to tie up a plant in the living room, and it bloomed right there in the house."

"Well, enjoy yourself," Sam said, sure her sister would spend hours with the plants and flowers she loved. There certainly was a lot for her to do, since work inside the inn had kept Caroline and her busy.

Sam quickly found the bucket she used to carry cleaning supplies, added the flashlight they kept for power emergencies and went upstairs. Now that she was alone in the inn, there was no hurry to make up the bed or clean the guest room. She simply couldn't resist having another look at the hidden room.

When no one else was in the house, it took on a life of its own. Like any building 170 years old, it moaned and creaked—sounds that were muffled by human voices when people were around. Gracie had been a bit creeped out when they first bought the house, but Sam had always felt in sync with the historic structure. Generations had come and gone, leaving an imprint of their lives, and Sam fancied she could listen to their stories in the solitude of empty rooms.

"Am I getting weird or what?" Sam said out loud to herself.

She didn't expect to see a ghost or be startled by mysterious shadows. She was much too grounded and practical to imagine things that weren't there, but she could hardly wait to explore a room forgotten by time. She didn't have visions of lost treasure or valuable antiques waiting to be found, but she wouldn't be happy until she satisfied her curiosity.

Her decision was made, and she didn't waste any time on cleaning. The chores would wait.

She opened the closet door, feeling like an intruder with the honeymooners' clothes hanging on the rod. Fortunately it wasn't necessary to touch or move them to have access to the wall panel. She got a firm grip on the flashlight and gingerly opened the movable part of the wall. Then, as an afterthought, she closed the closet door, although she didn't expect anyone to come into the bedroom. She didn't need the light from the windows, and a person who was snooping couldn't be too careful.

A quick survey by the light of the flashlight revealed a bulky chest and other objects harder to identify. The dust of ages coated every surface, but Sam was wearing her oldest jeans and a big shirt with the sleeves rolled up. If she got too dirty, she was wearing a tank top so she could slip out of the shirt and conceal it with the cleaning rags in her pail. She wasn't proud of scheming to fool her sisters, but they weren't the ones who'd discovered the secret room. They'd be as curious as she was if they'd had a sneak peek into a time capsule.

Her biggest worry was the floor. How sturdy were the boards after years of concealment? During the renovation, she'd been impressed by thick beams that exceeded modern requirements, but did the builders use the best lumber in a concealed room? What had motivated them to hide the space? Was it originally meant as storage for luggage, or did it have a more important function? A hideout for runaway slaves came to mind, but nothing she knew about the inn supported that usage. The fact that the secret room existed was nothing if not odd. And exciting.

With the panel at her back, she took one cautious step into the room. The board squeaked but held her weight when she placed the other foot beside it. She tried not to imagine the ceiling under her feet. If the board gave way, was there anything besides plaster to keep her from plunging to the floor below?

"Think like that, and you are going to spook yourself," she whispered.

In order to get a good look at the contents, she had to move toward the center of the room. She steeled herself to step on the next board, testing it as best she could with one foot. The only thing that encouraged her was the presence of the heavy-looking chest. The floor was strong enough to support it, so maybe it wouldn't give way under her weight in spite of the warning squeaks.

She moved forward gingerly, hoping she'd be safe if she didn't make any sudden moves. The flashlight made the space more eerie than she'd expected, and she was beginning to wish she'd waited until Jamie arrived. No one knew she was there, which made it an especially bad idea if she had a mishap.

She was looking for a handhold before she went farther when she heard a sound coming from the bedroom.

"I can't believe we forgot the camera." Erin's voice was muffled, but there was no mistaking it. The pair had returned for something they'd forgotten.

"I assumed it was in your backpack," Kyle said with a trace of impatience.

"Never mind. I'm glad we came back. It's warmer than I thought. Think I'll change into shorts."

Sam held her breath and eased the panel shut, dousing her flash so no hint of light escaped from the hidden room.

"What do you think?" Erin said, her voice much closer as she spoke from the closet. "Should I wear my new blue ones or go with the khaki?"

"Either," Kyle's muffled voice said.

"You know how long it takes me to decide what to wear."

"Okay, wear the blue. You look nice in them."

Sam had an almost overwhelming urge to sneeze as she breathed the stale air in the room. She clenched her hand over her mouth and nose and exerted every bit of control she could, but a muffled sound still escaped.

Holding her breath, she listened hard to find out whether she'd been heard. The couple was discussing the places they planned to see, deciding whether to picnic on the beach or in one of the island's nice parks. Would they never make up their minds and get going?

Sam was afraid to move and scared to breathe for fear she'd sneeze again. *What's taking them so long?* She didn't dare back up or go forward for fear of being betrayed by the squeaky floor. Of course, she was an owner. She had a perfect right to go anywhere in the inn, but her sisters were right about waiting until the room wasn't occupied. It could be a disaster if the guests knew there was a secret room. They might be tempted to explore it themselves and end up badly hurt.

Besides being almost unbearably stuffy, the room was much warmer than she'd expected at this time of year. There was no insulation, so it had heated up quickly on this sunny day. The back of her shirt felt damp, and beads of perspiration trickled down her forehead. The flashlight was slippery in her hand, and she willed the couple to leave—leave soon. She was afraid to stay where she was when the slightest movement made the board creak ominously, but she was even more afraid to move.

The darkness was overwhelming. She knew she was alone in the space, but her imagination ran wild. She was afraid rats and spiders were creeping up on her, although the rational part of her mind knew the inn had been thoroughly fumigated.

For several long minutes, she didn't hear a sound coming from the bedroom. How long did it take Erin to change? Had they left? She had no way of being sure, and she couldn't imagine anything more embarrassing then emerging from the closet while they were still there.

She rubbed the sleeve of her shirt over her moist face, and the board under her feet seemed to sway. Regardless of risk, she had to see if the floor really had moved. She looked over her shoulder at the closed panel and hoped they wouldn't see a slice of light coming from beyond the closet wall.

Shading the light with one hand, she was poised to turn it on when it slipped from her moist grip and landed somewhere at her feet. She stooped to search for it and made another unsettling discovery. The floor sloped, and the flashlight had rolled away beyond her reach. Now she was stranded in the darkness with no clue whether the guests were still in their room.

She crouched down, feeling a bit safer when she wasn't standing upright, but no less uncomfortable. Fifty-three-year-old knees weren't designed for long periods of stooping, but she was afraid to move to a more comfortable position. Would those people never leave on their bike trip? How long would it be before one of her sisters tried to find her? Could she stifle yet another sneeze? The next time she came here, she was going to wear a mask, but that thought didn't reassure her while she crouched in the black hole.

Her knees began to hurt big-time, but she didn't dare stand. Would they lock in that position so she couldn't get up without something to grasp?

"We'd better get going," Erin at last called out. "Before we change our minds."

"I wouldn't mind staying here all day with you," Kyle said.

Sam's heart sank. That was the worst idea she'd heard in eons.

"Silly, we came here to see the island. We can always stay inside if it rains, which it may do tomorrow."

Erin giggled, and a few moments later Sam was pretty sure she heard the outer door close. Before she could move, it opened again.

"I don't believe it!" Erin said with a peal of laughter, obviously returning to the room. "We came for the camera and nearly forgot it again."

"That's because you distract me," Kyle said.

The door closed again, and Sam took a deep breath, only to sneeze so violently she had to grasp at the floor to keep from lurching forward.

Her curiosity had definitely dissipated. She didn't care if Blackbeard's treasure was stored somewhere in the murky depths of the room. She was out of there.

It was easier said than done. She managed to stand upright—albeit with trepidation—and she was disorientated in the unrelieved darkness. She felt in all directions for the moveable panel, feeling a sharp stab on her palm when she finally connected with it.

Grasping with her fingernails, trying to ignore the pain in her hand, she finally pried the panel open, tugging desperately to get an opening large enough to step through.

"Thank heavens," she said fervently when she reached the solid floor of the closet.

Her hand hurt—a lot. When she stepped into the welcome light of the bedroom, she saw a wicked-looking splinter protruding from the fleshy area below her thumb. She caught sight of herself in the dresser mirror and scarcely recognized the dusty, disheveled creature reflected back at her.

She peeled off the shirt, but it was going to take more than a change of clothes to look normal again. Her eyes were pink and swollen. There must be a particularly vile form of dust in the hidden room. Blood was trickling out where she'd partly dislodged the splinter. Mostly, she was mad at herself. Not only had she been trapped in the hidden room, she hadn't learned a thing by being there. She was as curious as ever but considerably more reluctant to investigate again on her own.

Sam hurried down to the family quarters, eager to repair the damage to her clothes and person before one of her sisters demanded an explanation. Truth to tell, she was embarrassed to tell them about her misadventure, although she would have to come up with an explanation for red eyes and a stab wound on her hand.

Rather than lie, which she hated, she endured the pain of taking out the splinter and then treated it with antiseptic but decided not to call attention to it with a bandage. Then she took an allergy pill, squeezed eye drops in her eyes, and made herself as presentable as possible.

Gracie breezed into the kitchen a few minutes later carrying a small bouquet of daffodils.

"They won't last much longer outside," she said. "I thought we should enjoy a vaseful while we can."

"Lovely," Sam said, casually concealing her hand at her side. "You're back already with the Packard?" How long had she been trapped in the secret room?

Gracie laughed. "No, I haven't even left yet. I somehow got caught up in my gardening first. I was just going now. Then I'll work on our chart if you don't have any other jobs for me."

"No, nothing." Sam belatedly remembered leaving her cleaning supplies behind. She hadn't started to do the guests' room, let alone check to see whether she'd left dusty footsteps on the rug. "I'll make lunch when you and Caroline get back."

She hoped that wouldn't be until she had time to clean the room. Her hand ached, her eyes itched, and she felt wretched deceiving her sister. Was there anything in the hidden room that would compensate for being trapped there? She could only hope.

CHAPTER
Twelve

Caroline peered outside, watching as a vintage Bentley pulled up in front of the inn. The burgundy paint was polished to a glowing sheen, and even the wheels looked clean. She was pretty sure it came from an island rental agency that specialized in older but classy cars, and she could hardly wait to see who was inside it.

"What are you doing?" Gracie asked, coming up behind her.

Caroline whirled to face her sister. "You startled me!"

"Sorry. What *are* you doing?" she asked, craning to see what was so interesting outside the door.

"Shh," Caroline said, knowing she should at least have the grace to look sheepish for spying on a visitor. She smiled weakly at her sister and took another peek out the window.

"What on earth are you looking at?" Gracie said, moving in to get a closer look.

Caroline edged over and whispered, "That!"

"Oh, no wonder. That car's a beauty. I guess that explains why they didn't need to be picked up in the Packard," Gracie whispered back as she took another look. "Wait, why are we whispering? They can't hear us through the door!"

Caroline slumped against the wall, frazzled from a morning of eager anticipation and preparations for their new guest.

"The occasion just seemed to call for lowering our voices," she said. "It's not every day we get a famous actress at the inn."

Gracie frowned, clearly growing impatient with her sister. "I guess any guest is a cause for celebration. I was surprised at how quickly she booked for a month. She must have had her plane tickets before she decided where to stay."

"Yes, I was expecting Sophie Davis to check out other accommodations and get back to us in weeks, at the soonest. I guess she was impressed with Misty Harbor Inn."

"What's her name again?" Gracie asked. "She isn't someone I've heard of, but maybe it's because she's British."

"Lorraine Clayworth. She had quite a following at one time, although she was never as famous as Vivian Leigh or Elizabeth Taylor. I think she was better known as a serious actor, although I'm not quite sure what that means."

"Who's the man driving the car? He doesn't look like anyone I've seen on the island. Unless I'm mistaken, he looks like an English butler—at least the movie version of one. I like the tweed cap better than that awful thing you made me wear," Gracie said.

"Next time I'm in London, I'll get you one," Caroline said with a trace of irritation. "Anyway, the driver must be her personal assistant, Albert Grayson. I understand he goes everywhere with her."

"Sounds convenient," Gracie said. "If I had a personal assistant, I'd never drive that Packard wagon again."

"Don't you think it's so old-fashioned—a legendary actress traveling with her faithful assistant?"

"No, I think it's convenient," Gracie said.

Sometimes, Caroline thought, *Gracie doesn't have any flair for the dramatic. Actually, she never did.*

"Look," Gracie said, gesturing at the arrivals. "See how much luggage he's unloading. I've never seen a steamer trunk like that. It must hold dozens of outfits."

"That's vintage Louis Vuitton luggage," Caroline said. "Those aren't the pieces you'd expect to see on an airport carousel. Three, four, the little makeup case makes five. No, he's taking out another one. They've brought enough to stay a year."

"They booked their suite for a month, so I guess she'll be changing clothes a lot," Gracie said. "Why is she staying here for such a long time? Not that I'm complaining. She took another clandestine look. "We hardly know anything about her. Only that she's British and used to be an actress."

Carolyn watched as her sister pursed her lips as though about to say something more and then thought better of it.

"I can understand why people want to be here in Nantucket, although she's here a bit early in the season. We've been lucky on weather, but there's no guarantee May will be sunny and warm all month," Caroline said.

"What are you two doing?" Sam asked, joining them by the front entrance.

"Our guests are here," Caroline said unnecessarily.

Sam let out an exasperated sigh. "Shouldn't one of us go out to welcome them and help carry their luggage?"

Caroline felt like a dunce. She'd been so busy 'spying' on the new guests, she had forgotten her duties as hostess.

"Of course, I got carried away watching them unload. Will you help me welcome them, Gracie?"

Another sigh escaped her sister's lips. "Of course, I'm getting to be a pro at hauling luggage. If I had an assistant, he'd also serve as a bellhop."

"You're funny," Caroline said.

"I wasn't trying to be," Gracie grumbled.

The two went out together, and Caroline took the lead in greeting the older man who was managing the luggage while his employer remained on the backseat of the automobile. She was only a shadow behind the tinted window, which made Caroline even more curious to meet her.

"I'm Caroline Marris, proprietress of the inn, and this is my sister, Gracie Gold. We have another sister, Sam Carter, who will also be your hostess," she said.

He was a man of medium height and slender build, dressed in an exquisitely tailored gray suit, much more elegant then she'd expect on a servant. A fringe of white hair covered his forehead below the bill of his cap, and his face was impassive as he stood, surrounded by multiple pieces of stylish designer luggage.

"I'm so sorry, we don't have a luggage cart," she apologized. "There isn't a lift in the inn, so the pieces have to be carried up the stairs." She'd lived in England so long, she automatically said *lift* instead of *elevator*.

The man gazed at her with startlingly blue eyes, unfaded by age, which looked to be late seventies or early eighties. He gave her a sober nod and then took yet another piece from the trunk of the car.

"Of course, we'll see that your luggage is delivered to your suite," Caroline said, feeling a twinge in her back at the thought of hauling the bigger pieces up the steps.

The dapper man with ramrod posture finally spoke.

"Allow me to introduce myself. I am Albert Grayson, Miss Clayworth's personal assistant—for this and the last millennium."

Caroline shot Gracie a worried look, wondering if this was Mr. Grayson's attempt at humor or if he was dead serious. She suspected the latter from his subdued reverential tone.

"It's very nice to meet you," Caroline said, trying to get a glimpse of his employer through the Bentley's tinted window, obviously an aftermarket addition to the vintage vehicle.

"Likewise," he said, bending slightly at the waist, bowing to both of them in turn.

"I'd be happy to escort Miss Clayworth to her room," Caroline offered.

"Miss Clayworth prefers to wait in the car," he said.

Caroline thought she detected a slight note of disdain in his voice directed at the vintage Bentley. Maybe anything less than a Rolls Royce was below her.

"She will be exiting forthwith after I take care of the luggage," he said. "She would prefer not to be observed when she does so."

Caroline loved Albert's crisp British accent—such a contrast to his mild-mannered appearance—but why was his employer hiding in the car? She was concerned about his plan to carry the pile of suitcases into the inn. *Surely he doesn't plan to haul all of the luggage to the second floor by himself?*

Gracie came to his rescue—or so Caroline thought.

"Let me help you with those," she said, reaching for the handle on a valise.

The poor man looked mortified, Caroline thought.

"Thank you, madam, but I couldn't allow that." Gracie looked at Caroline, who could only shrug her shoulders at her sister. She knew it was too impolite to ask why not and was grateful Gracie didn't either.

She watched, along with her sister, as Albert slowly and painstakingly picked up each piece of luggage, transported it to the porch, and came back for more. His employer had not yet left the car, although Caroline's imagination went into high gear at the guest's failure to emerge from the car. *Does she have leprosy? Maybe not. Surely there's a cure for it now. Maybe she's been disfigured in a terrible accident or...*

"Why do you suppose he doesn't want any help?" Gracie whispered as he made another trip to the porch.

"I have no idea," Caroline replied in an equally hushed tone. "Maybe he's the only one allowed to touch her suitcases. Or maybe he doesn't want a woman doing what he considers a man's job?"

"I wish you and Sam felt that way about luggage handling," Gracie said, but Caroline could tell she was joking.

When all of the luggage was stacked on the porch, Albert proceeded to carry it inside and up the stairs. Caroline showed him to the suite.

"That will be all, thank you," he said politely but firmly. "If you wouldn't mind withdrawing now...."

"Yes, of course." Caroline went back to the foyer and herded her sisters toward the kitchen.

"What's going on?" Gracie asked.

"Apparently our guest doesn't want to be seen," Caroline explained. "I'll be in the parlor if you need me."

She was a bit ashamed for deceiving her sisters, but she intended to see their mysterious guest even if she had to spy from a front window. She found a spot where she could remain concealed but still see what was happening in front of the inn.

"I know what you're up to," Gracie said, covertly joining her by the window. "You can't stand not seeing who's in that car."

They had a rather long wait, since it took a while to carry the luggage up to the suite. It was well worth the wait when their guest finally emerged from the car, first giving her hand to Mr. Grayson who practically bowed over it.

The elegant woman who gracefully stepped out from the backseat of the vehicle took Caroline aback. Despite the warmth of the day, the actress was dressed in an ultrastylish black crepe dress that reminded Caroline of high fashion in the 1950s. Her narrow, pointy-toed high heels made Carolyn's feet ache. She was imagining how they would hurt her feet even though she was much younger than their guest. Perched atop the woman's elegantly coiffed white bob was a black pillbox hat with a half-veil covering her eyes.

"If I looked that good in a hat, maybe I wouldn't complain about the commodore's cap you and Sam expect me to wear," Gracie grumbled, still whispering.

Caroline could only nod mutely. She'd traveled the world but never in all her experiences had she seen a woman with such regal bearing, not even real royalty. Caroline imagined that when they finally met face to face, she would be inclined to curtsy to her the way Albert had bowed.

"Shouldn't we go out and meet her?" Gracie whispered. "She *is* a guest in our inn."

"Her butler—assistant—made quite a point of privacy," Caroline said, although she was as eager as Gracie to meet their guest. "I guess we'll have to wait until we bump into her accidentally during her stay. We have a whole month to do it."

"I guess you're right," Gracie reluctantly conceded. "But it is odd, a guest we're not supposed to meet. At least I didn't have to haul any of their luggage. She brought enough to stay a year."

Caroline watched, mesmerized by the couple approaching the front entrance. Mr. Grayson tenderly took her arm, a gentle gesture that went beyond kindness or courtesy, while he cradled a small dog with his other arm. She was intrigued, and it took all her willpower not to waylay them in the foyer. She held back because the elegant former actress was too regal to be greeted by a grubby innkeeper. Caroline had never suffered from a poor self-image, but she was horribly underdressed to welcome stage royalty. She definitely had to rethink her wardrobe when it came to welcoming guests. Her favorite pair of khaki shorts and military green T-shirt made her feel like a safari guide, even though it was perfect acceptable attire for a late spring day on the island. She glanced at Gracie in her yellow Capri pants and crinkle-cloth tunic and suspected she was thinking the same thing.

The two Brits disappeared from sight, but she could hear the cultured tones of their voices through the door separating them. Now that they were this close, Caroline felt uncomfortable spying on them, but her curiosity was by no means satisfied. She's been prepared to welcome tourists from all over the States and perhaps even Canada, but the actress was different from anyone she'd expected. She was going to have to rethink her role at the inn—and her sisters'. Maybe the idea of a weekly meeting to discuss management of the inn was a good idea.

Then it hit her. They'd brought a Yorkshire Terrier, a breed she recognized because a friend in England owned one. She wasn't too enchanted to remember the inn's rules: Pets were forbidden, except, of course, assistance dogs.

Sophie Davis hadn't mentioned a dog when she made the reservation for her great aunt. Was it possible she'd overlooked the prohibition against pets on their Web site? Caroline felt helpless. There was no way they could refuse to let her occupy the room because Miss Clayworth had a Yorkie. After all, she had Max with her, and it was unlikely the little pooch would be given free rein of the inn. Max was strictly confined to the family quarters and his fenced play area in the back.

When she got over her surprise, Caroline had to admit the Yorkie was show-worthy, its long coat brushed to a silky sheen. His—or her—fur was the traditional tan flowing into shades of dark steel blue. A black bow kept hair from blinding him.

She smiled to herself when she remembered that the pampered little pet was a descendent of nineteenth century rat catchers. Working class people would have owned its ancestors, not rich, cultured aristocrats.

Caroline hurriedly led the way back to the kitchen in case Mr. Grayson came back downstairs with requests. A few minutes later, there was a soft knock on the kitchen door; her caution had been well founded.

"If I might have a few words," he said.

"Of course." She led him to the library where she planned to sign him in.

As she would with any guest, Caroline asked if the rooms were satisfactory and started to explain about breakfast and bike rentals, although she doubted the latter information would be needed.

"Mrs. Davis indicated it would be acceptable for Miss Clayworth to dine in her suite," he said.

"Yes, of course, but we did mention that breakfast is the only meal we serve guests, except, of course, for box lunches, which are available with a day's notice."

"We understand. I'll come for Miss Clayworth's morning repast myself. I'll give you a written request concerning the menu as soon as I've settled her for a short nap. The trip was very wearing." He sounded worried and quickly left her to return to the suite.

It was no wonder Lorraine Clayworth was exhausted after a transcontinental trip. Caroline had traveled too much to underestimate how grueling it could be, especially getting through airports and all the security measures. Still, she felt a bit uneasy about catering to the woman's needs for a full month. Her fashionable garb didn't conceal her frail state, not unusual for a woman who had to be approaching eighty. If she became ill at the inn, would they be able to handle it?

"Did she like the room?" Sam asked when she returned to the kitchen.

Caroline shrugged. "I guess she found it acceptable."

"I wonder whether I should make something special for her breakfast tomorrow." Sam frowned and clicked her nails on the worktable.

"I think Albert will keep us informed," Caroline said with a sigh, feeling tired even though her day was anything but finished.

"I feel guilty, letting him haul all that luggage by himself. I offered to help, but he refused—very politely, of course," Gracie said.

"That poor man," Caroline said. "He certainly earns his salary. How old do you think he is?

"Maybe eighty," Gracie suggested.

"Well, he moves like a man half his age," Sam said. "He has to have a lot of stamina to carry all those bags."

"And to do Miss Clayworth's bidding," Caroline said in a disapproving voice. "It can't be easy, being at another person's beck and call twenty-four hours a day."

"Something tells me he doesn't mind," Gracie said thoughtfully. "In fact, he seems eager to be sure everything is just right for her."

"Go figure," Sam said dismissively.

"I have to admit, I'm curious about her," Gracie said. "I don't know what I expected, she's certainly different from anyone I've known—at least what I could tell from a quick peek."

Caroline had reservations about Lorraine Clayworth's monthlong visit. Would she be difficult to please? Or would she keep to herself and let Albert speak for her all the time? Either way, she was going to be an intriguing guest.

CHAPTER
Thirteen

Gracie smiled when she saw Miss Clayworth's assistant carrying the Yorkie down the stairs early Friday morning, their first full day at the inn. She hadn't expected to see their guests up and about, but apparently it was part of his duty to walk the dog before breakfast.

"Good morning, Mr. Grayson," she said in a cheerful voice, hoping he'd stop to chat for a minute.

"Please, call me Albert," he said, though the cultured tone used made Gracie feel like curtsying. "This is Wellington."

He put the dog on the floor and attached a leash made of blue velvet ribbon to a collar hidden under his long fur. A ribbon perched on top of Wellington's head matched the velvet lead, a touch that wasn't lost on Gracie. She assumed the Yorkshire terrier was male, since he was named after the British hero who had defeated Napoleon at Waterloo.

She stepped ahead to open the door and received a stiff "thank you" for her courtesy.

Gracie couldn't resist watching at the door while the elegantly attired Brit walked the tiny dog. This morning Albert was dressed in a charcoal gray suit with a silvery gray silk vest and a matching bow tie. His shirt—what little showed—was crisply starched and blindingly white, and his black wingtip shoes were as shiny as polished ebony. Gracie wondered how many pieces of luggage contained his wardrobe. It was going to be interesting to see what their guests wore. She suspected it would be a virtual fashion parade.

Albert took out a blue plastic bag, and Gracie was happy to see he was as fastidious with the dog as he was with his person. She'd been so interested in his morning routine, she'd forgotten to ask whether Miss Clayworth wanted breakfast in her room.

Sam was in the kitchen, preparing French toast and smoked turkey sausages for the newlyweds, who wanted to get an early start on sightseeing since their time on the island was nearly over. Gracie suspected her sister's hearty breakfast wouldn't suit the actress, but fortunately, Sam was flexible about what she served.

"You can pour this now," Sam said when Gracie came into the kitchen.

She handed her a pitcher of freshly squeezed orange juice. Sam refused to serve frozen, reconstituted juice, believing the inn should have high standards for the one meal they provided for guests.

"Albert is out walking the dog," Gracie said after she returned from the dining room.

"That's nice. Did you find out about their breakfast?" Sam rolled the sausages over to brown on all sides and flicked a strand of hair away from her face.

She was cooking in jeans and T-shirt, and Gracie smiled when she imagined the new guests' reaction to such casual wear. Maybe the sisters needed a white chef's jacket for occasions like this.

"No, sorry, I was so taken with the tiny dog, I forgot to ask. Maybe I can waylay him when he comes back in."

"I guess he'll let us know when her ladyship makes up her mind," Sam said.

It was unlike her sister to be sarcastic, so Gracie wondered what the guest had done to upset her. Sam quickly let her know.

"Albert insisted I change towels twice before Miss Clayworth was satisfied. First they weren't soft enough, and then she didn't like the peach replacements because the color didn't harmonize with the bathroom. Also I had to remove the pillows from the room because she travels with her own special ones. It's going to be a long month."

"Oh dear," Gracie said. "Maybe she won't be so particular once she's settled in."

"Well, she's certainly used to having things her way. We can only clean between the hours of ten and eleven in the morning. Albert will take care of most of it, but she would like us to change the sheets every day. And she will allow us to vacuum and scrub the bathroom floors. Oh, she brought her own sheets too. We won't have to launder them because they require special care."

"Which I assume Albert will provide," Gracie said, more amused than irritated as her sister was. She'd never met anyone like the actress and her assistant, so this was going to be a new experience for her.

Caroline came into the kitchen from the rear entrance bringing Max with her.

"Did you hear him barking up a storm?" she asked as she took off his leash and hung it up. "He went primal when he got the Yorkie's scent. I guess I either have to let him out earlier or wait until later. I have a feeling Wellington doesn't play well with others, certainly not a lowbrow cocker spaniel like Max."

Before Gracie could comment, she heard the newlyweds as they went into the dining room.

Sam was slicing the cracked wheat bread she'd made the previous evening. "I still need to make toast," she said. "Tell them breakfast will be ready in a couple of minutes, would you, Gracie?"

When she went back to the dining room, the couple was sitting side by side in the middle of a rather heated conversation.

"Gracie, you're just the person we need," Erin said. "Come sit with us."

"I'm supposed to tell you breakfast will be ready in a few minutes," she said.

They didn't have any rules about joining guests at the breakfast table, although it didn't feel quite right.

"We need to talk to you about something far more important," Erin insisted.

She looked even younger than she was in a bright yellow knit top and slender-legged jeans. Her hair was pulled back in a ponytail that bobbed when she moved her head.

"Yes, please sit down," Kyle said. "We need you to solve a weighty issue."

"It's only weighty because you're so obsessed with your BlackBerry, we never have time to talk."

"That's not true. I only do what I have to. What kind of a future will we have if I lose my job?"

"Like that's going to happen! You work 24-7 because you won't turn that thing off." Erin stood up, her cheeks pink with anger.

"A wife is supposed to support her husband." Kyle sounded more depressed than angry.

"Oh, I give up. I'm not hungry for breakfast." Erin flounced out of the room, and Kyle's face went pale.

"I should go," Gracie said, distressed by the newlyweds' quarrel.

"Please don't," Kyle said. "You were such a big help to Erin when you went to the beach with her. There were a lot of things we hadn't worked out before we got married. We'd done a lot of talking this week, and I thought we both feel better about our future together. But Erin still doesn't understand my point of view."

Gracie didn't like the sound of that, but she sat down opposite the young man and wondered what she could say.

"Erin had the wrong idea when she thought I didn't want kids," Kyle said. "I'd love to have a family, only I assumed we'd wait until we were financially secure. You have children, don't you?"

"Yes, Brandon and Paige. I'm also blessed with three grandchildren." She couldn't imagine where this was going.

"But there's nothing wrong with concentrating on a career for a few years before having them, is there? All I want is a secure future for us and any children we have."

"Children are a wonderful gift from God whenever you have them," she said.

"Erin already has names picked out for ours: Destiny and Dustin." He rolled his eyes. "I like plain names like John and Jane."

"Yuck," Erin said with mock distaste as she reappeared in the doorway. "I want special names for our children."

"You have to think about whether they'll like their names. My brother Julius hates his. He gets mad at anyone who doesn't call him Duke." Kyle said. "My parents had five kids. They named all of us after relatives. My sister Clara has never been thrilled with her name either. We mostly call her Sissy."

"At least you know about big families," Erin said.

"Big dysfunctional families," her husband said.

"I was an only child. My mother died when I was really young, so I hardly remember her," Erin said, speaking to Gracie. "My stepmother was always nice to me, but she wasn't very interested in children. I spent a lot of time with my grandparents while she traveled with my father."

"That's a shame," Gracie said. That could explain why Erin had opened up to her. Her heart went out to the young woman, but she wasn't sure what advice she should give the young couple.

"I want to be around to raise my children," Erin pressed, "but I'm beginning to doubt whether I'll ever have any. Kyle is married to his job and that infernal BlackBerry. He can't even give me his full attention on our honeymoon."

"You'll know when the time seems right to have your children," Gracie said. "The important thing is to be a loving, concerned couple. It's the best gift you can give your future children."

"You're right, of course," Erin said, walking around the end of the table to hug Gracie. "I hope someday I have your faith and special goodness. I'm not at all sorry we came here to honeymoon instead of going to Hawaii. Otherwise, we wouldn't have met you."

Kyle didn't say anything, but Gracie saw him flash her a grateful smile. She said a silent prayer for their future together.

"Help yourself," Sam said, coming into the room carrying a big tray that she put on the sideboard.

"Enjoy your day," Gracie said, feeling a little better about the young couple's prospects for happiness. It bode well that they were talking about their important issues—even it meant occasional flare-ups. If they bonded and came to some understanding, their honeymoon on the island could be counted as a success.

"What was that about?" Sam asked when they were back in the kitchen.

"They just wanted to chat," Gracie said, optimistic about their future together.

"At least they aren't demanding," Sam said.

Caroline sat on one of the wooden stools beside the work area, a bowl of bran flakes in front of her.

"I read over your list of jobs, Gracie," she said. "You did a really thorough job, right down to who shovels snow in the winter. But I noticed you only gave yourself summer jobs."

"It's only a tentative schedule," she said, not really wanting to talk about moving to the island full time.

"You put in jobs I hadn't even considered," Sam said appreciatively. "You're right about polishing the banister on the stairway, not to mention cleaning the silver plate."

"I hope we can afford to hire part-time help eventually," Caroline said. "I don't mind housework, but there's more to life than cleaning and scrubbing."

"That's why I suggested having the rugs commercially carpet-cleaned every spring," Gracie said. "And there's no way one of us should climb a ladder high enough to wash windows on the second floor."

"True," Sam said. "If we're really successful, I'd like to have help with the grounds. An upscale inn has to look sharp from the outside."

"I really don't mind gardening," Gracie said, hoping to avoid more conversation about staying there in the winter.

"I think this can count as a team meeting," Caroline said.

Gracie knew her older sister liked to fly by the seat of her pants, but they had to have an orderly plan to run a place as demanding as the inn.

Caroline still didn't seem like her old self, but Gracie didn't know if her apparent doldrums were caused by disappointment about George. Or maybe Caroline had changed during their long separation. Gracie and Sam had seen each other regularly over the years, but visits with Caroline had been few and far between while she was living and working abroad.

Gracie had often felt plain and uninteresting when she compared herself to Caroline, but she was gradually feeling more confident about herself. She was still trying to understand what role she would play at the inn. Erin and Kyle's friendship made her realize she did have a lot to offer others.

Could she live on the island year-round? Even now she missed her children and grandchildren, as well as longtime friends. She was active in her church at home and participated in several other activities. She was afraid she'd feel out of place and not really needed on the island once the tourist season died down.

The companionship of her sisters as they worked toward a common goal was important, but she prayed nightly for guidance on what she should do with the rest of her life. Was she meant to live on Nantucket, or was there another path in her future?

The women stopped talking when there was a soft knock on the closed door to the kitchen. Caroline slid off her stool to answer. Gracie admired her ability to sound charming at a moment's notice.

"Mr. Grayson, how are you this morning?" she chirped, greeting him as warmly as a longtime friend.

"Please, call me Albert," he reminded her in a solemn voice. "Miss Clayworth requests her breakfast now."

"We'll bring it right up," Sam said. "Our other guests had French toast, turkey sausages, and homemade bread. And, of course, freshly squeezed orange juice and coffee I grind myself."

"I'm afraid that won't quite do," Albert said stiffly. "Miss Clayworth always has yogurt in the morning, plain yogurt, not one of the artificially flavored ones."

"Fortunately, we have that," Sam said. "What else can I give her?"

"She has her own tea, specially imported for her," he said. "All we require is a pot of hot water, very hot water."

"Very well," Sam said.

Gracie didn't know whether Sam was relieved by the guest's simple needs or annoyed because she was just hearing about the plain yogurt.

"She sometimes indulges in a few toast points or a small serving of fresh fruit," Albert went on in a concerned voice, "but this morning she's a bit tired from the trip. The yogurt and hot water will suffice."

"What would you like for breakfast?" Sam asked.

"I never eat until Miss Clayworth has breakfasted," he said.

No surprise there, Gracie thought

"Then I would be most appreciative if I might have a boiled egg, exactly three minutes, and an English muffin, lightly toasted with marmalade. I'll require a pot of very hot water also."

Gracie could see how both of them stayed so slender.

"You know we only serve breakfast," Sam reminded him.

"Of course. I'll make arrangements for Miss Clayworth's other meals, and I'll take my tea and supper in the town when it suits her."

Gracie wondered whether the poor man ever ate without his employer's permission. He was a bit formal, stuffy even, but she sympathized with the way his life revolved around Lorraine Clayworth's demands.

The day dragged by for Gracie. Most of the jobs she'd put on her chart had to be done when the inn was full, or else they came under the category of annual maintenance. The garden hadn't grown much since she'd last worked in it, so a half hour of weed pulling and bush trimming was all it required. It did raise her spirits to see that some of her sunflower seeds had peeked through the soil already. If they grew as well as they did at home, it would mean she'd brought part of Art's garden to the island with her. The thought of their golden heads saddened and cheered her at the same time.

When Gracie returned to the house, Sam suggested cooking outside on the grill for their dinner, but a drizzly rain began in midafternoon and showed no sign of letting up. Instead, they made BLTs and ate early because the newlyweds were catching the last ferry of the day.

"I'll drive them if you want me to," Caroline offered. "I haven't done anything very constructive today."

"I'll do it," Gracie said. "Now that I'm used to the Packard, I don't mind. But I am *not* wearing the chauffeur's hat. It's too big and uncomfortable."

"I guess it wasn't a great idea," Caroline conceded.

Gracie was floored. It was totally unlike her sister to give up on one of her ideas. She would rather wear the hat than see Caroline so down in the dumps. She wondered whether she'd had any word from George but decided not to ask.

The newlyweds made a noisy exit, profusely thanking Sam and Caroline for their hospitality.

"Don't be surprised if you see us again some summer," Erin said as they were leaving, both handling their own luggage.

They chatted in the backseat and pointed out places they especially wanted to remember as Gracie drove them to the ferry.

"I think I'll make a memory book when I get home," Erin said, including Gracie in the conversation.

"That's a great idea. You'll treasure it forever," Gracie said, concentrating on rain-slicked pavement on her first drive in wet conditions.

"I wondered what you'd do with the five thousand photos we took," Kyle teased.

"It wasn't that many! Can I help it if I married a photogenic man? You're the one who insisted on all those shots of me."

Gracie smiled at their good-natured teasing.

She planned to wait with them until they had to get on the ferry, but Kyle insisted she get back in the station wagon after their luggage was unloaded. Before she did, he gave her a big hug.

"You've been wonderful," he said

"I don't know what we would've done without you," Erin said. "Thanks to you, I think we both grew up a little on the island."

She put her arms around Gracie and kissed her cheek.

"You've been a joy. We'll always remember our first guests at Misty Harbor Inn."

"Me too," Erin said, her eyes suspiciously moist under a souvenir cap with Nantucket embroidered on it. "We'll let you know when Dustin or Destiny make an appearance, but now I understand why Kyle feels he has to concentrate on making a success of his job first."

"It doesn't mean I love you any less," he said, putting his arm around his wife's shoulders.

Gracie couldn't help smiling, amazed at how fond she was of the inn's first guests.

"Hopefully, we'll be back another time," Kyle said.

"We've both fallen in love with the island," Erin said. "We can't thank you enough for all you did."

"I'm so happy you enjoyed yourselves. Please do keep in touch," Gracie said. "You know how to reach us by e-mail. And bless you both. It's been a pleasure to have you here."

She watched them walk off, pulling their suitcases behind them, hurrying to get out of the steady downpour. Had she really helped them, or had their love brought them closer together? She liked to think she'd given them a little nudge in the right direction.

Their first two guests disappeared from sight as she backed the Packard out of its parking spot. Would future guests be as charming and sweet as the honeymooners? She had her doubts about Lorraine Clayworth and her faithful retainer Albert, but she cautioned herself to keep an open mind and do her best to make their stay pleasant.

CHAPTER
Fourteen

Sam brought the minivan around to the front, eager to meet her daughter at the ferry Saturday afternoon. She was in such a good mood that she brought Max with her. The inn's mascot hadn't had his usual run of the place since Wellington arrived, and he was quivering with excitement at the prospect of riding to town with his head out the window. Sam planned to keep one hand on the leash whenever she stopped.

"No more running off," she admonished the buff-colored canine, smiling as she did so. *I wonder how Max would look with a velvet leash and a big bow on his head?* she thought. *Probably silly.*

At the landing, she had time to walk Max, pacing up and down in her eagerness to see her daughter. Even when the ferry arrived, the docking procedure seemed especially slow and tedious, but Jamie was one of the first passengers off, running toward her mother and trailing a small wheeled case.

"I couldn't wait to get here," Jamie said, her light-colored hair streaming around her face in the brisk wind as she hugged her mother. "I can't believe you found a secret room. You did wait for me to do more exploring, didn't you?"

"Absolutely! I wasn't at all tempted to go back by myself after getting trapped there. But the Emerald Room is empty now. We can explore to our heart's content."

"Isn't Aunt Caroline impatient to get into it herself?"

"You'd think so, wouldn't you?" Sam said thoughtfully. "Actually, she's been pretty reserved this past week since George didn't come for the parade. And Gracie thinks it's too creepy. It's all ours to explore."

"Wonderful," Jamie said, her face animated by the prospect.

She knelt and petted Max and was rewarded with one of his special kisses—wet but enthusiastic.

Sam filled her in on their guests and the happenings at the inn on the drive back, but their conversation kept coming back to the secret room.

When they got there, Jamie didn't waste time unpacking. After the four of them visited for a short time, Sam was ready to lead the way to the hidden room. This time she was better prepared. She covered her hair with an old headscarf and put an oversized denim shirt over her knit shirt. More importantly, she grabbed a handful of dusting cloths from the bag in the pantry and made sure she had two working flashlights. It wouldn't be nearly as scary going there with Jamie, but she wasn't taking any chances.

"Do you have the spare batteries?" she asked Jamie as they stood in front of the closet in the Emerald Room.

"Yes, Mother," Jamie said with loving exasperation. "You watched me put them in my pocket before we came up. I'm surprised you had the patience to wait for me to get here."

"Gracie was adamant about not exploring by myself again. I did have a fright when the guests came back, especially when I dropped the flashlight. Test yours before we go in."

"I already have."

"I know, dear, but better safe than sorry. You have no idea how creepy it was to be trapped in there in the dark."

She opened the closet door and let her light shine on the rough surface of the inner wall.

"I never would have guessed there was anything behind there," Jamie said.

"Be careful about touching it. I got a nasty splinter opening it in the dark." Sam took a deep breath and forced the panel open to reveal the hidden space.

"Oh, and the floor slopes," she said, leading her daughter into the stuffy space. "It held me, but I don't have much confidence in it. Maybe it would be better if we don't step on the same board at the same time."

"Wow, Mom," Jamie said, shining her flashlight around the room. "This is so cool. What do you suppose is in that old trunk and the chest of drawers?"

Sam let her beam of light hover on the pieces Jamie was talking about. "That's what we're here to find out. I didn't get a chance to look inside them before the guests came back and trapped me. I thought they'd never leave!"

"I'm glad you waited for me," Jamie said, crouching as a floorboard creaked beneath her. "Wow, I can't imagine being alone in here in the dark. You must've had nightmares about it!"

"Let's just say I wasn't eager to try it again on my own."

Sam gingerly tested another floorboard. It groaned under her weight but didn't give way. She made her made her way over to the trunk and motioned for Jamie to follow her.

Directing the flashlight beam at the bulky object, Sam could see it was an old steamer truck with a heavy brass latch and leather buckles encircling the domed top. Dust coated the outside, obscuring a brass nameplate. Peering closer, Sam pulled one of the cloths from her pocket and dusted the surface, sneezing several times in the process.

"Bless you," Jamie said, craning to get a better look over her mother's shoulder.

By squinting, Sam could just make out the name on the trunk. "Oh my!" She dropped the flashlight, narrowly missing Jamie's sneaker-clad toes.

"Mother! What's wrong?"

"This is…was…Hannah Elliott Montague's trunk," she said, stooping to retrieve her torch.

"The missing whaler's wife…oh, cool…oh, wait…," Jamie said, sputtering in midsentence. "You don't think…?"

"Yes, I'm afraid I do," Sam said, knowing she and her daughter were thinking exactly the same thing: *What if someone had murdered Hannah and secreted her body in the trunk all these years?*

"They never found a trace of her. What if…" The possibility was too chilling to put into words. Sam steeled herself for the worst; she wasn't at all sure she had enough nerve to open the trunk.

"We have to open it," Jamie said. "We might be on the verge of solving a historical mystery."

Sam shared her daughter's interest in finding out the truth about why the young widow vanished one night, but she wasn't prepared to face what could be her remains.

"You're right," Sam said, "I'll do it." Grimly, she knelt down in front of the trunk. The floorboards creaked again and so did her knees as she put her flashlight down beside her. "Shine your light on it so I can use both hands."

"Mom, let me do it," Jamie said, flipping her ponytail resolutely out of her eyes.

"You may have to. I can't seem to get these buckles undone." Gritting her teeth and squinting her eyes against more dust, Sam struggled with the closures. "There, got them," she said with satisfaction.

She hesitated, afraid of what she might find when she opened the lid.

"Let's do it together," Jamie said. "On the count of three. One...two...three."

She and Jamie lifted the heavy lid at the same time and peered into the deep recesses of the trunk—and gasped.

A pile of silken material was bunched together.

"Is it...Hannah Montague?" Sam said, afraid to look. "What are you doing?" she cried, as Jamie prodded the contents of the trunk with her flashlight.

"Mother, be reasonable, if there were a body in here we'd see bones," Jamie said matter-of-factly.

Sam heaved a big sigh of relief. "This is why you're the historian, and I was the elementary school teacher. Where is my head?"

Now that it seemed safe to look in the trunk, Sam joined her daughter at gently prodding the contents.

"Well, it's not Hannah herself," Jamie said, pulling out and holding up a dress of sheer fabric. "But this seems to be a tea gown, and quite a nice one in its day. Look, here's another dress under it. It looks like most of her wardrobe is in here."

"She must have disappeared with the clothes on her back," Sam said, mystified about why any woman would leave so much behind.

Jamie nodded her head in agreement. "Wherever she was going, she must not have needed—or wanted—anything from her previous life," she said.

"If she made it to where she was going," Sam added with a shiver.

Jamie laid down her flashlight and gently shook out the dress. "Shine your light on this, would you please, Mom?"

Sam directed her beam at the silken material. She couldn't tell if it was black, gray, or some other muted color in the narrow beam of the flashlight. The room was just too dingy.

"I can't tell if this has any damage or not," Jamie said, furrowing her brow as she tried to examine the dress in the dimness.

"Why did they call them tea dresses?"

"It was a hybrid between a ball gown and a wrapper," Jamie explained. "It usually had a train and long flowing sleeves. It was called that because the lady of the house could take tea in it and then wear it for dinner with her family."

"I wonder what else is in here," Sam said, still somewhat reluctant to dig too far.

"I'd love to be able to see everything," Jamie said, gingerly laying the dress she was holding aside and pulling out a sleeveless low-necked evening gown.

Sam shone her flashlight beam around the room, looking for something she and Jamie could use to put the trunk's contents on. The floor was much too dusty.

"Maybe there are linens or something stored in the chest of drawers, something we could pile all this clothing on," she said to her daughter. "I'll take a look."

"Sounds good, Mom. I'll wait on pulling out stuff to see if you find anything."

Making her way over to the heavy bureau, Sam trailed the beam of light across the dusty top and again dusted as best she could. The chest had two small drawers over two longer drawers that in the murkiness appeared to be well made. Sam suspected it might be cherry or possibly even walnut under the dark stain, but she didn't know woods well enough to be sure. Laying the flashlight on top of the dresser, she tried opening the top two drawers; they were locked. Next she yanked on the bottom drawer. Nothing budged. Doing the same to the next one, she was rewarded for her efforts with a flurry of dust motes scattering onto her face.

"Did you find anything?" Jamie asked, edging closer for a better look.

"Just more than a hundred years' worth of dust," Sam said, sneezing and coughing at the same time. "Wait, maybe this is something." She pulled out what looked like a tablecloth in the dimness. The hemmed edges were frayed and in some cases completely gone.

Jamie stepped carefully over to her mother and took the table covering. "This will work perfectly. We can use it to carry out the contents of the trunk. I think it's too heavy to move, but we can certainly unload it, she said excitedly. "Some of these pieces might be museum quality."

"The same can't be said of this old thing," Sam said, fingering the holes in the tablecloth as she handed it over to her daughter. "I hate to think what made these holes!"

Something clanked on the floor when Jamie took the cloth in her arms.

"What was that?" Sam asked.

"I don't know." Jamie focused her light on the floor where the sound originated. "Something fell out of the material. Let me put this down and feel around." Jamie laid the bunched up tablecloth on top of the things in the trunk and knelt, feeling her way around as she let the light play on the floorboards. "Aha! Found it!' she said after several moments of searching. "It's a key."

"Let me see," Sam said holding out her palm. "I bet it unlocks the top two drawers."

Jamie gave her mother the key. "Do you want to check it out while I put the clothes on this tablecloth and carry them downstairs? We may have to make two trips."

"Yes, good idea to take them to a place where we can see them better, but wait a minute. Let's see what's in the drawers," Sam said, still not convinced there wasn't something unsavory waiting to be found…at the very least a mouse corpse.

Shining the light on the drawer on the left, she put the key in the lock and turned. Then she carefully slid the drawer out and discovered—nothing.

"This one is empty," she said, turning to Jamie. She couldn't keep the note of disappointment out of her voice. She wasn't sure what'd she'd been expecting to find, but an empty drawer wasn't it. As she opened the next drawer and prepared to sweep the interior with her flashlight, the beam went out.

"Are you okay, Mom?" Jamie asked, flashing her light in Sam's direction.

"I'm fine, but the flashlight failed before I could see if there's anything stuffed in the back of the drawer." Sam's curiosity about the possible contents of the second drawer were at odds with her squeamishness at what she might find if she felt around the space.

Jamie made her way toward her mother. "I have the spare batteries right here. If we were superstitious, we might think the light failed because there's something we shouldn't see," Sam said.

"Of course, we're not," Jamie said, "but a hidden room does inspire some creepy thoughts."

In the dimness, Sam could see her daughter fishing around in her pocket for the spares. "Oh, Mom, I'm sorry. I grabbed the wrong size from the kitchen drawer. Take my flashlight."

"I'm being silly," Sam said, sticking her hand in the murky darkness of the drawer and feeling around. "Nothing's going to bite me...wait, there is something here," she said, pressing her fingers up against the back of the small drawer.

She felt cloth under her fingers, a wad with something hard stuffed into it. Sam tried not to let her imagination run amuck while she gingerly pulled it to the front and picked it up.

"What is?" Jamie asked, shining her light on the bundle in Sam's hand.

"I don't know, but let's take it and your cache of clothes downstairs. We can unwrap it in daylight. I think we've been in here long enough." A hearty sneeze punctuated her words. Even with her daughter's presence, the secret room was an eerie place to be.

"Good idea," Jamie said. "I can't wait to see what condition these gowns are in. We can leave the rest for another time. It's sort of like not opening all my birthday gifts at once so I have the anticipation of more to come."

Sam was buoyed up by her daughter's enthusiasm but still very eager to leave the confined space. Part of her felt like an intruder in someone else's life, even though her family owned the inn now. What secrets would they discover about the woman who had mysteriously disappeared so many years ago?

Sam helped Jamie carefully lay the gowns on the outspread tablecloth. The cloth-wrapped packet from the drawer was too heavy for her pocket so she held on to it, following Jamie to the moveable panel. They passed back through the secret opening and headed downstairs, eager to see what they'd retrieved so far.

Once they were back in their own living space, Sam was able to see what she'd taken from the small drawer. It was a yellowed handkerchief used to bundle up some hard, circular objects.

"Oh!" she cried, as she undid the tight knot and a shower of coins fell out.

Jamie stooped to help her pick up the coins that spilled off the edge of the worktable. "There's a lot of money here," she said, inspecting one of the coins. "I don't know the value of these coins today, but even in the late 1800s, this must have been a sizeable accumulation."

"Look at this, Jamie," Sam said, holding out the linen handkerchief to show her daughter. "There are three crosses embroidered on it. What do you suppose they mean?"

"I think we can assume everything in the room belonged to Hannah," Jamie said, slowly examining the intricate stitching. "At least until we find proof to the contrary. But why would she hide so much money before she disappeared?

"Oh my!" Sam said.

"Mom, what? Are you okay?"

"I'm fine, but we may have found proof Hannah Montague did steal the money from the lighthouse keeper, Robert Fenton. I so wanted her to be innocent."

"You think so, Mom? I hate to think she was a thief," Jamie said with a puzzled expression.

"Remember, I told you about the old newspapers Caroline found in the attic. They implied that she was guilty, and, of course, she was never seen on the island again. She became infamous in the annals of Nantucket history because she was blamed for the theft. This could be the stolen cache."

"We should get the coins checked out sometime soon," Jamie said. "They seem to be the right period, and who knows what the coins might be worth today."

"That's a good idea," Sam said, sounding a bit far away.

"Mom, you have a funny look on your face," Jamie said. "Are you okay?"

"I'm fine. I just don't want poor Hannah to be a thief. She lived such a sad life. Her father forced her to marry an older man she didn't love, when she very much wanted to be with her young suitor. Even though it happened a long time ago, I like happy endings."

"You know how much we love a good mystery too, Mom," Jamie reminded her. "I especially like it when there's an historical component. I bet we can get to the bottom of this. Caroline and Gracie will probably be interested in helping too."

Jamie's suggestion made Sam smile. She did love a good mystery, and with Jamie's researching skills, she thought they had a good chance to find some answers. But would she be happy with what they learned about Hannah?

CHAPTER
Fifteen

Gracie thought back over her first experiences as an innkeeper as she drove the minivan toward the business district of town. The honeymooners had seemed happier when they left than when they arrived. Lorraine Clayworth remained as reclusive as she had been on the day she arrived, but she hadn't turned out to be as demanding as Sam had feared. Albert was by her side whenever she left her room, whether it was for a short late-evening walk or an occasional drive in the rented Bentley. Otherwise, the woman seldom left her suite. Gracie found herself wishing she could at least meet their mysterious guest in person.

The May day was lovely, with a brisk but warm breeze whipping across the island. Because it was so nice, Sam and Jamie had elected to walk to town and treat themselves to lunch away from the inn. They'd invited Gracie to go, but she wanted to give them time alone. Instead, she was driving to meet them on their quest to find out more about the coins they'd found in the hidden room.

Gracie allowed extra time because parking could be a problem, but she was lucky to find a place on her first run through town. Sam and Jamie wouldn't be at the antiques shop yet, but she decided to go there alone. She loved browsing through Into the Past, a three-story business on India Street. She was eager for her sister and niece to get there. If coins could burn a hole in her pocket, that's what the cache from the old trunk was doing.

As she walked through the door of Into the Past, she felt a familiar twinge of excitement. The shop had the aroma of linseed oil and lemon oil polish used on period furniture, blended with an intangible scent of age. Gracie liked to think of it as the perfume of the past. It could only be found in stores filled to the brim with antiques, whether on the island or the mainland.

Gracie was admiring a new addition to the stock, a glass-fronted walnut bookcase, when Megan Folger-Wildes, the owner of the shop, came forward to greet her. The three sisters had been frequent browsers and occasional buyers while they furnished the inn, and they were on a first-name basis with the proprietor. Today she was wearing a long forest-green skirt and a blouse that made Gracie think of a gypsy queen, which complemented her copper hair.

"Sam told me about your secret room when she called to see if I'd be working today," Megan said. "It sounds terribly exciting. I'd love to see the contents if you're thinking of selling."

"We don't know quite what we want to do. Right now we're just looking for information, especially about some coins we found. My son Brandon has been collecting coins since he was a boy, so some of his interest has rubbed off on me. We're hoping you can help us."

"I'll do my best," Megan said, "although coins aren't one of my specialties."

Gracie noticed she wasn't alone with Megan. A pair of somewhat overdressed women in designer suits and excessive costume jewelry and makeup were handling the ceramics in an antique cupboard in spite of a sign that asked customers to ask for help instead of touching the items.

"I think this is a repro," the one in yellow said.

Gracie could tell by Megan's frown that the objects in question, a pastoral pair that could've been Meissen, were indeed a genuine antique.

"It's probably a modern knockoff from China," the other one sniffed, turning up her nose at the figurine. The pair looked so much alike that Gracie sized them up as sisters.

They wandered away from the collection of lovely old ceramics and started flipping through a box of old postcards. The henna-haired woman in black grabbed a handful and carelessly shuffled through it. Fortunately each card was in a plastic holder, so they had a chance of surviving the rough handling.

"Look at this," Yellow Suit said, picking up a cut-glass decanter and flicking her finger over the surface. "Waterford."

"Pretty, but they're still making ones just like it."

"Still, I need something fancy for brandy. Harold's boss won't drink anything else. What's your best price on this?" she yelled over to Megan.

The shop owner's raised her brows and looked at Gracie, and then hid her exasperation and went over to the critical customers.

Megan politely explained her pricing on the decanter, declining to reduce it.

"I could buy one like it any day in Ireland for half the price. Last time my husband and I were in Britain, we saw these all over the place."

"Look at this," the customer in black said, jingling from all the beads she was wearing. "Remember Nana's Satsuma vase? This looks a lot like it. Can you take a hundred off the price? There's a chip here."

Gracie cringed as the woman carelessly flipped the antique Japanese vase around in her hands.

"Yes, there is a tiny fleck on the base. I took it into account in pricing it."

"Let's try someplace else. Everything here is overpriced," the henna-haired customer said.

Megan stood, hands on hips, watching the pair stomp out of the shop.

"Rude," Gracie said sympathetically.

"They have a low-end shop in Boston. I have to keep my eye on them or they'll walk out with something. They try to look like classy customers, but most dealers have their number. Now, where were we?"

Before Gracie could bring out the coins, she noticed a familiar face descending the steps from the second floor.

"Hi, Bill," she said to her friend, who was carrying an old Mason jar full of metal odds and ends.

"Gracie, what a pleasure to see you!" His hearty greeting and sparkling blue eyes brought a flush to her cheeks.

"You too," she said. "What are you buying?"

"Some bits and pieces for a new metal sculpture, a sailing ship," he said. Beside his talent for practical things like carpentry, plumbing, and electrical work, Bill was an artist who sold his work on the island.

"Sounds interesting," Gracie said.

"What are you up to?" he asked.

She briefly told him about the discovery of the secret room and its contents. "I'm waiting for Sam and my niece Jamie. We're hoping Megan can tell us something about the coins."

"A secret room," Bill said thoughtfully. "That's pretty amazing since I was all over the place doing renovations. It must have been well hidden."

"Very well hidden. Sam accidentally found it when a closet wall moved."

"Well, good luck on the coins," Bill said, going to Megan to pay for his find. Gracie was happy to see he didn't haggle.

"Nice seeing you, Gracie," he said as he left.

"Sorry if we're late," Jamie said, hurrying into the shop just after Bill left. "I convinced Mom to try on a gorgeous sapphire blue cocktail dress."

"Something I might wear once in three years," Sam said. "Needless to say, I passed on it."

"Now that you're the proprietor of a Nantucket inn, you may need to attend some formal events on the island," her daughter pointed out.

"In your dreams," Sam said, although she was obviously pleased by the idea of a special gown. "I'll worry about updating my wardrobe when the inn is one hundred percent booked."

Gracie was pleased that they were alone with the shop's owner when she took out the coins. She carefully wrapped the intricately embroidered handkerchief and laid them out on a rubber pad Megan kept on the counter so none would roll away. She was eager to hear what Megan had to say about the coins and knew her sister and niece shared her anticipation.

"We're interested in anything you can tell us about them," Sam said.

Gracie watched the antiques expert carefully scrutinize the pieces.

"They're certainly old," Megan said, "but, of course, you know that from the dates. The important thing with coins is condition. These are obviously in well-circulated condition, but I'm not an expert on grading. A tiny flaw or wear spot can make a huge difference in the retail value. I have a price guide, but it's not terribly helpful when pricing well-worn coins. If you ever go to a coin show, you'll notice the really valuable ones are inside protective holders so people can see them without touching. Even the oil on our fingers can bring down the value."

"We're not expecting to make a lot of money on them," Sam said. "We would be thrilled to know whether they could be the money stolen from the lighthouse in 1880."

"That would be hard to determine," the antiques dealer said, "unless the coins you found exactly match the amount stolen. Also there couldn't be any dated after the date of the robbery. I'm a bit over my head here, but I know someone who might be able to help."

"We would really appreciate that," Gracie said, carefully scooping up the coins and wrapping them in the handkerchief.

"My grandfather knows more about Nantucket Island than anyone else I know. I can give Grandpa Folger a call and tell him I'm sending you to see him, if you'd like."

The sisters knew about Megan's grandfather, Harry Folger, or Grandpa Folger as everyone, related or not, called him. He was a teller of tall tales and an expert on Nantucket history. If anyone could tie the coins to an actual event, he could.

"That'd be great," Sam said, and Gracie nodded in agreement.

"Thank you," Jamie said. "I'd love to talk with him and hear some of his Nantucket stories, whether he knows anything about the coins or not."

Megan went to make the call, and Gracie and Jamie browsed around the shop while Sam waited at the counter. Jamie stopped to admire an ornate silver-plated dresser set. Besides the comb, brush, and mirror, it had delicate instruments, some with mysterious uses.

"I can imagine our Hannah using something like this," Gracie said, standing beside her niece.

"I hope she got away from the island and lived happily ever after," Jamie said in a wistful voice.

"Megan's finished with her call," Sam said, summoning them.

"Grandpa Folger would be happy to talk to you," Megan said, giving them directions to his house.

After thanking Megan, Gracie, her sister, and her niece headed off to see Harry Folger. In his eighties, the man had a reputation as an entertaining storyteller, which the sisters had seen at a clambake sponsored by Harvest Chapel. But he was also known as an expert on the history of the island, so the visit would be very helpful.

"Come in, come in," Grandpa Folger said upon their arrival, exchanging pleasantries and gesturing for Gracie and her companions to sit on one of the balloon back chairs in his cozy parlor. "Now, what can I do for you fine ladies on this lovely day?" he asked, after they'd politely declined his offer to make tea.

Sam briefly related how they had found the secret room. Gracie told him about the coins. She unwrapped the bundle for the elderly gentleman to inspect, and he laid them out on a small table beside his barrel-shaped easy chair.

"Always thought that inn had secret rooms," Grandpa Folger said with satisfaction. "There were rumors to that effect as long as I can remember." He picked up a coin and peered at it through the thick lens of a magnifying glass, which reminded Gracie of Sherlock Holmes. He did the same with each coin, looking at both sides and putting them in piles after he finished his scrutiny.

Gracie felt like squirming as he painstakingly examined each one. She could see that Sam and Jamie felt antsy too, but they had to be patient. They'd come for answers about the value and origin of the coins, and it obviously took some study.

Finally, Grandpa Folger sat back and laid the heavy magnifying glass aside. He brushed aside a wisp of thin white hair and blinked his faded blue eyes as though they'd just had a workout.

"Are any of them valuable?" Gracie asked.

"You have quite a tidy sum here," he began. "In the nineteeth century, it would've been more than a workingman would see in a year. Of course, a wealthy family would be worth considerably more, but it's still an amount to reckon with."

He thoughtfully scratched his head and picked up one of the coins again. "There are a few worth a fair amount today, but there's nothing really rare or special about any of these coins," he said in a tone suggesting it was bad news. They changed hands a lot of times, judging by the wear. Collectors want coins as close to mint condition as possible."

Gracie was disappointed at the news and could tell by the look on Jamie's and Sam's faces that they were too. They hadn't talked about what to do with the coins, whether to sell them or donate them to an island museum. None of them had expected the coins to be worth a fortune, but they had hoped they were special in some way. How could they trace the origin if they were common coins in circulation everywhere at the time?

"Sorry I don't have better news for you," he said.

Gracie was thinking of another approach when her sister beat her to it.

"Mr. Folger, we had another question for you. Do you remember anything about the robbery at the lighthouse where Robert Fenton was the lighthouse keeper about 130 years ago?" Sam asked.

Harry chuckled and drummed his fingers on the table he used to examine the coins. "I'm old but not that old," he said, chortling. "What's that granddaughter of mine been saying about me?"

Gracie could see by the twinkle in his eyes he was teasing them, but Sam blushed.

"I'm so sorry!" she apologized. "I didn't mean to imply you're that ancient."

"No problem, young lady," he said. "I'm just joshing you."

Sam sat back, and Gracie had to smile at her sister. Sam would never intentionally insult anyone, certainly not an elderly man who was trying to help them. Apparently he was comfortable with his age.

"I've read stories in old newspapers, but I don't think anyone ever found out why it was in the lighthouse in the first place or who the thief or thieves were. There were plenty of rumors, though. Maybe Robert Fenton was known to be a hoarder, although I can't imagine lighthouse keepers making much. Sure wish I could tell you more about what happened," he said.

"My aunt Caroline found a newspaper at the bottom of an old box in the attic during renovations on the inn. It said a significant amount of money disappeared from the lighthouse. Would these coins be called a 'significant' amount?"

"Could be. The average workingman didn't make much. Of course, the fellers who wrote newspaper stories back then tended to exaggerate. Sold papers. Did you check the archives of the local paper to see if there was ever a follow-up story?" Grandpa Folger asked.

Sam shook her head. "We've been so busy we haven't had time."

"That whaler's widow disappeared round about the time the money did, and folks back then thought she stole it. That much I do know. What you have here could be part of what the thief took. The coins match the time period perfectly," he said.

"We certainly appreciate all your help," Gracie said as she and Jamie got up to go. Sam remained seated, gathering the coins back up in the embroidered handkerchief.

"Have you been to the historical society to look through its archives yet?" Grandpa Folger asked.

"Not yet," Gracie said, but that's a good idea. "We only just found the coins, so we haven't exhausted all the places where we might learn more."

"I do have one other suggestion for you," Grandpa Folger said, rubbing his knees. "Got a touch of arthritis," he explained as he stood up to show them out.

"We appreciate your time and any advice you can give us," Gracie said, and Sam and Jamie echoed her sentiments.

"You could go talk to Bernie Bernard over in the assisted living facility at Bayberry Commons. He's a bit of a history buff when it comes to lighthouses. He's nearly ninety and kind of hard of hearing, but all his family is gone, so I know he'd appreciate the company. We play checkers twice a month or so. Beats me every time," Grandpa Folger grumbled good-naturedly.

"What a great idea," Sam said, adding, "Do you know the best time of day to visit him?"

"He's at his best in the morning. He likes to take a nap in the afternoon before supper. Try to catch him fairly early," Grandpa Folger advised.

They thanked Megan's grandfather again and promised to let him know if they discovered any interesting information.

"This island has more than its share of secrets," he said as they left. "Some good and some not so good. If you start turning over rocks, don't be surprised at what crawls out."

It seemed like an ominous warning from an otherwise genial gentleman.

Gracie drove home, lost in thought. She was more than willing to follow any lead. She knew her sister and niece loved a good mystery, and she liked loose ends tied up. She had never considered herself a particularly curious person. So what was it about Nantucket Island, with its secret rooms and unsolved mysteries, that called to her so powerfully?

CHAPTER
Sixteen

Gracie flopped down on a cushioned recliner on the inn's expansive back porch and kicked off her sandals. The sun was warm on her face, and she needed a few moments to sort out everything happening at the inn. They'd had extra guests on the weekend, and the couple had been very complimentary when they left, especially praising Sam's breakfasts. Her sister had gone out of her way by preparing eggs Benedict one morning and a breakfast pizza the next, a recipe she invented herself. It was loosely based on a fruity dessert pizza and served with cheesy eggs.

"A penny for your thoughts," Caroline said, coming out to join her and pulling up a wicker chair.

"Just mulling over the last couple of weeks," Gracie said. "I guess the highlight was Sam and Jamie exploring the hidden room. It's amazing how it remained hidden for so long. I don't care to go in there myself, but the things they brought out are fascinating."

"I wanted to talk to you about that," Caroline said. "Do you think we know enough about Hannah and the inn to plan our first history program?"

"We won't be doing the tea parties until later when the tourist season is at its peak, will we?" Gracie shifted in her chair to face her sister.

"No, but I thought we could plan ahead in case we get too busy later."

Caroline wasn't known for doing things before they needed to be done, so Gracie was a bit surprised by her suggestion.

"I guess we could get started," she agreed. "Unless you want to wait until Jamie gets back from her trip to town. She's really keen on history."

"As long as we have a little free time, I thought the two of us could go over everything we've learned so far. What do you think of displaying the gowns as part of the program?"

"People would love to see them, but we'd have to find a way to protect them. I wouldn't want people touching them," Gracie said.

"Maybe we could hang them on a portable rack and use plastic bags, the kind bridal shops use to protect their gowns," Caroline said. "There were enough items in the trunk to start our own little museum, maybe in the parlor since guests probably won't hang out there when there's so much to do on the island."

This was the kind of thinking Gracie expected from her older sister. She wasn't sure about leaving the fragile gowns on display, but it was good to hear a creative idea from Caroline. She couldn't help but wonder if George had contacted her. The last she'd heard, he was still in Europe—whether for business or pleasure Caroline hadn't said.

"Wouldn't it be nice if we could model them?" Gracie said wistfully.

"I don't think my waistline was small enough when I was ten," Caroline said with a light laugh. "The length might be right, but I'm sure they're too fragile to let out the seams. We're still not sure about commercial dry cleaning. An antique fabric specialist would know." She put her hands behind her head in a pensive pose.

"Why don't we have another look at them now?" Gracie suggested. "Sam's at the market, but she's been doing some online research about fashion in the 1870s. I think she printed out some information and left it in the library with the clothes."

"Why not?" Caroline asked, lazily rising and stretching. "I don't know what's the matter with me lately. I seem to be running on empty in the energy department."

Gracie had a pretty good idea why. Caroline had expected George to be a frequent visitor on the island, but so far he'd completely let her down. She wished there was some way to console her, but her sister wasn't like the honeymooners who had come to appreciate her counsel. In fact, it would be a very bad idea to give her sister advice of any kind. The success of the inn depended on the three of them working together in harmony. Gracie didn't want to cause dissension with unwanted advice.

They walked together to the library where the contents of the trunk were spread out on protective sheets.

"I have an idea too," Gracie said. "After we give a history talk, why don't we ask the audience to help solve the mystery? Chances are nothing would come of it, but maybe someone would know something."

"Good idea," Caroline said. "We might get lucky and have a descendent of a nineteenth century islander in the audience. I have an idea for a title. We can call our first talk 'The Unsolved Mystery of Misty Harbor Inn.'"

"I love it," Gracie agreed as they walked into the library. "Which dress is your favorite?"

"If I had to wear one, I'd pick the riding habit, mainly because it's tailored and doesn't have a bustle." Caroline walked over to a russet-colored jacket and the black skirt that had been folded next to it in the trunk."

"According to Sam's research, they wore a chemisette under it, a kind of high-collared shirt. Of course, the well-dressed woman would wear a hat. It's a shame we didn't find any in the trunk."

"They were probably kept in hat boxes," Caroline said, skimming through the sheath of information Sam had found about 1870s fashion. "What's your favorite?"

"If I were actually going to wear one, I'd pick the summer cotton. It's a little discolored with age, but I imagine it was originally a dazzling white. It's amazing how someone embroidered all those tiny lavender and yellow flowers on the skirt. It would be like wearing a garden." She gazed at the gown of her choice, trying to imagine how it would feel to wear yards and yards of material.

"We tend to think of the Victorians as prudish, but this silk ball gown is certainly cut low, even by modern standards," Caroline said. "Wouldn't it be fun to have a mannequin to display the dresses? We could change the gown from to time so none were exposed to light and air for a long period."

"It would be fun to hunt for suitable accessories in antique shops," Gracie said.

"We could add period accessories like a choker necklace or a jeweled collar."

"According to Sam's research, ladies wore gloves quite a bit, even inside. Sometimes they went to the elbow or even the shoulder.

We could do one of our tea talks on women's fashion when the inn was built." Gracie was getting excited about putting together their history presentations.

"Pardon me." Miss Clayworth's cultured voice interrupted their conversation, much to Gracie's surprise.

In the time she'd been a guest, the elderly actress had rarely made an appearance. Albert conveyed all her requests. She was only seen to leave the inn at dusk, when the pair walked the dog together.

After her initial spate of requests, she had turned out to be an ideal guest, asking little and never causing trouble. Gracie had wondered why she bothered to come all the way to Nantucket, when she obviously wasn't taking advantage of the many interesting things to do on the island.

"What can we do for you, Miss Clayworth?" Caroline asked before Gracie could get over the surprise of having their reclusive guest seek them out.

"May I come in?" she asked, still lingering at the library door.

"Of course, please do," Gracie said. "Let me clear a chair for you. We've been going over some clothing we found in an old trunk. We believe they belonged to a young woman in the 1870s."

"They certainly date from that period," the elderly woman said, ignoring Gracie's offer of a place to sit. "My, the Oriental silk is lovely. I wore something very like it when I appeared in *The Importance of Being Earnest* on the London stage. What memories it brings back. I was afraid the mauve would do awful things to my complexion, but it actually was flattering."

She ran beautifully manicured fingers over the bodice, her touch so gentle it didn't even move the cloth.

"The skirt was too long, even by period standards, and I was terrified I'd trip over it. Fortunately for my career, I got through the whole run without embarrassing myself. And I absolutely loved wearing the period finery. I grew up in a rather poor family and loved playing an aristocrat."

Gracie was dumbfounded. The last thing she'd expected was to hear the reclusive actress reminiscing over a stage role, but she was delighted to be able to talk to her.

"Was that before you came to America to make movies?" she asked.

"Yes, I was discovered on the London stage. I was young and terribly excited to be in Hollywood, but the stage remained my first love. I shudder when I think of some of the films I starred in. I would love to have done A *Streetcar Named Desire* or *The Glass Menagerie*, but my studio wasn't producing cinema of that quality."

"How many films did you do?" Caroline asked.

"Oh dear, no one has asked me that in such a long time. I did eleven I could be proud of, but there were others I'd simply rather not count. Can you imagine? Once they wanted me to appear in some dreadful wig and a dress my housecleaner wouldn't wear. Fortunately, my agent found a way to release me from my contract before I became a caricature of myself. I felt so sorry for Bette Davis, doing that dreadful horror piece after all her acting triumphs. I sometimes think Loretta Young was right to retire before they cast her in roles requiring frumpy costumes."

Gracie couldn't imagine Lorraine Clayworth looking anything but dignified and elegant. Today she was wearing a pale green sheath with a flowered jacket so transparent it seemed to float around her slender form. Her flat-heeled slippers perfectly matched the green of her dress, and, as usual, she was wearing a hat, a wide-brimmed straw adorned with a circle of silk daisies.

The elderly actress circled the room, apparently mesmerized by the display of period clothing.

"I see you have a very well-made corset," she said without picking up the garment. "They were originally made with whalebone, but I suspect this one has steel stays."

Gracie was impressed by Miss Clayworth's grasp of historical clothing, but she still wondered what had brought her out of seclusion.

"A dear friend of mine wore a jacket like this when she did *Hamlet* in a nineteenth century setting. It was a dreadful production. It closed in three weeks, but what it lacked in acting talent, it made up for in elegant costumes. Seeing these lovely garments has made me homesick for the theater."

Gracie glanced at Caroline, and it was obvious her sister was as intrigued by Lorraine Clayworth as she was. And what had made her so talkative after days of silence?

"Oh yes, I do have a request to make," the actress said, obviously tearing herself away from the antique garments. "Would it be possible to extend my stay? I was considering a tentative date of July first for my departure, if my suite hasn't been reserved for other guests."

Gracie wanted to jump up and down and shout *hurray*. Caroline's face showed how delighted she was. All three of them had been worried because no one had booked the suite beyond Miss Clayworth's stay. They couldn't afford to have their most expensive accommodations stand empty for the rest of the summer, and the sisters had grown to appreciate the elegant British actress and her assistant as guests. Even Wellington had behaved himself, although one accidental encounter with Max had shown he could hold his own in any barking contest.

"I'll have to check our reservations, but offhand, I'm pretty sure we can accommodate you," Caroline said in her best innkeeper's voice.

Gracie wasn't as good as her sister at hiding her feelings. "We'll be delighted to have you," she said.

"Splendid," Miss Clayworth said. "I underestimated how long it would take to write my memoirs. I started doing them in longhand, but Albert has convinced me to learn the computer. I have to admit my little laptop is efficient. Some names have faded from my memory after so many years, but the world I loved is right there, waiting to be rediscovered at my fingertips."

"You must have known so many famous people," Gracie said, feeling naïve as soon as she said it.

"It's not important how many celebrities you know," the actress said with the ghost of a smile. "It's how many know you."

"Who was your all-time favorite leading man?" Caroline asked.

"My dear, I was madly in love with all my leading men," she said. "Almost from infancy, I yearned to appear opposite Sir Laurence Olivier, but it was never to be. But I was privileged to know so many great performers: John Gielgud, David Niven, Alec Guinness, James Mason. My mind simply reels when I try to think of just one."

"Then we'll just have to read your memoir when it's published," Caroline said with her most winning smile.

"I'll instruct Albert to send you a copy as soon as it's published," she said in her regal voice. "Now I must get on with my work. I'm so pleased to be able to remain here until it's finished."

"It's our privilege," Gracie said as Miss Clayworth gracefully exited the library.

"She flows when she walks," Caroline said when their guest was out of hearing.

"I've never seen anyone so graceful, and she must be in her eighties," Gracie marveled.

"I thought I was familiar with English accents," Caroline said, "but I can't place hers. Her speech is so refined and melodious, I could listen to her all day."

"I wonder if she ever married?" Gracie said.

"No—well, actually, her niece told me that, but I looked her up online. She had a fabulous career and more male admirers than Elizabeth Taylor, but she never had a husband. On one site she was quoted as saying she was married to her career."

"I wonder where Albert comes in," Gracie said. "He seems to obey her every whim, but we've had hints that he's pretty strong-minded himself."

"He must have a good life working for her," Caroline said in an offhand way. She stood. "I'm going to go write her name in the reservations book."

"Or else he cares for her a great deal," Gracie said, hoping that was the reason for his devotion.

When Gracie was alone with the antique clothing, she wandered from item to item, visualizing them on a beautiful woman like Lorraine Clayworth. The actress was still a beauty. Unlike so many public figures who used artificial means to look young, the elderly actress wore her winkles like badges of honor and was more attractive for it. She had striking cheekbones and a perfectly shaped nose. She'd resisted the temptation to flesh out her thinning lips with injections or garish lip coloring. Her only makeup seemed to be the powder that softened the hallmarks of age.

Gracie stared at her favorite dress, what she called the flower-garden gown. It struck her that Miss Clayworth very likely could fit into it. The slender lines of her body wouldn't need help from the uncomfortable corset.

She picked up what she saw as an instrument of torture and wondered how anyone could breathe in it. If the corset had belonged to Hannah, as was almost certain, would the young wife have suffered when she wore it? Gracie tried to visualize her in the gowns she'd left behind. Certainly her rich husband hadn't spared any expense to let her dress fashionably in expensive clothing, but possessions could never compensate for the absence of love in a woman's life.

Gracie felt blessed to have had a husband who never wavered in his love for her. She still felt close to him, sometimes talking to him in her head. What would he have said about leaving their home to live on the island? Would he want her to put her all into this new venture, or was her place still in the house they'd shared? Maybe she would find the answer when the sunflowers bloomed—the most poignant reminder she had of the man she loved.

No doubt her children could manage well without her close presence, but could she make a permanent home away from them? Much as she loved her sisters, she missed Portland and the family and friends she had there.

Whenever she had difficult decisions to make, she liked to spend time in her garden. Prodded by thoughts of moving, she went again to the inn's flowery bower without bothering to get her hat or gardening equipment.

The spring flowers, especially the daffodils, were beyond their glory days, but everywhere she looked, there was a promise of summer blooms. Would her sunflower seeds grow to magnificent heights and spread their faces to the sun?

She silently prayed for an answer to her dilemma. Should she sell her house and move to the island year-round? She felt obligated to help her sisters but she wanted to live close to her grandchildren too.

Was Sam happy with her new responsibilities? She'd loved teaching. Could inn-keeping give her the same satisfaction? And what about Caroline? She'd been wildly enthusiastic while they were renovating the inn and preparing to open. Now she was much more subdued. Was it only because George was staying in Europe instead of coming to the island? Or would Nantucket be too small after her years of traveling and writing?

Gracie looked up at the upper floors of the pale yellow inn and wondered if the unhappiness of the past could be erased by new energy and purpose. Why had Hannah been so miserable there that she'd disappeared, never to be heard from again? Or had she left the island of her own volition?

Gracie wasn't going to be content until she knew the fate of the young widow.

CHAPTER
Seventeen

Caroline went to the foyer before breakfast to check the reservations for the first week in June. Guests had trickled in during May, but she had hopes that summer would mean a full house most of the time. The success of the inn was weighing heavily on her lately—something she never would have expected. In fact, nothing had gone quite the way she'd expected, least of all that George would stay away so long.

He'd finally called the night before, but their short conversation hadn't told her any of the things she wanted to know. Did he still care about her? Would he visit the island before the end of summer? Had she made the worst mistake of her life when she turned down his proposal?

At least she knew where he was: London. Why he was still there or when he would come back to the States was a mystery to her. The last thing she needed was one more puzzling thing to worry about. Along with her sisters, Caroline had been drawn into the mysterious disappearance of the inn's early resident, and now she thought about it constantly.

Before she could go to the kitchen for her breakfast, she saw Albert coming down the stairs. For a change he wasn't carrying Wellington, although he faithfully walked the Yorkie before his own breakfast every morning. He was dressed in a very formal-looking black suit and gray striped tie without his signature vest. Besides one of the pair's smaller suitcases, he was carrying a rain garment over his arm, no doubt because the weather report called for scattered showers throughout the day.

"Miss Marris," he said, hurrying up to her. "I have an urgent matter to take care of for Miss Clayworth. It requires me to be in Boston overnight. I should be able to return on the first afternoon ferry tomorrow."

"Would you like a ride to the dock?" Caroline asked.

"No, thank you. I'll avail myself of the Bentley. There are two things you can do, if you would be so kind. Could you prepare a light repast for Miss Clayworth's tea? She won't require dinner, but a cup of soup and perhaps some toast would be very welcome. She generally likes it around 4:45 in the afternoon."

"Of course, we'll be happy to," Caroline agreed. "And the other?"

"It's difficult for her to carry Wellington down the stairs, and they are a bit steep for him to negotiate on his own. Do you know a dog walker who could take him out at least three times today and once tomorrow morning? They needn't be long walks, but he does need a bit of exercise. We would expect to pay for the extra service, of course."

"That won't be necessary," Caroline said. "We'll be happy to see to Wellington's needs."

"Very kind, I'm sure," he said, although the frown creasing his brow grew even more pronounced. "I do hate to leave Miss

Clayworth, but she insists I see a literary agent in person on her behalf. She thinks perhaps her memoirs should be published in the United States since her film career was here."

Caroline smiled to herself at Albert's concern. He looked immensely unhappy about leaving his employer, and she remembered Gracie's theory that he served the aging actress out of love.

"We'll take care of everything," Caroline assured him. "Have a pleasant trip."

"Yes, yes, thank you. I'll be back before teatime tomorrow. Miss Clayworth will be most grateful for your help."

As he walked out, Caroline still wondered why he was so edgy. Was he jittery about the interview in Boston? Or was he upset about leaving Miss Clayworth alone?

When she got to the kitchen, Sam was loading the dishwasher after the guests' breakfast. They had one couple staying in the Periwinkle Room. The inn wasn't fully booked until the weekend. This was one of the days when Caroline doubted whether they should have purchased the inn, although neither of her sisters seemed overly concerned. Even Gracie, who wasn't an optimist by nature, hadn't been fretting over the empty rooms. Were they just sparing her because they felt sorry about George?

"I have a few cinnamon buns left if you'd like one for breakfast," Sam said.

"No thanks. I'm going to gain weight if I eat too much of your baking."

"Like you would," Sam teased. "I bet you don't weigh any more than you did in high school."

"I wish!" Caroline said. "By the way, Albert just left for the mainland. He'll be gone overnight."

"Really! He never leaves Miss Clayworth alone for more than an hour, as far as I've noticed," Sam said. "It must be something important to take him away from her."

"I don't think he was keen on leaving her now. He's going to Boston to talk to a literary agent on her behalf. He did ask us to give her a nice tea, maybe soup and toast, but she doesn't care for dinner."

"I can do better than soup," Sam said. "Maybe chicken a la king on toast or a soufflé."

"Maybe you should check with her first. She likes to eat at around 4:45," Caroline added. "Also, Albert needs us to take care of Wellington. I'll do that."

"You'll do what?" Gracie asked, coming into the kitchen.

"Albert will be gone until tomorrow afternoon. I assured him we'd take care of Miss Clayworth and her Yorkie."

"No problem," Gracie said. "I can't imagine guests who are less trouble. I wasn't sure when they first came, but they really don't ask much of us."

"You two can take care of your own breakfast," Sam said. "I managed to get an appointment for a haircut. It seems none of us ever has time for life's little necessities."

"Enjoy yourself. Get a manicure too," Caroline said. "You've been slaving away lately."

"It's my own fault for putting so much time into my baking. I have a tearoom owner interested in buying my cranberry bread on a regular basis. I need to firm things up with her while I'm in town. Is there anything either of you need?"

Gracie shook her head. Caroline did have one request: "Would you mind buying a stamp while you're there? I think I'll write a letter to George."

"No problem. Should I ask how much the postage is to England?"

"Yes, I guess so. Thanks."

Gracie brought out a box of cereal and poured orange juice for both of them, quickly setting the table for their breakfast. Watching her go through the simple routine, Caroline wondered what was on her mind. She looked unusually preoccupied.

"Have you talked to your kids lately?" she asked.

"Yes, Brandon called last night, and Paige texts or writes long e-mails when she can. Brandon and Stacy are hoping to visit before the summer's over, and, of course, I'd love to see the grandkids."

"Is something bothering you?" Caroline knew her sister too well to be fooled by her artificial cheerfulness.

"No—well, yes, sort of. Living on the island is a big decision for me. I'm still not convinced I belong here."

"Of course, you do! What could be better than the three Marris sisters fulfilling Mom's dream of living on Nantucket Island? We had such wonderful times here when we were young," Caroline said in her most persuasive voice.

"Yes, we did," Gracie agreed, "but I have a family now. Maybe I should live closer to them."

"Maybe," Caroline said, deflated by her sister's doubts about the island. "I hope I didn't rush you into something that's making you unhappy."

"Not at all. I made the decision on my own. You're not to blame in any way. I've just been wondering if I'll be happy staying here year-round."

Caroline poured out a serving of cereal and then realized she had absolutely no appetite.

"Sometimes things don't turn out the way we expect," she said thoughtfully.

"I haven't wanted to ask. I hate to see you looking so unhappy," Gracie said. "When is George coming back to this country?"

"I've no idea," Caroline said, holding back an impulse to cry. "I don't even know why he's staying in London so long. This is his busy season at the boat yard, the one time I'd expect him to be here. Sometimes I think he's doing it to avoid me."

"I don't believe that," Gracie said, walking over to her sister and putting her arms around her shoulders.

"I didn't take his marriage proposal seriously enough. I thought we could work things out when I wasn't so busy with the inn. The last thing I expected was for him to take it as rejection. That's why I want to write a letter. Maybe I can explain how I feel. I am a good writer, so maybe I can better explain why I said no to his proposal. The few times he called, he didn't want to talk about it."

"We're a sorry pair," Gracie said with a sound halfway between a laugh and a cry. "Middle-aged with no idea what we really want for the rest of our lives."

"I guess all we can do is put our faith in the Lord and pray that things work out for the best," Caroline said. "It's just that I can't imagine a life without George in it. We're such a good fit. He's calm and understanding—at least he used to be. I've never known him to do an unkind thing, and he's fun to be around. We joke that we complement each other, since we're practically opposites."

"I always thought he cared a lot for you, even though I don't know him well. I suspect things will work out between you. He may be in London working on some big deal," Gracie assured her.

"He may have too much on his mind right now to deal with your relationship, but he loves you. I'm sure of it."

"Do you think so?" Caroline caught a tear making its way down her cheek. "I had a hard time being around our first guests, the honeymooners. They made me wonder what I'd missed by not getting married when I was young. I had offers, you know, but the time never seemed right. There were so many other things I wanted to do."

"You've had an adventuresome life," Gracie said. "It never would've suited me. All I ever wanted was a husband who would love me all my life and, of course, children and grandchildren."

"You're a born caregiver," Caroline said with a small smile. "Now I may be the one who needs you the most. I don't know when I've ever felt so—unsettled."

"I want to be there when you need me," Gracie said in a soft voice.

Caroline threw both arms around her sister. "Thank the Lord, I have you and Sam. I don't want to live alone anymore."

"I understand how you feel," Gracie said, her eyes tearing. "Now, do we have to take Wellington out?"

"Let's do it together," Caroline said. "I can't remember the last time we had a really good girl-talk."

Sam had brought the stamp when she got back from town, but Caroline wasn't sure what she wanted to say to George. She didn't even know if the letter would catch up with him before he came back to the States. All she knew for sure was that sisters were a blessing she'd overlooked most of her life. Her long talk with Gracie had given her spirits a badly needed lift. She hoped all three of them would become year-round residents of Misty Harbor Inn, but if her sister felt compelled to return to her family in Portland, she would understand.

Caroline was the last one to go to bed, although she hoped for a better night's sleep than she'd been having lately. She still didn't know where she stood with George. Gracie's counsel had given her new hope, if not for reconciliation with the man she loved, at least for future happiness at the inn.

When the lights were out, she lay in bed for a long time, tired but not sleepy. She toyed with the idea of getting up for hot milk, but it wasn't her favorite beverage. Eventually she had to doze off, didn't she?

Cuddled in the light blanket that was still needed on a cool island night, she thought of all the wonderful times she and George had shared. He'd taught her to love the sea, and she'd brought out his sense of humor.

Just when she thought she was ready to drop off, she heard a thump above her head. The inn could be a creaky place with noisy plumbing and the house settling, but this seemed to be a new sound. It wasn't the wind in the eaves or the distant slap of waves on the beach. She sat upright and listened hard until she realized it had come from Miss Clayworth's suite directly above her.

Albert was away for the night. Had something happened to their elderly guest? With her heart in her throat, she stuck her feet in the slippers by the bed, pulled on her lightweight cotton robe, and raced to get the duplicate key to Miss Clayworth's room.

Everything was silent in the foyer. She hurried up the stairs, driven by anxiety for the welfare of their elderly guest. When she reached the door, she knocked softly, then more insistently.

"Miss Clayworth, are you all right?"

"I think so."

"May I come in? I have a key."

For several long moments she didn't hear anything from inside the room, and then a weak voice gave her permission to enter. She unlocked the door and opened it as quickly as possible, touching the light switch on the wall as she went in.

"My dear, I'm so glad you heard me," the elderly woman said from where she sat in the wicker chair. "I did a foolish thing. I couldn't sleep, so I wanted to find the book I've been reading. Unfortunately, I tripped and fell."

"Are you hurt? Should I call an ambulance?" Caroline asked, trying not to panic.

"No, please no. I don't seem to be injured. It's all my fault. I threw my robe around my shoulders instead of putting it on. It got twisted around my feet, and I fell. Albert's going to be very upset with me. Usually, I ring a bell when I need something in the night."

"Would you like me to help you back to bed?" Caroline asked, stooping beside the guest.

Caroline tried to figure out the easiest way to help her out of the chair. She guided Miss Clayworth's arms into a lovely ivory silk robe with embroidered vines and flowers. She still had the problem of getting the woman to her feet without doing any damage to her frail body.

"Maybe I should call my sisters to help," she said. "I don't want to hurt you."

"You won't. I believe I can walk now. It's only my dignity that's injured. I promised Albert not to wander in the night. He most certainly will be upset with me if he finds out I've fallen."

"He won't find out from me," Caroline said, a little surprised by Miss Clayworth's concern about her assistant. "Now take my arm, and I'll try to ease you out of the chair."

Caroline helped her up, surprised because she seemed to weigh little more than Gracie's eight-year-old granddaughter Evelyn.

"You are a dear," the actress said when she was safely sitting on the side of her bed.

"Now, tell me honestly, do you hurt anywhere? I'm sure I can get a doctor to come check you out."

"It's totally unnecessary. I can't thank you enough for coming to check on me. Oh, come here, my little darling," she said to Wellington who nuzzled her feet and begged to be lifted.

"I rely on Albert so much," Miss Clayworth said. "I don't know what I would do without him. I never married or had children, something I think about more and more as I grow older."

"You must have had many opportunities," Caroline said, meaning to be kind.

"Oh yes, but I was married to the theater, heart and soul. My suitors never would've understood why I couldn't put them first in my life."

"Do you have regrets?"

"Regrets?" The actress had a faraway look that Caroline couldn't read. "Lorraine Clayworth lived to act. I don't know if I'm that person anymore. My parents are long gone—they never did completely approve of my career. My only living relative is Sophie. I'm afraid my great niece and I don't share a close bond, although she was kind enough to find your lovely inn for me. To answer your question, the elderly woman you see before you does regret never finding a soul mate. Growing old is so much harder when you do it alone."

Caroline helped settle the fragile actress back into bed and made sure Wellington was in his cushioned dog bed. She brought water for both of them and then turned out the bedroom light.

"I'll leave the table lamp on in the sitting room and crack your door a bit," Caroline said. "Here's my cell phone number written on this pad. If you need anything at all, use your bedside phone to call me."

"I can't thank you enough for your kindness," Miss Clayworth said in a weary voice. "I do believe I'll be able to sleep now."

"Good night," Caroline whispered as she backed out of the room.

Would she end up an elderly woman with only a paid companion? Had she ruined any chance of happiness with George? Caroline quietly returned to her bed, but sleep was elusive.

"This isn't the way I wanted it to be," she said, wishing more than ever that George would come to the island to be with her.

CHAPTER
Eighteen

"It's a shame we couldn't visit Bernie Bernard sooner," Gracie said. The promise of summer radiated in the early June morning as she and Sam drove to Bayberry Commons.

"Yes, it's a shame he was too ill to see us, but the director of the assisted living facility said he's much better and eager for company," Sam said.

"Maybe we'll finally talk to someone who can shed light on Hannah's destiny," Gracie mused, although she wasn't optimistic. The days of bustles and forced marriages seemed so far removed from the present. It was a lot like reading a book and having to search for a missing chapter.

"Jamie really wanted to come with us. Unfortunately, she scheduled the video chat with her major professor weeks ago. She needs help with some research before he leaves on the student tour of Great Britain he leads every year," Sam said.

Gracie knew Jamie was disappointed she couldn't join them on this leg of the investigation. Still, she would be eagerly awaiting the results.

The sound of children singing filled the air as Gracie and Sam entered the lobby of the assisted living facility. A Brownie troop was serenading residents who were scattered around an inviting commons area. A few were in wheelchairs while others were sitting on overstuffed couches or straight-backed padded chairs.

They didn't know how to recognize Mr. Bernard, so they made their way toward a reception desk, hoping he was in his room waiting for them.

"Oh, look," Sam said, pausing to listen to the singers for a few moments. "Aren't they sweet?"

"Yes, they are," Gracie agreed. "I didn't know Brownies had activities year-round. Guess I'm out of touch with those kinds of things."

Gracie couldn't help but notice the wistful look in her sister's eyes.

"You miss teaching, don't you?" Gracie asked.

"Sometimes I miss it a lot," Sam admitted. "Don't get me wrong. I'm very happy with my life the way it is, but it meant a lot to me to be able to get children off to a good start in school. Every new class had its challenges." She smiled. "I loved each and every child, even the naughty ones. What I don't miss is the staggering amount of paperwork. It got worse every year until I hardly had time for teaching."

"Maybe you can find some volunteer opportunities here," Gracie suggested. "Once the season is over, the inn won't take so much of your time.

"I've thought about it," Sam said just as they reached the reception desk where a woman was talking on the phone. "But I must say I'm enjoying my baking. I think it has a good chance of growing into a profitable side business."

The receptionist gave them an apologetic shrug and motioned for them to sit at two chairs in front of her desk.

Gracie was about to say something more when the receptionist hung up the phone.

"I'm sorry," the curly-haired woman said to them. "How can I help you?"

"We're here to see Mr. Bernie Bernard," Gracie said. "He's expecting us."

The receptionist smiled. "He'll be delighted to have visitors. We're so happy about his recovery. He's one of our favorite residents, always cheerful even when he isn't feeling well.

"Where can we find him?" Sam asked.

The woman consulted a chart.

"This morning Mr. Bernard should be in the recreation room. I don't see him listening to the Brownies—aren't they cute?—so you should find him there. He's the reigning checkers champion, so he'll be defending his title. We run a competition once a month."

With an air of polished efficiency, the woman issued visitors' badges and gave them directions to the area.

"Just a formality," she said. "We don't allow solicitors or anyone who might prey on the elderly."

Clipping the identification badge onto the pocket of her pink and white striped polo shirt, Gracie led the way while Sam followed.

"I hope he can shed some light on this mystery," Sam said as they walked down a tiled hall with immaculate black and white squares.

Paintings by local artists hung every few feet, most of them landscapes of the island or the sea. Gracie was interested to see that most had price tags discreetly placed on the frames. A sign indicated that proceeds from the donated art would be used to enhance the facilities

Gracie agreed with her sister about finding some kind of solution. She wasn't the mystery aficionado her sister and niece were, but the coins and their connection to the missing whaler's widow had piqued her interest. She always preferred books and movies with happy endings. She fervently hoped Hannah's story would have a "happily ever after" conclusion.

"Here we are," the receptionist said to Sam, who was looking around the room for someone who met the description Grandpa Folger had given them.

Bernie Bernard wasn't hard to pick out among the checker players in the pleasantly furnished room. Unless she was very wrong, he was the round-cheeked, balding man with a fringe of snowy white hair encircling his pate and standing out in feathery tufts.

"Checkmate," crowed the winner of the game, taking the last red checker on the board.

"Checkmate is only in chess, and you know it," his lanky opponent said, gathering up the red and black checkers and slipping them into a bag.

"I just like saying it." The winner of the game chortled. "Let's play another game just for fun."

"No, you've won another championship. That's enough for me today," the defeated player said.

Gracie could tell both men took their play seriously, and the loser had had enough. It looked like the perfect time for Sam and her to introduce themselves.

"Mr. Bernard," she said loudly, hoping he could hear her over the din of the two televisions turned on at different ends of the room.

"Eh?" he said, turning to her and Sam as his friend went off to watch a spirited game of Monopoly.

"I think Grandpa Folger called you before your illness," Gracie said after they'd introduced themselves. "He said no one knows more about lighthouses than you do."

"He said that, did he?" the elderly gentleman said with a chuckle. "Well, I know a thing or two. What is it you want to know?"

"We're interested in Robert Fenton," said Gracie. "We understand there was a robbery when he was the lighthouse keeper. We're the new owners of Misty Harbor Inn."

"Quite by accident, I discovered a hidden room," Sam said. "When we explored it, we found a cache of coins wrapped in an embroidered handkerchief. We wonder whether they have any connection to the money stolen from Robert Fenton."

"We have all kinds of questions," Gracie said, getting into the spirit of inquiry. "Why would a lighthouse keeper have a sizeable amount of money? Is it possible the whaler's widow really stole it, and if so, why not take it with her when she left the island?"

"So you see, Mr. Bernard, we're hoping you can shed some light on this, no pun intended," Sam said.

"Please, ladies, call me Bernie," he said. "Why don't we go back to my room where it's quieter, and I'll be happy to answer your questions."

"That would be wonderful," Sam said.

Gracie offered her arm to Bernie, who rose stiffly from the chair. Grasping a cane with an ornately carved top, he ushered them toward the door.

"Is that a whalebone carving on your cane?" Gracie asked, intrigued by what she could see under his thick-fingered grip.

"That it is. It's called scrimshaw. Belonged to my grandfather before me, and still as sturdy as a hickory tree. He moved his hand to show her an elaborately carved female head reminiscent of the figureheads on sailing ships.

After Gracie admired it, Sam said, "It's really nice of you to see us. We've hit a dead end so far when it comes to the stolen money."

"My pleasure," he said, chuckling mischievously. "I can't wait to see what it will do to my reputation around here if I'm seen escorting two such lovely ladies as yourselves to my room. You wouldn't happen to be checkers players, would you?"

"I wouldn't be any competition for you," Gracie said. "My grandchildren clobber me, and they're still little."

Gracie thought she wasn't sure what she'd been expecting Bernie to be like, but it certainly wasn't a nonagenarian ladies' man! Still, his flirting was fun, and she liked him already. Maybe she would continue to drop in to see him from time to time—that is, if she decided to become a permanent resident of the island. Her mind kept bumping against her dilemma, even when she was concerned with something entirely different.

Once they were settled into comfortable upholstered chairs in his cozy sitting room, Gracie waited expectantly while Bernie went to a little dormitory-sized refrigerator and pulled out a bottle of lemon-lime soda. He located three glasses and poured the bubbly liquid into them, handing one to Sam and one to her.

"I'm supposed to watch my sugar intake," the round little man said, "but sometimes I like a treat. A man can't live on cafeteria food and watery coffee."

He took a sip of the soda and leaned back. "Now what can I do for you two?"

Gracie exchanged a look with Sam, who gave her an imperceptible nod and pulled out the bundle of coins, wrapped just as she'd found them. Sam explained to Bernie how and where she and her daughter had come across them.

"We took them to Megan at her antiques shop," Gracie said. "She said coins aren't her area of expertise, but she referred us to her grandfather, Harry Folger."

"Terrible checkers player, but he knows a lot about Nantucket history," Bernie said thoughtfully, taking another sip of the bubbly drink.

"Is it possible these coins could be part of the money stolen from the lighthouse?" Sam asked, holding several of them on her palm to give Bernie a better look.

"As far as I know, from all accounts I've read and heard about, it was a pretty large sum stolen from the lighthouse keeper, Robert Fenton," Bernie said, warming to his subject.

"Old Fenton was also the organist for the church at that time. The money came from donations parishioners had made over the years. It was earmarked for a new pipe organ Fenton was appointed to travel to Boston to buy it. The way I understand it, he had the cash because he was taking a ship the next day. Whoever stole it must have known his plans and known when he went into town for his supper. Broke in and took the money. Saved him a trip I guess, but folks were mighty upset, stealing from the church and all."

"So the money was never recovered?" Gracie asked, glancing at Sam who was listening raptly to Bernie's story.

"No, it wasn't. Broke Fenton's heart, being as he was the organist and the person responsible for the money. Coincidentally the wife of one of Nantucket's wealthiest whalers attended church there. She was a recent widow, and the money disappeared right around the time she did. Never heard from again."

Gracie looked at her sister again, knowing they both were aware Hannah Montague's disappearance had been somewhere around the same time as the theft from the lighthouse. They just hadn't been sure of the exact date.

Feeling a heaviness in her heart, Gracie looked away from Sam. She knew none of them—Caroline and Jamie included—wanted to think poor young Hannah had been a thief, even though that had been the accepted notion ever since she and the money disappeared at roughly the same time more than 130 years ago.

"Ahem," Bernie said, clearing his throat and gesturing at his empty glass. "Don't look so unhappy. Pour me another glass of soda, please, and let me tell you why I think our poor young widow has gotten a bum rap over the years."

Bernie's words made Gracie feel hopeful as Sam went to refill his glass with sparkling soda.

"Thank you," he said, taking a drink. He paused for a moment with his eyes closed, and Gracie wondered if their elderly host had drifted off.

Gracie cleared her throat. "Mr. Bernard, I hope we're not tiring you out too much," she said, glancing at her watch.

"Nonsense," he assured her, opening his eyes with a twinkle. "I'm just gathering my thoughts, but thanks for your concern."

Sam smiled at her and Gracie smiled back. Being a historical detective was wearing. She might just need a nap herself after they coaxed all the information they could from Bernie.

"Now, Hannah's father…something Elliott…Isaiah or Isaac maybe…owned the old Elliott farm. He was a self-righteous old codger, if my history serves me correctly," Bernie said. "Practically disowned his own daughter when she fell in love with someone who didn't meet with his approval. Instead, he married her off to old Jedediah Montague, a cagey old character who'd been married before. If I recall rightly, his first wife died, and he was left with two sons. Can't remember their names right now. I think his young second wife, Hannah, had a good heart. Her husband was stingy, but she managed to help the poor folks on the island as much as she could," he said. "Legend had it she sold jewelry her grandmother left her to help sailors crippled on the whaling ships. It was a dangerous calling at best, and a bad captain could make it much worse."

Gracie was touched at the thought of Hannah's helping the destitute, probably in spite of her husband's objections. The more she learned about her, the more sympathetic she felt. Bernie's narrative suggested that he felt Hannah was treated poorly by both her father and husband, but there was still a question about the money. Would a good person, as Hannah seemed to be, steal money belonging to her church, even if she intended to give it to the poor? Or was she so desperate to get away from the island that she put aside her scruples and took the money?

Bernie was beginning to ramble and repeat himself, obviously starting to fade. He seemed to be struggling to remember details. Probably the checkers tournament and their visit had sapped his strength. She knew she and Sam should leave so he could have his lunch and a nap.

"Sure wish I could think where I learned about Hannah's good deeds," he said, his brow furrowed in concentration. "Probably just a local legend, but I must have heard or read it somewhere. Are you planning to go to the historical society?"

"Yes," Sam answered, "that's another place Grandpa Folger suggested we go to. But he said you were the expert on lighthouses."

This made Bernie smile. "That old flatterer," he said, perking up a bit. "Old Harry's just hoping to beat me in checkers someday," he said with a grin, draining the last of his lemon-lime soda.

He let out a satisfied belch then reddened.

"Excuse me, ladies," he said, sheepishly. "I'm not used to visitors of the fairer persuasion."

His comment made Gracie smile broadly.

"It's been delightful talking to you," Sam said.

"Bernie, thank you so much for all your help," Gracie said, shaking his hand.

"Next time you see Harry Folger, tell him to bring me another liter of soda," Bernie said to them as they thanked him again and left.

"Whew, Bernie certainly has a feel for island history," Sam said, as they went down the hallway and past the lobby where the Brownies were munching on cookies and drinking fruity punch now that their singing was over. Tired-looking troop leaders were trying to hurry their charges.

"I agree," Gracie said. "He's certainly not at all what I expected."

"Me either," Sam said. "He was actually much more interesting and informative than I could have hoped for."

Gracie agreed with her sister, adding, "I just hope we didn't wear him out too much."

"Or ruin his reputation." Sam giggled.

"I think we were supposed to be enhancing his reputation," Gracie said, laughing along with her sister.

Growing serious, Sam asked, "Speaking of reputations, do you really think Hannah Montague deserves the bad one that has plagued her all these years?"

Gracie saw her sister grip the bundle of heavy coins tighter. "I really don't know," she said. "I want to believe Hannah is innocent of the theft. Bernie certainly believed she was, but I wish we could find proof. We'll just have to do some more research."

Sam nodded. "I agree with you. Both Jamie and I want to believe Hannah's innocent of the crime. More investigation might prove it, although it won't be easy this long after the event."

Heading out the door of Bayberry Commons, Gracie noticed the pensive look on her sister's face.

"A penny for your thoughts, Sam?" she asked.

"Several pennies and then some," Sam answered, hefting the bundle of coins.

Her sister's comment made Gracie laugh, but then she grew serious again. "Why do you suppose we care so much about Hannah Montague?"

"I've been wondering that very same thing myself," Sam said thoughtfully. "I imagine Hannah wasn't that much older than Jamie when she disappeared. I'd like to think her story had a happy ending."

"Me, too, Sam. Me too," Gracie said, linking arms with her sister the way they had as children.

If nothing else came of the summer, they were sharing a quest to clear the name of a wrongly accused young woman. Gracie felt surer of her innocence than ever, even though the coins in the bureau drawer seemed to be damaging evidence.

Even if she did take the money, Gracie thought, *why did she leave it behind when she left the island?*

CHAPTER
Nineteen

Sam felt in a whistling mood, not that she could produce much of a tune, but the sun was shining, the beaches were crowded with vacationers, and a new guest was expected as soon as Gracie came back from meeting the ferry. It was mid-June, and even Caroline had finally gotten in the swing of things, thanks to Gracie's meticulous job chart.

After trying to whistle a few bars of a girl-group song she'd recently heard on the radio, she gave up on her anemic musical interlude and hurried up the stairs with fresh towels for Miss Clayworth and Albert. The assistant took the towels at the door, blocking her view of the room. He looked particularly chipper this morning. Apparently, even somber English butlers weren't immune to a really beautiful Nantucket day.

After the delivery, Sam checked her watch, surprised Gracie wasn't back yet. The ferry was reliable about arriving on time, and she only had to find a lone male guest. Whenever one of her sisters was late, Sam worried about the reliability of the Packard. It had been perking along just fine since the oil cap debacle, but it came off Detroit's assembly line a long time ago.

Never one to waste time waiting, Sam found the outdoor broom and started sweeping the front porch. The one constant irritant in keeping the inn immaculately clean was sand. If the wind didn't carry it to their front door, their guests did, not that she was complaining. She was grateful for each and every person who came to stay with them.

The Packard purred up to the front entrance with their newest guest, so Sam temporarily abandoned her sweeping to welcome him. She knew his name, Nathan Billingsley, and his home address—a small town in the Berkshires—but his reason for coming to the island wasn't clear. He'd been a last-minute booking, although she knew that the local Parks and Recreation Department was paying for his two-week stay.

"Welcome, Mr. Billingsley," she said as he climbed out of the rear door of the station wagon.

"I want to carry my own portfolio," he said without acknowledging her greeting. "Be very careful with the long black case. It's packed with supplies I'll need for my class."

He unfolded his impressive length from the car seat and looked up at the inn as though he were memorizing it.

"Good light," he muttered, not to himself but to the person on the other end of his cell phone. "No, I probably won't have much time to paint, but you know me. My fingers itch when I'm not holding a brush."

It seemed an odd thing to say, but Sam did notice his exceptionally long fingers with greenish stains under his nails. He was wearing a navy blazer with only one brass button left, and the holes in his jeans were either signs of wear or high fashion. She suspected the former.

He pushed a mop of reddish orange hair away from his forehead, although it immediately fell back, and concluded his call with "Love you."

"My wife," he said by way of explanation, although he seemed to be talking to the air.

Sam looked over at Gracie, who rolled her eyes before starting to unload the guest's luggage.

"No, no, I'd better carry that myself too," he said, grabbing a corrugated cardboard box away from Gracie. "You have no idea how much trouble I had bringing that on the ferry."

"Mr. Billingsley is an artist," Gracie said. "He's here to teach a two-week class in the summer arts program for children."

"Nate, call me Nate," he said, attempting to carry the box and bag at the same time. "Mr. Billingsley is my father, and believe me, I'm nothing like him."

"I'm Sam Carter. You've met my sister Gracie. We have a third sister, Caroline, who runs the inn with us."

"Nice," he said in a voice that made it clear he couldn't care less. "Now, what exposure does my room have? I prefer morning sun, but I suppose I'll have to settle for what you have. Hank Goshen at Parks and Recreation, my boss for the summer session, said I was lucky to get a room here. Of course, I'll probably do most of my painting outside on the bluff or down on the beach."

"Won't you be teaching most of the time?" Sam asked, a little surprised by his cavalier attitude.

Why's he planning where to paint when he's here for the children? she thought. She'd spent too many years crafting meticulous lesson plans to have much patience with a teacher who didn't take his calling seriously.

"I don't have my schedule yet," he said a bit impatiently. "Now, where's my room?"

"Follow me," Sam said, picking up a battered canvas backpack and an easel.

Behind her Gracie scooped up an overnighter and a garment bag, what seemed to be the remainder of his luggage. Judging by the battered appearance of his pieces, he either traveled a lot or traveled rough.

"I'll have to make another trip for your canvases," she called to his retreating form.

Hurrying to catch up, Sam tried to keep an open mind about her new guest. After all, the quarrelsome newlyweds had turned out to be real sweethearts, and far from being haughty, Miss Clayworth and Albert were kindhearted and appreciative. She could understand why the new guest was a bit harassed after riding the ferry with so much baggage.

"We call this the Emerald Room," she said, catching up with him at the top of the stairs and putting down his bags to open the door.

Wouldn't he be surprised if he knew what was behind the wall in the closet? They'd decided to keep it their secret. Even if they talked about the secret room in their history presentations, there was no way they wanted a guest to know the location.

"Breakfast is served from seven to nine," she said, going through the spiel that had become so familiar to her. "Bike rentals are available, and if you need one, there are several places to rent a car on the island."

Before she could ask if he had any questions, his cell phone rang. He snapped it open so fast, she hardly saw his hand move.

"Yes, dear. No, I don't think so."

"Do you have a swimming pool?" he asked Sam.

"No, I'm sorry. We don't."

"No pool. I'll probably get enough exercise walking. Or I could rent a bike. I don't know. Let me ask."

He turned to Sam again. "My wife wants to know how much the bike rental is."

After quoting him a price, Sam tried to back out of the room.

"Just a minute," he said to her. "Do you serve vegan?"

"We can prepare a breakfast for you with no meat or eggs," Sam assured him. "Breakfast is the only meal we serve, although box lunches are available."

"No problem," Nate said into the phone. "Yeah, love you too."

"My wife is a swimming instructor. She's doing Red Cross classes this summer. That's why she couldn't come with me. What do you think of this?"

He held up a pad of art paper and displayed a partially finished painting. At least Sam thought it was incomplete because it looked like a purple hen riding a sleigh across a sky with several quarter-moons.

"I really don't know much about modern art," she said.

"I'm mostly inspired by Kandinsky," he plowed on, ignoring her comment. "My wife thinks I'm more like Picasso, but he left such a huge body of work, there wouldn't be any point in trying to emulate him. What I'm really about is listening to one's inner self. I really don't care if students make a muddy mess as long as they're following their own muse."

"That's nice," Sam said, although she didn't see any point in giving art lessons if the children didn't learn something about technique. "Will there be anything else?"

His cell phone rang again before he could answer, and she took the opportunity to leave.

Gracie was in the kitchen having tea with Caroline, and they both had questions about their new guest.

"Any special requests?" Caroline asked.

"His wife wants him to eat vegan," Sam said. "That won't be a problem, since we only serve breakfast. He's going to be teaching a two-week summer course, but I have a bad feeling about his skill with young children. The art teachers I've known have either been very, very good or terrible. One woman who worked in our school was fired. She sat at the front of the classroom making dollhouse miniatures for a club project while the kids ran wild."

"You should write a book about your teaching experiences," Caroline suggested.

Sam arched one eyebrow and poured a cup of tea for herself.

"If I ever write a book, it will be about baking. In fact, that might be a good idea. I could call it *Baking with Berries* and include my favorite cranberry and blueberry recipes. Of course, you're the writer in the family, Caroline, I could give you the material and let you whip it into shape."

"It's a little more complicated than that," Caroline said with a broad smile. "You need an agent and a publisher, and then you work with editors. I admire Miss Clayworth for taking on such a big project at her age."

"I'll be first in line to buy her memoir when it's published," Gracie said. "What a glamorous life she's led."

Sam noticed a strange look flit across Caroline's face, but her older sister said nothing. Was it possible she thought the life of an actress was anything but glamorous?

Once both she and Gracie had believed the career of a travel writer was exotic and exciting, and then Caroline had given it up without a backward glance. The big question was whether Caroline was happy as an innkeeper on quiet Nantucket. Sam hoped so, but she had her doubts. How long had it been since her sister had mentioned George? Was he ever coming back? More importantly, would he visit the island before the summer was over?

More than anything, Sam wanted her family—Jamie and her sisters—to be happy. That was her hope for the future, but she still couldn't tell if the inn was the answer for any of them.

CHAPTER
Twenty

$\mathcal{G}$racie tried to keep the disappointment out of her voice as she listened to Caroline's excuse for not accompanying her to the historical society that morning.

"Yes, I know that updating the inn's Web site is a priority," Gracie agreed as she cleared away their breakfast dishes, "but I thought you wanted to be involved in researching the history of the inn and the mysteries surrounding Hannah Montague."

Gracie knew she should be happy her older sister was following her list of appointed tasks, but Gracie had been hoping for company on her trip to see the society's historical librarian, Elizabeth Adams.

"Couldn't we do it another day?" Caroline asked.

"Afraid not. Elizabeth has been out of town, and she'll be leaving again soon for a conference in New York City. We have to catch her while we can."

"I'd really like to go," Sam said, answering the unspoken request, "but as you can see, I'm up to my elbows in flour. I thought I'd be able to finish this cranberry quick bread, but I left it in the oven too long and burned it. It's hard to keep up with everything and still find time to experiment with new recipes."

Gracie didn't doubt that Sam really wanted to go with her, but it seemed important for Caroline to go too. She would be writing their history presentation and might have questions of her own. And it just wasn't like Caroline not to drop everything and go off on an adventure.

"Well, I don't envy you the job of getting those bread pans clean," Gracie said, looking at the charcoal rims on the pans in the sink.

"I thought Jamie was going with you," Caroline said, studying the text on her laptop's screen. "Take a look, would you? What do you think of this to advertise the mystery night?" she asked.

Peering at the screen, Gracie frowned. "There won't be anything to talk about for this event if I don't get over to the historical society and get some research done. Jamie said she absolutely needed to get some work done on her thesis, so she's out."

Just then her niece hurried into the kitchen. "Aunt Gracie, I got enough work done to be able to go with you," she said, breathlessly. "I really didn't want to miss this opportunity to learn more about Hannah."

"Wonderful," Gracie said, pleased she would have a second set of eyes and ears to confirm what she learned.

"Good," Caroline said, hardly looking up from the computer. "Now I don't feel so bad about not going with you.

Gracie was actually thrilled history-loving Jamie was able to go with her rather than Caroline, but she didn't want to say anything to hurt her sister's feelings. Plus, she had been sincere in wanting Caroline's eye for detail on this trip to the historical society.

"Well, then, let's go," Gracie said to Jamie.

"Just let me grab my purse," Jamie said. "I wasn't sure if you'd left already or not."

Checking her watch, Gracie was happy they still had time to get to the appointment on time. "Your chauffeur—that's me—already brought the Packard around to the front." While the sisters most often drove Sam's minivan when running personal errands, they also realized that their beautiful 1941 Packard was one of the best advertising tools for the inn.

After more than a month of practice, Gracie finally felt comfortable driving the classic station wagon on the island's roads. She'd also lost the hat Caroline had found for her. They were running an inn, not a carnival!

Thanks to the influx of tourists, there was more traffic on the road, but Gracie managed to park close to the renovated colonial home housing the historical society. Before she and Jamie entered the venerable old building, she admired the well-kept facade, reminding her as it did of Misty Harbor Inn. As they entered, she could see several rooms with antiques on display, but they weren't there this morning to view the museum portion of the building.

"When I called to set up an appointment with Elizabeth Adams," Gracie said, "the historian told me there are rooms set to store old records, especially maps, newspaper clippings, and journals left by earlier islanders."

"I'm excited to get access to them," Jamie said.

"They can only be seen when the historian is present," Gracie said. "We're lucky to catch her between her vacation and her conference. That's why we couldn't wait for your mother to finish her baking."

"I can't believe how much she's enjoying herself," Jamie said with a smile. "I never thought she'd do anything but teach, but she's having a ball with the inn and her baking."

A tall, slender woman who appeared to be in her late twenties or early thirties came to meet them before they had a chance to look for her. When they'd talked on the phone, Gracie had pictured her as older and more formal, but she looked like a person who enjoyed life and her work. Her outfit for the day included a vintage bolero jacket with a pair of cropped pants. An unusual brooch made up of several old watch parts was pinned on her lapel. It reminded Gracie of something Bill Dekker would make if he designed jewelry instead of sculptures.

"I'm Elizabeth Adams," the woman said warmly, and you must be Gracie Gold," she said, extending her hand. "We spoke on the phone."

"So nice to meet you in person," Gracie said, shaking the younger woman's hand. "This is my niece, Jamie Carter. She's working on her master's thesis in American history."

The librarian's face lit up. "What's your area of interest?" she asked Jamie as she ushered them into a room near the rear of the building.

As the two younger women talked about their academic backgrounds for a few minutes, Gracie looked around a room decorated with reproduction period furniture and a few real antiques. The ambience in the room was perfect for their visit—a serious quest to learn more about the original inhabitants of Misty Harbor Inn. She hoped Elizabeth Adams could help them prove or disprove the anecdotal information gleaned from Grandpa Folger and Bernie Bernard. Gracie had no idea where real historical research would lead, but she was excited to find out.

"I'm sorry, Mrs. Gold," Elizabeth said, "I get so carried away when I talk to people who've chosen the same field I did."

"It's not a problem," Gracie said. "And, please, call me Gracie."

"I'm sorry, Aunt Gracie," Jamie said, "I'm just as eager as you to get going on our research."

"Please tell me what I can do to assist you. You mentioned something on the phone about Hannah Montague," the historian said.

"Yes, my sisters and I are interested in learning more about the background of Misty Harbor Inn, especially Jedediah Montague and his second wife, Hannah. We're planning mystery nights—talks and possibly historical re-enactments—and would like to confirm what we already know with solid historical information. We've gotten some wonderful anecdotal stories from local history buffs, Harry Folger and Bernie Bernard," Gracie said.

Elizabeth smiled. "There's a lot of information to be gleaned from oral histories."

"It was actually Grandpa Folger who suggested we come here to look at newspapers from the period," Gracie said.

"I'm happy to help you all I can," Elizabeth said, motioning for Gracie and Jamie to follow her. "Newspapers from that time period were often preserved in scrapbooks and organized according to topics. During the Great Depression of the 1930s, the Works Administration gave grants to libraries and organizations like ours to sort through and salvage historical information. They literally put people to work cutting and pasting. The society has quite a large collection housed in this room."

She led them beyond the first room into another room off-limits to tourists.

"Do you have newspaper articles dating back to when Jedediah Montague owned the house that is now our inn?" Gracie asked.

"Certainly we do," Elizabeth said. "The *Inquirer* and *Mirror* have been around since the 1800s. We keep the older material in fireproof files."

Gracie watched as the historian scanned the neatly lettered labels affixed to each filing cabinet drawer. The cabinets in this room were larger than most, perhaps specially ordered to hold large-sized scrapbooks.

"As I recall, Jedediah Montague was the son of a ship's captain," the historian said. "Montague made the family's fortune by whaling. He built your house for his first wife. She died at the end of the Civil War, leaving him with two sons."

"Yes, we'd heard that," Gracie said, noticing that Elizabeth seemed perplexed by something as she opened and closed drawers. "Is everything all right?"

"Some of the scrapbooks seem misfiled," she said, frowning, "but I'm sure I can find the one you need."

"We also know his second wife, Hannah, disappeared not long after she was widowed in 1880," Gracie said

"She was about my age," her niece said with a quiet sigh.

"Oh, good. Here's the one I've been looking for," Elizabeth said, lifting out a large buff cardboard-covered book.

Gracie couldn't wait to get a closer look at the contents of the book, and she could practically feel Jamie's eagerness.

"Let's take this volume over to a table," Elizabeth said, indicating a heavy golden oak library table with utilitarian chairs on either side. She carefully laid the scrapbook on the polished surface and produced several pairs of white cotton gloves for herself, Gracie, and Jamie.

"We can't be too careful," she said as she pulled on her pair. "You have no idea how corrosive the oil in your skin can be. We're in the process of transferring all the articles to the computer, but we're always a bit understaffed and underfinanced to get the job done very quickly."

She carefully leafed through it until she came to the clippings she was looking for.

"Here's Jedediah Montague's obituary!" Jamie exclaimed, moving close to see better.

"Yes, it is," Elizabeth smiled with satisfaction and invited them to sit for a closer look as she turned the book to face Gracie and Jamie.

"It confirms what we've already heard—that Jedediah was preceded in death by his first wife, Mehitabel, mother of his two sons, Lachlan and Fitzwalter," Jamie said.

"What I thought you'd find particularly interesting are the clippings on the next page," Elizabeth said, carefully turning a thick page with heavily glued articles.

"Oh my," Gracie said, reading the fine print.

"What is it, Aunt Gracie?" Jamie strained to get a better look.

Sitting back on the hard chair, Gracie pushed an errant strand of hair out of her eyes and took a deep breath. "It says here Jedediah Montague died owing half the businessmen in town. It doesn't explain why he was overextended but he clearly was."

"Oh, wow," Jamie said.

"Read on," Elizabeth said, pointing to another clipping. "There's more."

Gracie scanned the story, and when another strand of hair fell across one eye, she ignored it. "Interesting! It says in this story dated months later that Hannah's grown stepsons were able to pay off all of their father's bills, helping to restore his name and standing around Nantucket."

"Does it say anything else?" Jamie asked.

Gracie read further, then actually harrumphed. "Well, I never…"

"What is it?" Jamie leaned over to read for herself.

Gracie could tell by the look on the historian's face she knew what the next article revealed.

"It's more gossip and innuendo about poor Hannah," she said indignantly. "According to this story, her stepsons said they hated to disparage their stepmother's good name, but their late father had been an upstanding citizen who always paid his creditors in a timely way until he remarried. His second wife was a spendthrift who squandered his fortune."

"That certainly seems to track with the reputation Hannah carried down through the years," Jamie said sounding morose.

Gracie glanced at the article again and sighed. "Those sanctimonious stepsons are quoted as saying they hoped God would forgive Hannah for her misdeeds, as the people of the church have done." She read on then said, "The article also mentions Hannah disappeared sometime after the evening service at her church. Her stepsons are adamant she never returned home that night after attending church."

Gracie could see how much Jamie shared her frustration. Hannah's name had been blackened, and the reporter who wrote the story hadn't included her side of the story.

"Her stepchildren accuse her of stealing the money from the lighthouse without coming right out and saying so directly," Jamie said.

"Exactly," Elizabeth said. "I read those accounts a while back and knew you'd find them interesting."

"I guess tabloid journalism has been alive and well in America for centuries," Gracie said, feeling dejected from what she and Jamie had just learned.

Gracie watched Elizabeth shut the heavy scrapbook and carried it back to the filing cabinet where she efficiently slipped it into its proper place and shut the drawer. The action made Gracie feel as though a chapter on the mystery of Hannah Montague was being closed too—and not with the resolution anyone had been hoping for.

Rising to go, she thanked Elizabeth for all her help.

"History always holds some surprises, doesn't it?" Jamie said. "It was a pleasure to meet you. Thanks so much for your help."

"My pleasure," the librarian said. "I wish I could tell you more about Hannah's fate, but the written record is silent."

"That didn't tell us anything we wanted to know," Gracie said as they drove home.

"No, but it gave us more leads. I wonder what happened to the Montague brothers. They certainly had a poor opinion of their stepmother, but maybe they were the ones who drove their father into bankruptcy."

"I'd like to believe Hannah was an innocent victim," Gracie said thoughtfully, "but so far we have no evidence."

When they got back to the inn, Gracie was surprised to see Caroline still glued to her chair in front of the computer.

"You've certainly have been working a long time on that Web site," she said. "Are you promoting our mystery talks?"

"Oh, hello, Gracie…Jamie. Believe me I got up to take breaks," she said, stretching. "Tell me what you found out. I can't wait to hear."

Gracie exchanged a look with her niece.

"You two don't look very happy," Caroline said.

"We'll tell you all about it," Gracie assured her sister. "But first, where's Sam? We can tell both of you at the same time."

Gracie watched Jamie go off to find her mother, but she didn't have to wait long.

"At least I got those pans cleaned," Sam said as she entered the room. "But there's a stain on our second best tablecloth that defies my best efforts."

"We don't exactly have good news about Hannah," Jamie said.

"Please, tell us what you found out," Caroline said.

Gracie told them what she and Jamie had discovered with the help of Elizabeth Adams. Once in a while, Jamie would add a few more details.

"I see why you two have such long faces," Sam said, giving her daughter a hug.

"Well it certainly gives us lots of material for our mystery night," Caroline said thoughtfully.

Something in her older sister's tone of voice made Gracie pay closer attention. "What are you thinking, Caroline?"

"Well, you'll laugh that this is coming from impractical me—but maybe being an innkeeper is rubbing off on me," she said.

"What is it?" Gracie asked.

"Where did those stepsons get the money to pay off some of their father's debts?" Caroline paused for a moment before continuing. "What if they stole the money from the lighthouse and blamed Hannah? If she learned the truth and wanted to clear her name, she might have been in serious danger."

"What if they murdered Hannah and disposed of her body to keep Hannah from telling the people of Nantucket the truth?" Sam suggested with a shiver.

Jamie laughed. "Mom, maybe you weren't so far off wondering if there was a body in the trunk. The brothers could've had a reason to hide her in the secret room. Speaking for myself, I'm awfully glad they didn't."

"Caroline, maybe it was a good thing you didn't go with us after all. You've brought a fresh perspective to all this. Thank you!"

"You're welcome," Caroline said, smiling. "Who would have thought I'd be the practical one today?"

"And you know," Gracie said, "Bernie mentioned the old Elliott farm. We need to visit out there. Maybe Hannah's father left something there that will provide more clues about her."

"You're turning into a regular Nancy Drew," Sam said with a giggle. "Next you'll want a deer stalker hat and a magnifying glass like Sherlock Holmes."

"I'm afraid we'll need a master detective to unravel the web of intrigue associated with the inn," Gracie said. "And my curiosity has definitely been piqued. But I would feel so much better if we could clear Hannah of nasty suspicions. I've felt sorry for her since we learned she was forced to marry a man she didn't love."

"You're a closet romantic," Caroline teased. "But I love the way you care about people, past and present."

CHAPTER
Twenty-one

Caroline sat staring at the computer without really seeing what was on the screen. A gentle June breeze ruffled her hair, and the sun was warm on her face, but she was in her own world, worrying about George's last e-mail message. Two days ago she'd received a cryptic note saying he was back in the States but would be tied up for a while.

What did "tied up" mean? She'd been hoping for a phone call, but none had come. After nearly thirty years of friendship, she knew that George wasn't acting at all like himself. Was he angry? Hurt? Or maybe he was tired of her and had found someone else.

"How are reservations coming?" Gracie asked, startling her by suddenly appearing beside her.

"Oh, I haven't checked yet, but we do have several more for our mystery event. I'm glad we decided to have it at night instead of making it a tea party. Visitors have too much else to do during the day."

"Yes, it's been perfect beach weather. If we weren't so busy, that's where I'd be." Gracie pulled up a chair and looked at the computer screen. "Let's see if we have any new hits."

"Here's a family of five. They want to come in August, but they insist on bringing their two dogs, one a German Shepherd and the other a Doberman. I don't think we need a team meeting to decide that one," Caroline said. She started typing in a refusal.

"Imagine, taking two huge dogs on vacation and expecting to keep them in one of our lovely rooms," Gracie said with a shudder. "They'd probably want us to dog-sit while they enjoyed themselves on the island."

"Yes, we have to be firm about no pets after Wellington leaves." Caroline reached for the iced tea on the table beside her and took a sip.

"The little Yorkie has grown on me," Gracie admitted. "He seems to be a good companion for Miss Clayworth."

"Unfortunately Max hasn't warmed up to him," Caroline said. "Whenever they get a scent of each other, it's a hate-hate relationship."

"Males!" Gracie laughed, sounding lighthearted and much happier than when she first arrived for the summer season. Caroline was glad for her sister's sake but wished she could enjoy the inn and its guests more than she was.

"What else do we have?" Gracie leaned forward to view the screen for herself.

"We can say yes to this one," Caroline said, scrolling down to a perfectly reasonable request. "An older couple wants to celebrate their fiftieth anniversary on Nantucket. They honeymooned here, so it will be a sentimental visit."

"That's lovely. Be sure to confirm it right away. Wouldn't it nice if the inn became known as a honeymoon haven?"

"Romantic, but we're not likely to fill all our rooms if we try to emphasize one group," Caroline said, not at all charmed by the thought of newly married couples making a pilgrimage to Misty Harbor Inn.

"Erin and Kyle were sweet, though," Gracie reminisced. "I'm glad they were our first-ever guests."

"Hey, you two, I need you," Sam called from the doorway.

Caroline bounded up, not wanting to hear any more about romantic couples. Gracie didn't realize what a sore subject it was. Her sisters both knew she was upset by George's absence, but she preferred to hide the depth of her disappointment. There was nothing they could do to help, and she didn't want either of them trying to patch things up. Gracie was a born matchmaker, and Sam's practical approach to matters of the heart would only irritate her.

"What is it?" Gracie asked.

"I need one of you to run into town and buy up all the blueberries you can find. My blueberry muffins were such a hit at the teashop, they've ordered ten dozen for tomorrow. What I don't need today, I'll freeze for future orders."

"That's great," Gracie said, "but are you sure you have time to bake on that scale?"

"It won't be a problem. I'm having the time of my life! But don't worry; I can still do all my jobs in the inn. Your work chart has helped immensely, Gracie. No more wasting time wondering who will do what."

"I have to admit, your system does work," Caroline said. "And much as I hate doing things by committee, it is helpful to have a team meeting once a week. I didn't anticipate all the little decisions that have to be made."

"Like who washes and polishes the bikes," Sam said. "I don't know how the red and blue ones got so muddy. We haven't had that much rain."

"Maybe we're happier not knowing," Caroline said, wishing she didn't feel so cynical this morning. She was the family optimist, the "can-do" Marris. Lately, Sam was providing the enthusiasm, and Gracie seemed increasingly energized by the challenges of inn-keeping.

As hard as she tried to keep up her end, Caroline was afraid she was failing her sisters. Part of her wanted to rush to George and make things right, but her responsibilities lay on the island. She had been the one who pushed her sisters to buy the inn with her. They had to make a success of the first season if Misty Harbor Inn was going to have a good future, and things were certainly looking good. The June weather was cooperating, and reservations were slowly but surely coming in.

"I guess I could go get the blueberries," she volunteered.

If George didn't call her soon, she would try contacting him. This was something she wanted to do in the privacy of her room, but first she had to work up the nerve to do it. What could she say? He must have reasons of his own for being aloof. If he didn't want anything more to do with her, was there really any way to change his mind?

"That's okay, I'll go," Gracie said.

"Thanks," Sam said. "I have a short list of other things I need. And Caroline, Albert brought a message from Miss Clayworth. She'd like to have tea with you when it's convenient."

"With me?" Caroline was surprised. Their longtime guest had gone back to her reclusive ways since the evening when she'd fallen, and she'd never invited any of them to her suite. They still had to clean during specified hours, although it was an easy accommodation to make. Albert handled most of it, although it was hard to imagine him holding a duster in his tailored suits and tasteful vests.

Caroline had no trouble keeping busy until it was time to go to Miss Clayworth's room. She took a tray with very hot water, using the inn's best bone china teapot decorated with violets and touches of gold.

Before she could set down the tray and knock on the door, Albert opened it and motioned her inside with a theatrical gesture. Was it possible he'd been an actor himself before he became Lorraine Clayworth's assistant? Caroline hadn't thought of it before, but he was playing the part of a loyal butler to perfection.

"My dear, please come in," Miss Clayworth said.

The actress was wearing a long blue silk robe embroidered with Chinese dragons over a shimmering white floor-length gown. The costume would have looked much too theatrical on anyone else, but Miss Clayworth pulled it off with grace and charm. Her long white hair was piled on her head today, and Caroline had to wonder if hairdressing was one of Albert's skills. His employer never went farther than a hundred yards from the inn, so she certainly hadn't visited any of Nantucket's beauty salons.

"It was nice of you to invite me," Caroline said, setting the tray on the small table between two chairs.

"Do have a seat. Albert will prepare our tea. I hope you like anise biscuits."

"Oh yes, very much," Caroline said. "I enjoyed them in England. I lived in the Cotswolds for many years while I was a travel writer."

"I didn't realize that. What brought you back to the United States?"

"I guess after traveling for so many years, I was ready to finally put down some roots," Caroline said with a light laugh. "It seemed time to reconnect with my sisters."

"How nice that the three of you are working together in your lovely inn. I can't tell you how helpful it's been in working on my memoirs."

"That's wonderful to hear." Caroline watched with interest as Albert went through a tea ritual that seemed more Oriental than English. The tiny cup he handed her was so delicate, she was afraid to hold it too firmly.

Miss Clayworth took her cup in both fragile, heavily veined hands and daintily sipped. Caroline tried to do the same, but the brew was still much too hot for her. She put it down and bit into a small cookie, finding the taste of anise strong but not unpleasant.

Albert had disappeared so silently, she only then realized he was gone. This was certain to be the most unusual girl-talk she'd ever had, but Miss Clayworth fascinated her. How could a woman her age be so beautiful? She was excessively thin but without looking bony or emaciated. When she was young, she must have been stunning. Now she'd had the wisdom to age gracefully without facial surgery or Botox. She made wrinkles look beguiling.

"I cannot tell you how much I appreciated your help the evening I fell," the actress said. "It's sad to be alone at my age, although I'm greatly blessed to have Albert."

"He seems very faithful."

"Yes, more so than I deserve, I'm afraid," she said wistfully.

She sipped her tea. "I made a sad mistake when I rejected all my suitors," she said with regret in every word. "For a long time, I didn't admit it, even to myself. A woman shouldn't grow old without a man to love her."

Her admission was so deeply personal, Caroline wasn't sure how to answer. She opted for rapt silence, wishing she'd seen the actress when she was still performing on the London stage.

"Forgive an old woman for her reflections," she said, moving her lightly rouged lips into a faint but warm smile.

"I feel honored to be here with you," Caroline admitted. She'd never met anyone quite like the actress. It was tempting to ask about famous people she'd known, but she sensed this wasn't what Miss Clayworth wanted to talk about.

"I'll regret leaving when my memoirs are finished." She put down her teacup, and Caroline noticed a slight tremor in her hands. "I couldn't have done them without the tranquility of your lovely inn."

"I'm so happy we could provide the atmosphere you needed." Caroline shook her head to decline more tea, which was too bitter for her tastes.

It soon became obvious that Miss Clayworth was tiring. Albert came back into the sitting room and hovered over them. Caroline took it as a signal to leave and stood. Her hostess looked up at her.

"Miss Marris, please forgive me if I am being too forward," Miss Clayworth said as Caroline stood to leave. "But I hope you'll find your soul mate before love passes you by."

There was no answer to that. Caroline thanked her and backed out of the room, totally forgetting to bring the tray with her. She felt as though she'd been in the company of royalty.

For the rest of the day, Caroline thought of little other than her "audience" with the regal actress. One thing kept running through her head: *Find your soul mate before love passes you by.*

Was George destined to be with her, or had she ruined any chance of growing old with him? He certainly was the only man she'd ever loved with her whole heart and soul. The thought of losing him forever made her tremble with fear.

Her sisters were kind and understanding, but this was something she couldn't share with them. She didn't want sympathy or advice. Either would make her feel even worse.

Bedtime came early for the Marris sisters. Sam was up at dawn preparing her special breakfasts for the guests. Gracie followed her younger sister's lead in beginning her workday early, and truth to tell, Caroline was exhausted that evening. Worries and regrets disturbed her nights, and she was glad to retreat to her bedroom, the only room in the inn that was totally hers.

As usual, she put her cell phone on the bedside table to recharge, but tonight she had another reason for bringing it with her. For better or worse, she was going to call George. The suspense about his intentions was becoming as hard to bear as the separation.

He answered on the fifth ring.

"I hope I didn't wake you," she said, forgetting the clever words she'd intended to say.

"Caroline, it's not even ten o'clock. I have a couple of hours of work to do yet."

"Sorry. Is this a bad time?"

"No, no, it's okay." His impatient tone said far more than his words. "I've been meaning to call you. How are things going at the inn?"

"We're gradually getting into the swing of it." This wasn't what she wanted to talk about, but she gave him a quick rundown on their recent guests. "I miss you, though."

"How is that old Packard doing now?" He didn't react in any way to her confession.

"Fine. Gracie seems to like driving it."

They chatted for a couple of minutes, but he avoided anything personal. She had questions racing through her mind, but in the end, she couldn't bring herself to ask the important ones: *When will I see you? Do you still care about me?*

"Well, get some sleep," he said. "Sounds like you're pretty busy."

It was a dismissal, not concern for her well-being.

"Yeah, we are."

They said good-bye like two strangers.

Caroline couldn't believe how wretched, how empty she felt. She wished she hadn't called at all. Was this the end of their long friendship? He hadn't said anything to make her believe otherwise.

Max strolled over from his doggy bed in the corner of the room and put his paws up on her blanket as though he knew she was hurting.

"I have you, don't I?" she said, scratching under his chin the way he liked. "Well, come on up. We'll make an exception about not sleeping on my bed—just this once."

The curly-haired cocker spaniel wasn't a soul mate, but Caroline needed any comfort she could get. Where was her life going without George as a part of it? Max snored, making the little buzzing nose she usually found amusing, but Caroline lay awake for hours, wide-eyed and miserable.

CHAPTER
Twenty-two

The mail was waiting to be sorted on a small table in the foyer, and Gracie was delighted to see an envelope addressed in her granddaughter's large but neat printing. Inside a folded sheet had a picture of the birdbath in their backyard with a note that said: "I love you, Grandma" on the back. A large, somewhat fierce-looking robin sat in the middle of the bath.

Smiling broadly, Gracie took a minute to admire Evelyn's efforts. Her granddaughter loved nature, and already she was planting a small plot of flowers and caring for them herself.

It took a minute for Gracie to recognize the names on the return address of a second envelope addressed to her.

"My goodness, it's from the honeymooners," she said with pleasure, taking out a note card with chubby-cheeked children on the front. When she opened it, there was a photograph of the happy pair taken on the front porch of the inn.

Dear Gracie,

We can't tell you how much it meant to both of us to spend our honeymoon at Misty Harbor Inn and getting to know you. Thank you for all you did for us. We hope to see you again in the near future.

Love, Erin

Gracie's eyes grew moist when she thought of her first and favorite guests. She hoped they would have a long, happy marriage and someday return to Nantucket.

An unexpected thing had happened since she'd returned to the inn for the summer. She discovered their guests could be fascinating. Each and every one had a special story to tell. Some were frank and open like the honeymooners, and others were more guarded and private. Miss Clayworth never ceased to mystify and charm her. She wouldn't grow tired of speculating about her if she stayed a year, which, alas, she wasn't going to do. Their British guests would be gone by the Fourth of July, only a couple of short weeks away, and Gracie felt sad to see them go.

She heard a soft creak from the stairs and saw Albert descending with Wellington in the crook of his arm, his second trip of the morning. Perhaps not realizing he was observed, he looked melancholy, his face reflecting deep unhappiness. Was he bored with his endless trivial duties? Did he miss home in England, not finding much to entertain an elderly man in Misty Harbor Inn? Or did his unhappy expression come from another reason?

"How are you today, Albert?" she asked, stepping up so he noticed her.

His face underwent a sudden change, reverting to his accustomed formal expression.

"Quite well, thank you."

Albert wasn't one for chitchat, but one subject always seemed to awaken his interest.

"How is Miss Clayworth today?"

His eyes came alive, and he smiled. "She's a bit fatigued from finishing her memoirs, but her health is satisfactory."

"I'm sure that's reassuring to you. You wouldn't want her to have health problems so far from home."

"Oh no, that would be terrible," he said with conviction. "She's fragile, you know. I do my best, but her well-being is always a worry."

If a bolt of lightning had hit the roof of the inn, Gracie couldn't have had a more startling revelation. Albert didn't stay with Lorraine Clayworth because he liked walking the Yorkie and running her errands. The man was in love with her. It made so much sense, she didn't know why she hadn't realized it before.

Gracie nodded, feeling tongue-tied by her insight and the absolute certainty with which it struck her.

"I'll just be going," he said, walking around her to reach the front door.

Watching him leave, Gracie's mind was racing. Did the actress know how he felt? Had he ever told her? Did he feel the distance between them was too great for him to speak? She understood the English were still class conscious in the twenty-first century, and Miss Lorraine was a celebrity, perhaps someone beyond his station in life.

Was there anything she could do to help the poor man realize his dreams? Her heart ached at the thought of unrequited love, but perhaps Miss Clayworth had suppressed feelings for Albert as well.

In the past, her children had needed her as a sounding board when they were facing a dilemma, but she'd always thought helping them as part of being a mother. Paige was far from home in her job as a national park ranger and occasionally felt a tinge of homesickness so that she had begun to think of returning to Portland. And of course, Brandon and his wife Stacy appreciated it when she helped with their twins and Evelyn from time to time. But she was beginning to accept what she'd hidden from her consciousness for such a long time: They were self-sufficient and didn't really need her anymore.

Here at the inn, she could use her God-given gift of empathy to make a difference in people's lives. It held amazing possibility, and something she'd have to ponder. She'd have to make a distinction between interfering and helping, not always an easy call.

Another guest thundered down the circular stairway. She looked up to see the art teacher and quickly moved out of the way, not sure he wouldn't just bowl her over in his haste. He was loaded down with an easel and painting supplies, although she understood he had an appointment with his supervisor to talk about the workshop starting Monday.

"There's a bulb out in the bedside lamp," he said without preamble.

"I'll take care of it," Gracie said, changing her mind about fascinating guests. Nate Billingsley was more annoying than interesting. She'd had his number since she picked him up at the ferry, and he hadn't done anything to change her initial opinion.

"Oh, I'll need a box lunch and a bungee cord to fasten my easel to the bike."

"We take orders for box lunches the evening before they're needed," she reminded him.

"I'll settle for anything—maybe a peanut butter sandwich," he said, giving her a hangdog look with his pale blue eyes. "I'm easy to please."

"All right, I guess I can put together something."

He didn't mention vegan, not surprising since he'd put away half a rasher of bacon at breakfast. Apparently he was only vegan when he was on the phone with his wife.

After she took care of the lightbulb and the lunch, Nate was easily forgotten as Gracie went through her list of chores for the day. But she couldn't get Albert out of her mind. He looked terribly vulnerable in unguarded moments. Her heart cried out to help him, but what could she do without violating a guest's privacy?

At least she had one happy prospect. Brandon, his wife Stacy and their three children, Evelyn and her twin brothers Zachary and Jacob, would be arriving to stay at the inn for the weekend. Gracie planned to room with Caroline while they were there so the family could use her room. Fortunately, the kids thought it was a lark to bed down in their sleeping bags on the floor.

She could hardly wait to drive the station wagon down to meet the last ferry of the day, although her son probably would want to drive back to the inn. He loved the idea of a vintage Packard to chauffeur guests.

After an afternoon of clock watching, Gracie announced she was leaving to pick up her family. In her eagerness to see them, the trip to the ferry had never seemed longer. She arrived before it docked, pacing up and down beside the station wagon until they debarked and ran toward her.

"Grandma! Grandma!" Evelyn shouted as soon as she spotted her. "I didn't even get seasick."

"Thank heavens," Stacy said, approaching with a firm grip on both her two-year old sons.

"We didn't lose one overboard either," Brandon said, giving Gracie a big hug. "How're you doing out here on the island, Mom?"

Eager as she was to talk to her son, Gracie didn't have a ready answer. She certainly wasn't unhappy, and her newly discovered sense of purpose added a whole new dimension to running the inn.

But was she ready to rent or sell her house in Portland and move to Nantucket year-round?

"Can we go swimming, Grandma?" Evelyn excitedly asked. "I have a new swimsuit. It's yellow with green stripes. I picked it out myself."

"Maybe in the morning," her mother said.

"Can I drive, Mom?" Brandon said.

Gracie hesitated. She was surprised to find that she was reluctant to hand over the wheel to her son. She had grown to love the big old Packard.

"The clutch can be a little tricky," she warned him, but she handed over the keys and went around to the passenger side. Brandon slid behind the wheel while his family settled down in the vehicle.

One thing was sure, Gracie thought. It was going to be a wild and wonderful weekend. The only sad note was her worry about Albert, but she hardly saw him on Saturday.

By late afternoon she wished she could say the same thing about Nate Billingsley. He seemed to pop up continually, coming and going and always leaving a trail of sand. He took over the parlor, setting up materials for his classes, although they would be held at an elementary school.

Evelyn discovered Gracie and him when she returned from walking Max. She sat cross-legged on the carpet and watched him fuss over a box of shells, driftwood, and odd objects he'd picked up on the beach. Gracie was trying to protect the antiques in the room and keep him from leaving a snail trail wherever he went. It was pretty much a hopeless cause, and she was resigned to vacuuming as soon as he left the room.

"What's that for?" Evelyn asked when he pulled out a long, ropey vine and shook sand from it.

"There's more to art than dabbing paint on canvas," he said impatiently. "Don't you have somewhere you need to be?"

"But what's it for?" Evelyn repeated, never one to be easily dissuaded.

"I think Mr. Billingsley is going to teach the children how to do assemblage art," Sam said, coming into the parlor and wrinkling her nose at the mess. "That's means taking discarded and interesting objects and combining them into a meaningful artworks."

"Oh, we did that in kindergarten," her granddaughter said dismissively. "I used dry leaves and Popsicle sticks."

"I won't be teaching Popsicle art," Nate said defensively. He glanced at Max. "Is that dog supposed to be in here?"

Max was sniffing overtime, perhaps deciding whether he approved of the flotsam and jetsam in the parlor.

"My grandma doesn't care," Evelyn said indignantly. "You're the one getting sand everywhere."

"That's enough, Evelyn," Gracie said. She agreed with her granddaughter but couldn't let her be rude to a guest. "Why don't you take Max to the kitchen for a drink of water?"

As soon as she left, the twins came in from playing with their mother on the front porch. Zach made a beeline for the box of found objects while his brother climbed up on the chair next to the artist.

"Don't you kids have anyplace else to go?" he asked impatiently.

Stacy hurried into the room and claimed her boys, but Gracie thought the guest was unnecessarily cross with all three of her grandchildren. Apparently Sam felt the same way. She jumped to their defense as soon as the twins were gone.

"It's a good thing when children are curious," she rebuked him.

"They can be curious someplace else. It took me hours to find all this stuff when I could've been painting."

Nate held up a small piece of pale green sea glass and put it in the pocket of his khaki shorts. Apparently the good bits weren't going to his class, Gracie thought.

"You don't much like children, do you?" Sam said.

It was unlike her sister to be so confrontational, but Gracie could see she was upset by Nate's dismissal of her niece and nephews.

"They're okay in their place," he grumbled. "Where can I throw this away?"

He handed Gracie a clump of sea grass, apparently rejecting it for his purposes.

"I thought you were a teacher." Sam sounded more puzzled than angry now.

"I teach at a junior college. Once in a while, I even get a student who knows which end of a paintbrush to use."

Gracie wanted to ask how he got a job teaching young children. Perhaps he knew someone employed by Parks and Recreation. She wasn't naïve when it came to the ways of the world.

His cell phone rang, a jarring noise that he responded to immediately.

"Yeah, sweetheart, I got my class schedule. I'll be spending more time teaching than I thought." He listened for a few moments, then ended the call. "Love ya."

Did his wife call every hour on the hour? Gracie was beginning to believe she did.

Sam was frowning, obviously upset by the would-be teacher's attitude. "Will you have any teacher's aides helping you?"

"Nope. It's all my problem." He'd finished sorting and closed the lid of the corrugated cardboard box.

Evelyn wandered back into the parlor with a serious expression on her face.

"What's up, sweetie?" Gracie asked, drawing her over to where she was standing.

"Mom and Dad said I could stay here until they come for the Fourth of July if it's okay with you, Grandma."

"I'd love to have you," Gracie said, hugging her granddaughter.

"Just me, not the twins," Evelyn emphasized.

"No, they're too young to stay alone," Gracie assured her.

"Mom said maybe I could go to art classes. I really like drawing."

Evelyn sounded a bit unsure, but Gracie thought it was a good idea to keep her entertained. The busier she was, the less likely it was she'd get homesick.

"That's a great idea, Evelyn," Sam said. "I'll be happy to take you to one of Mr. Billingsley's classes.

The artist gave the eight-year-old a sour look.

"Since I'll be taking Evelyn anyway—if there are still openings— maybe I can give you a little volunteer help, Nate. I was an elementary teacher for many years before we bought the inn."

"Thanks, but I really don't need help. My plans are made."

"Most teachers find they're more effective if they have an assistant to help with managing the classroom."

Sam had a stubborn look. Gracie knew she wasn't going to take no for an answer.

"The classes are nearly at capacity," Nate said.

"I'm sure you can make room for Evelyn if you have a volunteer helper."

"I guess."

Gracie grimaced inwardly. His lack of empathy with her grandchildren didn't bode well for successfully teaching youngsters.

"It's settled then," Sam said. "I'll take Evelyn to Parks and Recreation and enroll her after breakfast Monday morning."

"I insist on doing things my way," Nate said, carrying his box to the parlor door. "You can help with cleaning up and such, but don't try to give art lessons."

"I wouldn't dream of it," Sam said in a sweet voice that didn't fool Gracie.

Her sister had been teacher of the year in her district, and she'd also spent quite a few years working with student teachers in her classroom. The quirky artist was going to learn a few things about relating to the children in his classes.

"Thanks, Aunt Sam," Evelyn said when Nate was gone. "You can be my special teacher."

Gracie couldn't stop grinning. If anyone could make Nate Billingsley a better teacher, it was her sister.

Now, she thought, if George would just come to see Caroline—and if she could just find a way to help Albert.

CHAPTER
Twenty-three

Sam didn't mind getting up earlier than usual to prepare breakfast and start her baking Monday morning. Gracie helped her serve breakfast to their guests, including Nate Billingsley. The artist asked for extra sausages with his blueberry pancakes, and they both suspected he was making up for the vegan meals he got at home.

Brandon and his family had left, and Sam was glad she was going to help in the art program. She wanted Evelyn's stay on the island to be fun for her, but she had doubts about Nate's teaching ability. Was he scared of kids, or did he just not like them? Either way, his own art came first with him, and he'd spent the weekend sketching and painting away from the inn. He came back Sunday evening carrying a canvas splattered with great blotches of electric blue and sunflower yellow. She wasn't sure which end was up, but then, she'd never been a fan of modern art.

"What can I do for you while you take Evelyn to the art class?" Gracie asked.

"Hold the fort!" Sam joked, remembering it was their grandfather's favorite expression. "I just hope I can still enroll her. She really draws well for her age."

"I hope Mr. Billingsley doesn't put her off art for life," Gracie said with unusual scorn. "Really, I don't understand how he got the job."

Sam only nodded. They'd exhausted that topic of conversation. Was that what happened when sisters lived and worked together? Would they get tired of talking to each other?

"I wonder when Caroline is getting up," Sam said. "She gets her work done, but sometimes I think she must be working in the middle of the night."

Now that she thought of it, she certainly hadn't talked to Caroline very much lately. Her older sister was putting up a brave front, but she wasn't her usual cheerful, chatty self.

"It was nice Brandon could come for the weekend," Sam said.

"Yes, I loved seeing them. I hope Evelyn has a good time and doesn't get homesick."

As if on cue, Gracie's granddaughter came into the kitchen dressed for the day in white shorts and a frilly lavender and yellow top. She had a short, perky haircut she could manage by herself, so she was ready to leave for town as soon as she finished breakfast.

Sam had phoned ahead to be sure there was room in the class for her niece. When they arrived at the elementary school, children were already lining up to get into the building, the younger ones escorted by parents or nannies.

"The door should be open by now," the fair-haired mother of a boy said. "Class is supposed to start in five minutes."

Most schools allowed around ten minutes for children to settle into their classrooms. Nate should've unlocked the door by now, but she tried to cut him some slack on his first day.

At five minutes past the starting time, he rode up on one of the inn's rental bikes with a cell phone pressed to his ear. He seemed to be doing more listening than talking, but it irritated Sam. A crowd was waiting for him, and he didn't seem in the least concerned.

When they did get inside to the designated classroom, Nate wasted more time laying long strips of newsprint on the tables while the children milled around, some of them getting into mischief. She broke up a shoving match and assigned seats roughly according to age, which ranged from six to ten. So far Nate hadn't said a word to any of his students.

Most of the supplies were furnished, but the class description had called for a paint shirt. Since Sam had no idea whether they'd need them the first day, she had the children hang them on the backs of their chairs. Tomorrow they could use the cubbyholes on one wall to store them.

"Okay, you'll need pencils," Nate said, putting a handful on all three tables.

Sam noticed that half or more had broken leads, which led to a rush to the pencil sharpener beside the chalkboard. The teacher didn't seem to notice that few pupils were listening when he started telling them what to do.

"We're going to practice circles," he said in a pedantic voice. "A good artist has to be able to make perfect circles. You can use the paper on the table."

After some confusion, Sam checked that every child had a sharpened pencil, but only a few actually began making circles. Within a few minutes, they were drawing cars, crooked houses, and big-headed people. Some were making images using their hands as patterns.

Nate sat on the edge of the teacher's desk at the front and took another call on his cell phone. Sam was gradually progressing from annoyance to outrage. How could this man expect to be paid for such slipshod teaching practices? She was ready to take control of the class herself when he ended the call and started paying attention to the children, albeit half-heartedly.

When she leaned over Evelyn to see what she was drawing, her grandniece whispered, "He's not a very good teacher, is he?"

Out of the mouth of babes, Sam thought, trying to decide what to do. She could find out who was in charge of the summer programs and complain about him, but if he were fired, Evelyn and the other children might be deprived of the opportunity to learn more about art. Or she could treat him as one of her student teachers and try to teach him something.

When he started to draw obscure symbols on the chalkboard, maybe expecting the children to imitate what he did, Sam passed out the wooden boxes of crayons stored on a nearby shelf.

"Now everyone draw and color a picture of your favorite thing to do in the summer. Mr. Billingsley will come around and see what you're doing." She hoped.

Meanwhile, she interrupted Nate's rather meaningless monologue and asked him to come out to the hallway with her.

"What is your lesson plan for today?" she asked.

He shrugged nonchalantly. "I don't think art should be structured. The kids can find their own way if they have the time and materials."

"Wrong!" Sam said emphatically. "Their parents expect them to be inspired, to learn new techniques and exercise self-discipline to complete projects."

He shuffled his feet and looked uncomfortable.

"You don't have a clue how to teach young children, do you?"

"Hey, it's a job. My aunt works in Parks and Recreation. She told me to apply online, and here I am."

She could hear the children getting restless and noisy behind the closed door.

"Two things can happen," she said, trying to be patient. "You can take the next ferry back to your wife, or you can put some effort into planning and carrying out a worthwhile workshop."

She expected an argument, but Nate only looked pale and confused.

"You're afraid of the kids, aren't you?" she asked in a soothing voice. "You wouldn't be the first teacher to feel intimidated, but give them something worthwhile to do, and you'll earn their respect."

"We could play the color wheel game, I guess."

He explained that he'd indicate a color on his chart, and the students would try to match it as closely as possible with the big set of markers he had to distribute.

"I got to buy them with part of their fees," he said.

"These children need a variety of activities each day. Six-year-olds don't have the attention span of an adult, so you can't expect them to stick with one activity during a two-hour workshop. They'll need a break for refreshments and another to play outside for about fifteen minutes."

"No one told me about snacks," he protested.

"When I registered my grandniece, they gave me a green sheet with an overview of the class. It clearly stated that parents can donate crackers or juice boxes if they like—and you'll find that most will be happy to. Did you even read your copy?"

"It must be somewhere in my room at the inn."

"Have you ever made a lesson plan?"

"I borrowed something like that from another art teacher. I'm only teaching junior college art until my work catches on. Money is pretty tight right now."

"Mr. Billingsley, you have a lot to learn before you can call yourself a teacher."

"I have a feeling you're the person who's going to teach me," he said. Sam glanced at him and was met with the ghost of a smile, a nice change from his usual scowl.

"Yes, and you'd better learn fast, or you'll lose control of your class." She could hear a commotion through the closed door. "I hope you have a good idea for the rest of the time. I'll run to the market and get some juice boxes and graham crackers. After today you'll have to sign up parents."

When she got back to the school, Sam was relieved to see the children busy with scissors and colored paper, cutting strips to make a paper weaving. She was pretty sure Nate had a lot he could teach them, and she felt hopeful he'd get organized and make the workshop fun and instructive. She'd sit in on the beginning of the next session, but maybe he could manage on his own now that he knew what was expected of him.

He was in the middle of a demonstration when his cell phone sounded. Much to her satisfaction, he turned if off and shoved it in his pocket without answering.

After the class ended, Evelyn rushed to show Gracie what she'd made. Sam found herself looking forward to seeing Nate's other projects. He wasn't an ideal teacher—or the ideal guest—but she had hope for him.

CHAPTER
Twenty-four

*I*s that a new pin, Shirley?" Gracie asked as their octogenarian neighbor came up to her just as Gracie was getting ready to go to town.

Gracie could tell Shirley was pleased she'd inquired about the glittery rhinestone piece pinned on her lapel. Gracie honestly couldn't tell if it was a giraffe or a horse, but she knew how fond Shirley was of her trademark rhinestone pins.

"How nice of you to notice," Shirley said, tucking a strand of snowy white hair back into her bun. "It's a zebra, and I just acquired it."

Good thing she hadn't complimented the elderly woman on what a nice giraffe it was, Gracie thought.

"Where are you headed?" Shirley asked.

"I have some errands to run," Gracie said, trying not to check her watch. She had a long list of things she wanted to accomplish today, but it wouldn't slow her down that much to talk to their neighbor.

"So what's new at the inn?" Shirley asked.

Gracie wanted to think of something quickly so she could get going. The first thing that popped into her mind was the planned

Mystery Night. Briefly she went over what she and her sisters were planning and how they'd been gathering information on the background of the inn.

"We're especially interested in the story about the whaler's widow, but I don't think we have the whole story yet."

She didn't mention how close they'd become to the century-old mystery and Hannah, the unfortunate widow who'd disappeared.

"*Mmm*," Shirley said, "no doubt you've visited the new owners of the old Elliott farm. Isaac Elliott, Hannah Montague's father, was the original owner of that place. A sheep farmer he was. 'Course, the land has change hands many times over the years."

"Actually no, not yet, although it was suggested that my niece and I go out there," Gracie said, suppressing a small giggle because she knew that the "new" owners of the old farm had actually been living in it for about a decade. It was so telling of how people thought on the island.

Shirley harrumphed. "*Tsk tsk*, I'm sure that place is a goldmine of information. I'm surprised you haven't gone by there yet."

"The new owners have been out of town for a while, and its been pretty busy around inn," Gracie said, knowing the excuse sounded lame even to her own ears.

She and Jamie had talked about getting out to the farm on a research trip, but there had been a lot going on lately. If Gracie were totally honest with herself, she and Jamie had been disheartened by the information they'd gleaned at the historical society. The stepsons' accusations about the missing widow had been upsetting since they were inclined to be sympathetic to Hannah. She and Jamie feared any additional research they turned up would corroborate the Montague sons' disparaging words rather than exonerate Hannah.

"Well," Shirley said, leaning in conspiratorially toward Gracie, "I have it on good authority they're home now. He was a longtime summer resident who turned island dweller when he retired from lawyering. She's…"

Shirley lowered her voice even more, causing Gracie to have to lean in to hear whatever the elderly woman was about to reveal.

"She's what?" Gracie encouraged.

"She writes those books." Shirley lowered her voice to a whisper.

"Those books?"

"She's a romance writer!" Shirley said triumphantly.

Gracie could tell her neighbor expected some kind of response, but for the life of her, Gracie didn't know how she was supposed to react. Did the revelation call for shock, surprise, excitement—or possibly condemnation?

"She calls herself Delinda Dryer," Shirley added, with a knowing look. "Won't put her real name on them."

"Wow, I'm impressed," Gracie said, genuinely taken aback. Delinda Dryer was a *New York Times* best-selling author who wrote complex family sagas. Gracie had left a phone message for a Mr. Jonathan Crester, the current owner. Apparently Crester was the married name of the famous writer.

Shirley nodded knowingly. "She's been on a book tour—he always goes with her—and they're just now back on the island."

"Thanks much, Shirley. I'll give them time to settle in before I try to contact them again," she said.

She knew better than to ask Shirley how she knew. Their neighbor always seemed up on everything happening on the island. In fact, Gracie was happier not knowing who Shirley's sources were.

"You know the hymnal I gave your sister Caroline, the one that belonged to Hannah Montague when she was a girl? I bought it for a pittance from the folks who owned the inn a while back. They were selling things right and left. I knew then they must be in over their heads."

Gracie remembered the hymnal Shirley had bought some time ago and given to the sisters at their open house.

"Yes, I know the one you're talking about," she said.

"Folks back in the day didn't throw anything away. I wouldn't be surprised if old Elliott squirreled away journals or such in that old house. I ran into Mr. Crester when the renovations started and asked him if they'd come across anything like that when they moved in. He said no, not so far, but they'd only just started doing the place over. You know how folks kept diaries and such back in the day. Not like today when we're so busy with other things," she said with satisfaction.

Gracie thanked Shirley for the information about the author and her husband. She was definitely going to call Mr. Crester again. Her errands could wait. She hurried back into the inn to find Jamie and tell her what she hoped was good news about the current residents of the old Elliot farm.

With Jamie by her side and hanging on every word, Gracie made the call and found Mr. Crester to be a gracious gentleman who invited them to visit as soon as they could. He had a deep interest in the history of the old house and its original inhabitants and was eager to share information.

Several hours later Gracie found herself staring at the old Elliott farm in wonder, admiring the long graceful porch, shuttered windows, and sweeping view of the ocean beyond the tree line.

"Oh, Aunt Gracie, it's gorgeous, isn't it?" Jamie said, getting out of the Packard and shutting the door resoundingly.

"Breathtaking," Gracie agreed, still feeling a bit rattled from the rutted country lane she and Jamie had had to traverse to get to the house once owned by Isaac Elliott, Hannah's father.

A few moments later, Gracie knocked on the front door using an ornate, old-fashioned doorknocker. She exchanged excited glances with Jamie as they stood waiting for someone to answer. It was hard to believe Hannah Elliott Montague had lived in this house as a girl. How much of the old house had survived modernization over the centuries? What clues about the life of the original inhabitants had turned up in the course of the renovations?

The woman who answered the door was much smaller and prettier, even with her face devoid of makeup, than the author photo Gracie had seen on the jacket of a book she owned. She was casually dressed and probably close in age to Gracie.

"Come in, come in," Delinda said, greeting them warmly. "You'll have to excuse my appearance." She laughed as she pulled her oversized sweatshirt down over black yoga pants. "The glamorous life of a writer is only an illusion, especially when we're trying to unpack and settle in from being on the road."

"Thank you so much for letting us come over so soon after you're back," Gracie said, introducing herself and Jamie.

"No problem," the author said smiling. "I'm thrilled someone wants to come take a look at the old papers and things we pulled from the attic. They've just been sitting around since we renovated ten years ago. I think we should have donated them to the historical society right away, but Jonathan wanted to study them and do some research before we did. Of course, some other project always got in the way," she said, ushering them into a sitting room.

"What a lovely room," Gracie said, admiring the controlled clutter in the space. It wasn't her style, but a plentitude of personal mementoes mixed with antiques and a collection of old dolls in a cupboard reflected the personality of the owners and had a charm of its own.

"My husband loves history," Delinda explained. "And, of course, it seems natural to be surrounded by reminders of the past. I prefer to work with the most up-to-date equipment, though, so my office is totally modern to the point of minimalism."

Gracie loved the antique hatboxes strewn casually around the room, some occupied by dolls with china heads, although she suspected their placement was actually very deliberate. Instead of looking stuffy, the contrast of the antique wallpaper and striped Victorian loveseats played against a corner stand with glass Christmas ornaments nestled among a collection of seashells. It was a cozy, homey room that made her feel at ease.

"You must be the ladies from Misty Harbor Inn," a tall, smiling man of about sixty said as he entered the room.

"I'm Jonathan Crester," he said, extending his hand to Gracie and then Jamie. They exchanged pleasantries while Delinda excused herself to get back to some revisions on her latest book.

"Would you like a tour of the house?" he asked.

It was a tempting invitation, but Gracie didn't want to impose, especially since they'd come on such short notice. Mostly she and Jamie were eager to look at any journals or diaries that may have been uncovered during the renovations of the farmhouse.

"That's so kind, but we know you just returned to the island. Perhaps another time?"

"I do have some things that need doing today," he admitted. "But I was eager to meet some fellow history buffs. Suppose I give you a rain check on the tour, and I show you what you've really come to see?"

"What we've seen of the house so far is wonderful," Gracie said. "I'd love to come back for a tour when it's more convenient."

"This house is fantastic," Jamie said with enthusiasm. "It still has an eighteenth century ambience. Most places lose that when they've been renovated."

Jonathan beamed. "We really tried to keep the authentic feel of the original farmhouse, but we wanted it to be comfortable and livable by our modern standards too. We had the floors sanded and stained, installed energy-efficient windows, and updated the plumbing, which hadn't been done since the 1930s. My special project was replacing the grout in all five fireplaces."

"I know how much work it is to bring an old house up to modern standards. It seemed to take forever to make the inn ready for guests," Gracie said.

"It's wonderful you did," their host said. "I hated to see the old place deserted and ravaged by age. We drove by a while ago, and it looks great."

"Thank you so much," Gracie said, pleased that a resident of the island appreciated what they'd done to the inn.

"The papers you came to see are in my office, if you'll follow me. It was a parlor in Isaac Elliott's time, and I believe he worked on his accounts there."

They followed their host to a room beside the commons area. The showpiece of the space was a huge roll top desk that dwarfed all the other furniture in the room.

"This desk is late nineteenth century. Old Isaac's desk was too small for me, but I had it repaired by a genius of a refinisher to use in the upstairs guest room. He knew not to touch the patina, thank heavens. Nothing ruins a piece of antique furniture more that stripping off the old surface." Gracie and Jamie stopped to admire the stunning antique.

"The journals I have were actually discovered in a secret compartment when he started work. We were fortunate it had never been stored in the barn with other original furnishings. The dampness on the island can ruin furniture quite quickly when it's exposed to a leaky roof and an invasion of vermin.

Gracie nodded sympathetically. "We salvaged all we could, but some things in the attic were beyond help."

"But I digress," Jonathan said, opening a cupboard on the side of his massive desk and extracting an old filing box. "Here you go."

He placed it on a small table situated between two balloon back chairs. "Please take your time and peruse the contents for as long as you want. If you need anything just press this button," he said, going to what looked like a cold air return. "It's an ancient intercom system installed decades ago, but it still works. Now, unless you ladies would like some tea, I'll take my leave."

"No, we're fine, thank you so much," Gracie said, eager to see what was inside the box.

An hour later, she and Jamie had sifted through page after page of ledgers recording every household and farm expense incurred in Isaac Elliott's time, all detailed in Isaac Elliott's cramped handwriting. Gracie could see their historical value but the contents so far were disappointing. There was nothing personal in the business accounts.

Stretching, she looked over at Jamie. Her niece put down the ledger she'd been carefully going through.

"Oh, Aunt Gracie, this is really hard to read. The ink has faded, and Isaac's penmanship leaves something to be desired," she said.

"Unless you're interested in the price of flour and the wages of a farm hand, there's not much in the books I've gone through," Gracie said.

"This one is much more interesting," Jamie said. "It's a daybook, a sort of diary but with very short entries. Isaac mentions his son going off to sea. He reported that in one sentence. Hannah got half a page when she wanted to marry a man he didn't approve of. He threatened to disown her—I can practically read his anger in the way the words are scratched into the paper. Look at this."

Gracie took the cardboard covered journal and read the portion Jamie pointed out.

"Goodness, he bartered her hand in marriage to that wealthy whaler, Montague, for land he wanted to graze his sheep. This is so sad. What a cold-hearted father he was. He treated Hannah like one of his possessions."

"I know," Jamie agreed. "Read the next passage."

Gracie's eyes grew moist as she read of the patriarch's cruelty. "He says his daughter and son were both dead to him because his daughter is a thief, and his son disobeyed him. He doesn't even mention what the son did. This is so heart wrenching."

"He doesn't even mention his son by name!" Jamie said. "You'd think he was talking about a lost sheep."

"In a way, I guess he was. Obviously, he was pious without understanding the true message of the Bible," Gracie said as she continued reading. "There's no hint of love or forgiveness in his entries."

"Have you come to the part about the Great Fire of 1846?" Jamie asked, leaning over to read see where she was.

Gracie stretched and rubbed her back. "I'm just getting to that part."

"It really devastated the area, leaving a hundred families homeless," Jamie said.

"This is interesting," Gracie said. "I've never heard of sheep storms. Apparently the fog would come over the moors this time of year and drench the sheep. After the hot sun dried their coats, it was sheep shearing time."

"I've read enough about sheep to last me a lifetime!" Jamie said, which made Gracie laugh and nod in agreement. "Isn't it sad? Isaac devotes pages to sheep, but only a few sentences to his own children. It makes me want to cry for Hannah's sake."

"Me too! Look. There's just one more journal," Gracie said, pulling it out of the box and starting to gently turn the pages. "Yes, more household and farm accounts," she said, sighing. She paged through the whole journal while Jamie watched her expectantly.

"Nothing here," she said disappointedly. She examined the book again but found nothing of interest. "Wait a minute," she said, noticing a small tear on one edge of the journal's cover.

"Did you find something, Aunt Gracie?" Jamie asked.

"I'm not sure," Gracie said, picking carefully away at the tear with her thumbnail. "Oh, I hope I'm not damaging historical documents," she lamented as she continued to gently peel away the cover.

"I think you're okay. It's just a ledger of old household accounts," Jamie reassured her. "And you're being careful."

"Well, would you look at this," Gracie said, feeling her excitement build as she extracted a sheet of paper from between the cover and its backing. The handwriting was shaky and larger than in the ledger entries.

"What is it?" Jamie asked with renewed enthusiasm in her tone.

"It's what we've been looking for," Gracie said. She began to read out loud what Isaac Elliott had written on the paper he'd secreted away. It sounded like a prayer—or maybe a confession.

"This is the first time he's mentioned his son by name," she said excitedly. "His name was William, and he became a minister on the mainland, although Isaac didn't know where his church was."

"William?" Jamie said, sharing her excitement. "As in Hannah's mysterious William?"

"Yes!" Gracie said, thrilled she and Jamie had just discovered a piece of the 130-year-old puzzle.

"What else does he say," Jamie asked.

"Let me see," Gracie said, scanning the cramped handwriting. "He says he saw William and Hannah a time or two when his son came to the island to see his sister. They didn't see their father, and it was for the best, according to Isaac. What a breathtaking entry!"

"Wow," Jamie said. "Talk about a dysfunctional family—although they wouldn't have called it that at the time."

"Oh my," Gracie said as she read on, feeling misty-eyed. "Isaac Elliott writes here he's asked God for forgiveness for the hurt he caused his family. He doesn't know how or why his daughter disappeared, but for years after she did, he prayed she was still alive and had found happiness. And best of all, by this point he no longer believed she was a thief," Gracie added triumphantly.

"Well, he belatedly shows some compassion for her," Jamie said.

"He also writes he believes her stepsons stole the money from the lighthouse and used it to pay off their father's debts. Otherwise they would have lost the house," Gracie said, continuing to read. "Isaac didn't have any proof but he claims he wasn't alone in his suspicions. He's distressed because he can't clear Hannah's name, but he believes she was innocent in the eyes of the Lord."

"I hated believing Hannah was a thief," Jamie said. "I'm really glad we got to read Isaac's journals."

"Me too," Gracie said. "I guess we have Shirley to thank for prodding me into calling Mr. Crester again."

"Wasn't he nice to let us come here and have access to the journals. Historically speaking, they're priceless," Jamie said.

"They certainly are." Gracie returned the loose sheet to its hiding place inside and cover and carefully placed the journals back in the box.

"Should we mention the secret page?" Jamie asked as Gracie and over to press the antiquated intercom button.

"Yes, I think we should."

"Did you find anything interesting?" Mr. Crester asked when he came into the room.

"One of the back covers had separated a bit," Gracie said, retrieving it and holding it out for his inspection. "There was a sheet inside. I hope you don't mind that we took it out and read it."

"Not at all. I can't wait to read it myself." He extracted the sheet and silently read it, smiling when he got to the end. "If you'd like, I can make a copy of this page for you to keep."

"Oh, that would be wonderful!" Jamie said. Their host took the old paper to another room and returned shortly with a duplicate.

"This is great," he said. "I'm so happy you found this page. I guess we didn't look carefully enough."

"It wasn't that easy to spot," Gracie said, "but isn't it marvelous? It's wonderful to learn Hannah's father came to believe she didn't steal the money for the church organ. This is exactly what we need for the history nights we're planning at the inn."

"They sound interesting," Mr. Crester said. "I'm glad I could help. I might be interested in coming to one of your presentations, if they're open to the public."

"They certainly will be. We'll put a notice in the paper when we start them. But I'd also be happy to give you a call. You and your wife can come as our guests." Gracie said.

After thanking their host for his generosity in letting them look at the journals, Gracie knew it was time for her and Jamie to go home and share the news with the others.

"Say good-bye to Mrs. Crester for us," Jamie said, adding her thanks to Gracie's. "It was a thrill to meet her."

"She's sorry she couldn't visit, but deadlines can be intense," he said.

When they got back to the inn, Gracie could hardly wait to share their findings with her sisters and show them the photocopy of Isaac's note. She called for an impromptu team meeting that even Caroline attended with enthusiasm.

"Even though Isaac Elliott didn't have proof of Hannah's innocence, he believed she was innocent. I don't believe she wasn't a thief either," Caroline said.

"I feel a lot better about finding the money in the secret room, now that I'm pretty sure Hannah didn't steal it," Sam said.

"I feel the same way," Gracie said, "especially in here." She put her hand over her heart and smiled at her sisters and niece. "Maybe some day we can clear Hannah's name in the eyes of the world—or at least in the island's historical records. She doesn't deserve to be seen as a villain."

CHAPTER
Twenty-five

The sun shining off the rented Bentley was so bright Gracie had to shade her eyes. She was sweeping the front porch, although it really didn't need it, and watching Albert polish the vehicle to a brilliant sheen. For the first time since his arrival at the inn, he was wearing a faded polo shirt and trousers without a crease.

Grinning to herself, Gracie went on with the unnecessary sweeping until Caroline startled her by coming up behind her.

"I just swept yesterday afternoon," her sister said. "You don't need to do it again."

"*Shh*," Gracie warned. "I'm watching Albert polish the Bentley."

"Why on earth is he doing that? They'll be leaving tomorrow. The rental agency doesn't expect to get the car back in pristine condition."

"It has nothing to do with being a rental." Gracie motioned her sister back into the foyer and closed the door.

"I know that expression," Caroline said in a suspicious voice. "That's how you used to look when you were keeping a secret from me. What are you up to?"

"You'll just have to wait and see." Gracie headed to the kitchen and left the broom on its hook over the cellar steps.

"What on earth!" Caroline watched with one hand on her hip, a sure sign of exasperation. "There's something you're not telling me."

"Yes, there is. I do have a secret. If you want to know it, sit out on the front porch around seven-thirty this evening."

"You're playing a game with me," Caroline accused her in a good-natured voice.

"Wait and see."

Gracie hadn't felt in such high spirits all summer, not even when Brandon and his whole family were there. She was having a wonderful time with Evelyn and looked forward to her son's return for the Fourth of July, which fell in the middle of the following week, but her excitement had another source.

When her chores were done—the ones that really needed doing—Gracie went the kitchen where Sam was finishing a batch of chocolate chip cookies.

"They're for Brandon and his family when they come back," Sam said. "I've made out a menu of things I think everyone will like. Aren't you excited? They'll be here five days including the Fourth. We can watch the fireworks from our own back porch. Mom would've been thrilled."

"Yes, she would have," Gracie agreed. She'd been counting the days until her son returned, but today she had something entirely different on her mind. "Why don't you join me on the front porch around seven-thirty this evening? Bring a book or something to make it look like you just happened to be there."

"You have that look," her sister said.

"What look is that?"

"You know, your eyes are sparkling, and you have a little grin. You're not planning a practical joke, are you?"

"No, nothing like that, but you'll be sorry if you're not here." Gracie grinned to herself, enjoying her secret.

The evening was perfect with a light breeze cooling the island. Gracie loved the long days of summer almost as much as the time she'd spent on the beach with Evelyn during the afternoon. Her granddaughter played until she was exhausted, content to watch television inside the inn when her grandmother went out to the porch.

After making herself comfortable on a lawn chair, Gracie began to wonder whether her sisters would be curious enough to join her. Finally Sam came outside and pulled up a chair, just as Caroline was coming back from walking Max.

"Now what is your big secret?" Sam asked.

"You'll see in a minute."

Gracie tried not to stare at the front entrance or the big Bentley parked as close to the porch as possible. She didn't have long to wait. The door opened and Albert stepped through it with Miss Clayworth on his arm.

The actress was wearing champagne palazzo pants with a matching jacket and silver ballerina slippers. A long feather boa circled her neck, setting off her classically beautiful features. Her hair was piled high on her head and set off by a jeweled comb. She looked so stunning Gracie was dumbfounded for a moment.

"Good evening," Albert said as Miss Clayworth nodded a greeting.

When he actually winked at her, Gracie's jaw dropped. Was this the stuffy assistant who'd come to the inn back in May?

She watched with her sisters as he seated Miss Clayworth on the front seat of the Bentley, closed the door, and went around to the driver's side to start the car.

"How can a woman in her eighties be so gorgeous?" Caroline asked. She turned to Gracie. "Where are they going?"

"Wait. She sat in the back when she first came here," Sam observed. "Uh-oh, Gracie has that look again," she teased. "You were expecting them. What's up?"

"Mr. Grayson is escorting Miss Clayworth to the theater."

For a moment both sisters stared at her in amazement.

"You mean, like a date?" Caroline asked.

"Not *like* a date," Gracie said. "A date. Period."

"How did you even know about it? It's not as if either of them is exactly forthcoming." Caroline stooped to pet Max and gave Gracie a searching look.

"I learned the theater group here is doing *The Importance of Being Earnest*. Miss Clayworth appeared in it at the beginning of her career, so I bought two tickets and gave them to Albert."

"And?" Sam prompted.

"I may have casually suggested he invite the woman he loves."

Caroline's mouth popped open. "You've been playing cupid!" she said. "I can't believe it."

"What a wonderful way for them to end their stay at the inn," Sam said. "Do you think anything will come of it?"

"I don't know, but have you ever seen Miss Clayworth looking happier?" Gracie asked.

"When I had tea with her, she told me she regretted not marrying. Maybe it's never too late to find someone who loves you." Caroline sounded sad, and Gracie knew she was thinking of George.

"I'm so proud of you, Gracie. If nothing else, they'll both have a wonderful evening to remember." Sam stood and hugged her sister. "I think I'll go to bed early. Tomorrow's Saturday, and we'll have people coming and going all day."

"I will be sad to see our Brits leave," Gracie said.

"Two weeks ago I would've been happy to get rid of Nate, but he buckled down and did a good job with the art workshop after I helped him a bit," Sam said. "Now I'm a little sorry he'll be checking out in the morning."

"It was nice his wife Ingrid could come for a day before he left," Gracie said. "I hardly saw her, but I guess they rode bikes around the island and had a good swim."

"She was nicer than I expected, considering how often she called to check on Nate," Sam mused. "Guess I learned something about not prejudging people."

"There's something to be said for keeping in touch," Caroline said, not fooling Gracie, who knew she was thinking of George.

"Well, good night. Breakfast will be served at seven-thirty so our departing guests can catch an early ferry." Sam went inside, and Caroline followed her with Sam.

"Yes, I'd better get Evelyn to bed," Gracie said, following them, still charmed by the happiness she'd seen on the faces of the elderly couple.

Lord, if it's meant to be, grant them happiness together in their remaining years, she prayed.

Caroline came down early Saturday morning, although helping with breakfast wasn't on her list of duties. She'd had a restless night, unable to get Albert and Miss Clayworth's surprising date out of her mind. If a woman in her eighties could still be loved and courted, was there hope for her? Caroline couldn't imagine being with anyone but George, but hope for reconciliation had faded as week after week passed without seeing him.

"Good morning!" Nate said sticking his head into the kitchen. "Sorry I ordered vegan for Ingrid. She won't be eating breakfast this morning, but she would like some soda crackers to settle her stomach if you have any." He beamed. "Guess what! We're going to have a baby!'

Sam rushed over and hugged him. The young man who thought he didn't like children was going to be a father, and he was bubbling over with happiness.

"That's wonderful," Caroline said, adding her congratulations to her sister's.

After breakfast, the oldest Marris sister hovered in the foyer, waiting to send their departing guests off with gift bags Sam had filled with samples of her blueberry bread and homemade jam. She hoped to someday sell online, but for now, she wanted to send visitors home with a couple of flavorful reminders of their time at Misty Harbor Inn.

Gracie joined her in time to congratulate the parents-to-be, but Caroline knew she was hoping to say good-bye to Miss Clayworth and Albert. When he made his first trip down the stairs with luggage, he put it down and came over to them.

"I can never thank you enough," he said, taking Gracie's hand and touching it with his lips.

Caroline was amazed at his courtly gesture, and surprised when he did the same to her before carrying luggage out to the Bentley.

"I wonder what he meant by that?" Caroline said.

Gracie shrugged. "I suspect he's leaving here a happier man than when he arrived."

"The inn has that effect on people," Caroline said, hoping her sister would say more.

"Yes, it is a special place." Caroline saw an enigmatic smile cross Gracie's face.

She waited with Gracie until Albert finished loading the car and Miss Clayworth slowly made her way down the stairs, taking Wellington from him when she had safely reached level ground.

"Thank you, dear Gracie, for your kindness and insight. I've never had a lovelier evening at the theater." She planted a soft kiss on her cheek.

"And Caroline, I so enjoyed our tea together. Remember, it's never too late," She squeezed her hand and made her way to the car on Albert's arm.

"She's getting in the front seat again," Caroline said, awed by what she saw as the beginning of a new relationship. She turned to Gracie. "You can play cupid for me anytime."

"You're only saying that because you think I won't," Gracie teased.

Caroline was thankful for a busy day to keep her occupied, but by sunset she wanted solitude to think about the course her life was taking. When she'd convinced her sisters to buy the inn, she'd never dreamed George would go missing from her life. She thought she was adding something special to the rest of her life, not losing the person who meant the most to her.

The beach was nearly deserted when she reached the stretch below the bluff. Farther along the shoreline, a young couple was frolicking on the sand, dashing in and out of the waves, but they only made her feel more alone. She wandered farther away from them, not worried about returning to the inn before total darkness. Perhaps she'd even sleep on the beach and let the sun rouse her at dawn. She needed the sense of renewal a gorgeous sunrise could give, and even more, she needed time for prayer and meditation.

Much as she loved her sisters, she couldn't share her sorrow with them. She'd wanted them to be together after years of separation, but an important person was missing from her life. She wanted to believe Lorraine Clayworth, but in her heart she felt it was too late to love again. She'd lost George and had no one to blame but herself.

"Were you thinking of a swim?"

Her heart stopped at the sound of a deep male voice, and she jerked around, not believing her ears.

"George."

"Sorry if I startled you. Gracie told me where I could find you."

"When did you get here?" It was the only thing she could think to say.

"Late this afternoon. I brought my boat."

She remembered the *Caroline*, named after her, and wondered if he still had it. Would he change the name if they were through for good?

"Thought it would be convenient to sleep on board."

She could just make out his broad shoulders and handsome face in the fading light. His hair was windblown, still thick but showing white, and she yearned to see his familiar smile. But perhaps the time for smiling was over, and he'd only come to make their separation final. She was afraid to say anything that would lead him to break things off forever. It way typical of him to want to wrap things up neatly, even relationships.

"Have you been keeping busy?" he asked, falling into step beside her as she slowly walked farther down the beach.

"Very. Besides running the inn, we've had a little mystery on our hands. Do you remember us talking about Hannah Montague and her mysterious disappearance? We found some things of hers in a secret room." She wanted to talk about anything but the long time they'd spent apart—and whether he was there to make it permanent.

"Interesting." She could tell he was only being polite.

"We've started a series of historical mystery nights to tell people about the inn and the island. The first one was well attended, and not just by our guests. Even some locals came."

"That's nice."

She wished it were light enough to see the expression on his face. Or maybe not.

"I have some news for you," he said in a thoughtful voice, not reaching out to take her hand the way he used to when they walked. "I'm selling the business. It's taken a long time to finalize the details, but I'll be closing sometime next month."

"That is surprising news." She didn't know whether to congratulate him or not.

"I'm sorry I didn't put you in the picture sooner. It's a complicated deal, and I wasn't sure it would go through until just recently."

"I understand." It seemed an appropriate thing to say, but she didn't understand a thing.

"I'm not sure what I'll be doing next. I'll be officially retired, but I want to keep active, maybe sailing to someplace I've never been before."

She knew how much of the world he'd seen. How far did he plan to go? When would she see him again?

"Maybe we can make a voyage together," he said in a barely audible voice.

Her heart was thumping so hard, she thought it would burst. There was nothing she wanted more than to sail off on an adventure with George, but she suddenly felt as though she had the weight of the world on her shoulders: the responsibility of making a go of the inn she's convinced her sisters to buy with her.

"There's the inn…," she began, unable to articulate the full extent of her obligation to Misty Harbor Inn.

"Of course." He must have been expecting her to put the inn first. His voice was flat, totally without expression. "Well, maybe you can show me something of Nantucket while I'm here, anyway."

"Yes, I'd like that." She could hardly force the words from her mouth. How could she pretend to be a tour guide when she wanted so much more from their friendship?

Before she'd worried their relationship was over. Now she knew for a certainty, and it hurt.

"I'd better walk you back to the inn," he said. "If I know you, you didn't bring a flashlight."

He produced a small light from his pocket and used it to illuminate their way back up the bluff.

After he left her at the door, she went to the back porch and sat in the dark, feeling all chance of happiness slipping away forever.

CHAPTER
Twenty-six

Caroline glanced around the suite. It was in perfect order, ready for the next guests who were expected later in the day. Tourists and locals would be awaiting the spectacular Fourth of July fireworks display tomorrow, but Caroline couldn't muster any enthusiasm. She looked around the cozy sitting room, knowing there was nothing else to be done there but reluctant to leave it.

Tea with Miss Clayworth had been a lovely interlude in an otherwise depressing summer. Caroline closed her eyes and could see the elderly woman, kindness radiating from her patrician face, as she presided over the tea table.

Was it possible the aging actress had discovered true love after all? Was it right under her nose, and neither she nor Albert had been able to break down the barrier between employer and employee until Gracie had seen what they could not?

Caroline smiled at the thought of her sister playing cupid, but it was a bittersweet reaction. Gracie could take the problems of the world on her shoulders, but there was nothing she could do for her own lovesick sister.

This was Caroline's last chore of the day. Her sisters had willingly agreed to get along without her so she could spend time with George. Now that the time was approaching, she didn't know if she could be with him. How could she pretend they were just friends?

Would he stay a day, two days, even a week? It didn't really matter. She knew she'd have to say good-bye without knowing when or if he'd return to the island. Was this the way early whalers' wives felt when they waved good-bye to their men, not sure whether they'd see them in a year, two years, or never?

One thing was sure: The longer she thought about life without George, the more depressed she became. The old Caroline wanted to throw caution to the wind and sail off with him today, but how could she leave her sisters to cope with running the inn? She'd convinced them to buy into it with her, even though she wasn't sure whether Sam would be happier teaching. Gracie still wanted to go back to her home on the mainland and her old life, even though she was doing her best to fit into life on Nantucket.

Dear Lord, what should I do? Caroline agonized in prayer.

Life had been much less complicated when she only had to think about herself. Now she felt weighed down by the need to help her sisters make a success of the inn. She loved Misty Harbor Inn even more than they did, but she loved George too.

Yes, she'd said it! Now that she'd admitted it to herself, she couldn't go on with her life without some kind of resolution.

Forty-five minutes later she was ready to bike around the island with him.

"That's a new outfit, isn't it?" Sam asked when Caroline came into the kitchen to pick up the special box luncheons she'd packed for their outing.

"I've had it a long time, well, a couple of years, but it never seemed my style."

"It's about time you wore something besides khaki shorts and peasant blouses," Sam said, continuing to admire the crisp white linen shorts and the navy and white striped boat-neck shirt.

"I have to ask you something," Caroline said, taking one of her sister's busy hands in hers and peering in her eyes. "Are you happy we bought the inn? Do you really like it here?"

Sam paused so long, Caroline dreaded hearing a negative answer.

"Yes," she said at last.

Caroline let out a pent-up breath. "That's it, just yes?"

"I could go on and on about how much I like being on the island. The responsibility agrees with me, and so does the challenge of making a success of the inn. As for my baking, I never had enough time when I was raising Jamie and teaching to really be creative. And now I do. Does that answer your question?"

Stepping forward and hugging her, Caroline whispered, "I love you, little sister."

She hurried to the front porch with the things she needed for their bike ride, only to find George waiting for her with both bicycles ready to go.

"Good morning," he said, his eyes shaded by tortoise-framed Ray-Ban sunglasses. "Ready to go?"

"Yes, completely ready," Caroline said, concealing her own eyes behind sunshades, not wanting George to read fear and uncertainty in them.

The day was hot, even with the ocean breeze, and she could feel herself wilting soon after they began their trip. Most of the time she followed George, making it hard to carry on a conversation. That was the way she wanted it. She needed time to think of what to say when they stopped for lunch.

By the time they descended to one of the more secluded beach areas, she was hot, parched and frightened. If things went badly today, she might never see George again.

He locked their bikes together and carried the lunches and a large beach towel down to the shoreline, picking an area where they could be relatively alone, seen but not heard. It was exactly what Caroline was hoping for.

"Is the inn doing well?" he asked as he spread the towel.

"We were off to a slow start, but it's definitely picking up." She wasn't there to talk about Misty Harbor Inn."

"Your sisters are looking well. Inn-keeping must agree with them."

"Sam is really taking to it," Caroline said, confident this was true. "Gracie... Well, she isn't quite sure yet about living year-round on Nantucket."

"And you?" George took her hand and pulled her down to sit beside him.

"I love the island." This, too, was true.

"Is it large enough for the woman who crashed an archaeological team in Egypt and interviewed one of Africa's bad-boy dictators?"

"I was younger then."

George was smiling at her, but she found it hard to smile back. George was acting so normal, so unconcerned. She glanced out at the ocean, watching the waves come in. Her whole future was riding on the next few minutes, and she was still groping for the right words.

"Well, what do we have in here?" he asked, opening the basket Sam had especially packed for them. He pulled out a bunch of green grapes and held one to her lips.

"Not yet." Caroline was pretty sure she'd choke if she tried to eat.

"You're probably parched." He twisted off the cap on a bottle of water and handed it to her as a pair of young men raced by with surfboards.

"Pretty calm for surfing today," George commented.

He looked especially handsome with the breeze ruffling his silvery hair. The white of his golf shirt emphasized his deeply tanned arms and face, and today he was the one wearing khaki shorts.

Caroline couldn't stand another moment of inane talk. She didn't care about food, drink, or young surfers. The moment was now, and she could only pray she wouldn't blow it.

"When you proposed to me…," she began.

He raised his hands, palms out. "Please, Caroline, no explanations. We've both lived separate lives for a long time. Maybe it's too late to change that."

He glanced out at the sea, but she wanted him to look at her. Gently touching his cheek, she turned his face toward her and went on.

"I was wrong."

That got his attention. He took off his sunglasses and focused on her face. It didn't make it easier for her to say what was on her mind.

"I thought we had plenty of time to be together, but we don't."

"What are you trying to say, Caroline?" Frown lines creased his forehead, making it even harder to say what had to be said.

George liked directness. She took several sips of water to ward off a woozy feeling and knew it was now or never.

"Will you marry me, George?"

Was it bad or good that he looked totally dumbfounded?

In a moment she had her answer. He wrapped his arms around her and sweetly kissed her, lingering over her lips as he whispered a definite, "Yes, darling."

Tears blurred her vision. "I don't deserve a second chance." The words spilled out in spite of the surge of happiness coursing through her.

"You're hard to get. I'll give you that," George teased. "But think how long Ahab chased Moby Dick."

"You're comparing me to a white whale?" She couldn't contain a girlish giggle.

"I'm comparing you to a rare, exotic creature who's never very far from my thoughts."

"You stayed away so long. I thought you must hate me."

"Never. Not once. I was trying to give you the needed space to decide what to do with the rest of your life." He leaned over and gently kissed her forehead.

"I can't desert my sisters."

"You won't have to. We'll work things out. I'm a pretty good handyman, if it comes to that."

Caroline smiled, remembering how he'd restored the Packard.

"We'll make a future together," he promised. "I love you, Caroline Marris."

"I love you too."

As delighted as she was to have Brandon's family back on the island on the Fourth of July, Gracie needed a few quiet moments in her garden. Stacy was a good mother, and Brandon helped her, but the twins were a handful on the best of days. Even Evelyn was acting a little hyper, glad to have her family back even though she'd enjoyed her stay with Gracie at the inn. One twin was afraid of Max, and the other couldn't get enough of the energetic cocker spaniel. Evelyn tried to mediate, and things descended into chaos until Stacy gave them all a short timeout.

"Whew!" Gracie said to herself. As much as she loved having Brandon's family at the inn, she badly needed a time out herself in the garden she'd lovingly tended for more than two months.

All her flowers and plants were flourishing, but it was the sunflowers—Art's sunflowers—that were her pride and joy. Their golden heads were shoulder high, and she was already thinking of harvesting the seeds and expanding their plot next year. She rarely thought of the garden she'd left behind these days, although it surprised her to realize it.

The return of her son to the island was the icing on her cake. Caroline came back from her day with George bringing wonderful news: They were going to be married. The three sisters had talked late into the night with Caroline confessing she'd been the one to propose this time. She promised not to desert the inn, but Gracie and Sam both assured her they could manage while she went on a honeymoon.

With things working out so well for her sisters, Gracie felt pressured to make a decision about living at the inn year-round. She wandered back inside and decided a short nap was in order. After all, the fireworks wouldn't begin until dark. Fortunately, the family could enjoy the display from the back porch of the inn.

The twins didn't last until dark, but Evelyn joined her parents, Aunt Sam, and Grandma for the spectacular fireworks.

Gracie always cringed a bit when the noisy ones boomed over the island, but she loved the great bursts of color.

"Quite a show," Brandon said in his usual understated way when the sky filled with red, white and blue rockets for the conclusion of the display.

Stacy hurried a sleepy Evelyn off to bed, and Sam went inside to put some finishing touches on the breakfast she'd serve to guests and family in the morning, so only Gracie and Brandon were left on the front porch, illuminated by a soft yellow light

"Are you enjoying the island and the inn?" her son asked, sitting beside her as a cool breeze chased away the lingering heat of the day.

"I've been asking myself that very question," she said, taking a few moments to think about everything that had happened so far this summer.

She thought of Kyle and Erin, and how she had been able to help the honeymooners get off to a good start on their marriage. They were lovely young people, and she hoped things would work out well.

And perhaps she'd overstepped her role as innkeeper when she gave Albert the theater tickets, but she still smiled when she remembered the elderly gentleman's happiness. Something had changed between Miss Clayworth and her assistant. A wall had come down, and Gracie hoped they would enjoy years together.

"I've been able to help some people, if only in a small way," she quietly told her son.

"You always were a born counselor," he said. "Remember when I was at loose ends, not knowing whether college was right for me. I couldn't have had a better listener. You helped me know my own heart."

Gracie could hear the smile in his voice, even though she couldn't make out his face in the darkness on the porch. She'd loved being a mother, but she knew neither of her children needed her care and attention. Her home on the mainland was an empty nest in every sense of the word.

A lone firefly flitted by like a tiny lantern. "I've been struggling with a decision," she said. "Should I sell or rent my house and live in the inn year-round?"

"I don't think you're asking me for advice, Mom," Brandon said with a chuckle. "I suspect you've already made you decision."

"I just feel I'm deserting you and Paige."

He reached over and took her hand, gently squeezing it. "You're with us in our hearts each and every day. I think of your wise ways whenever my children challenge me. Whatever you decide to do is fine with me. I'm sure Paige feels the same way."

Gracie's eyes were moist, and her heart swelled with love for her grown son, but she'd made her decision when the sunflowers nodded at her in the breeze. Most guests would come and go without touching her life, but she knew her place was here at Misty Harbor Inn.

Sam came onto the porch from the inn, followed by Caroline.

"I didn't know you two were still here," Sam said. "Wasn't that a great fireworks display?"

"The best I've ever seen," Caroline said in a voice that left no doubt about her newfound happiness.

"Mom has something to tell you," Brandon said, standing pulling her up by the hand.

"Good news, I hope," Caroline said. "This has been the perfect Fourth of July.'

"I've given it a lot of thought," Gracie said, feeling a little fluttery about her decision but eager to share it. "At first I didn't feel I was really needed here, but our guests have helped convince me otherwise."

"You were wonderful with the honeymooners," Sam said.

"And giving those theater tickets to Albert was a stroke of sheer genius," Caroline said. "That's what you do best: helping people. So what is your news?"

"I'm going to live here year-round. When the season is over, I'll make a decision about what to do with my house. I see now that my place is here with my dear sisters. And who knows what future guests might need my help?"

Sam hugged her, and Caroline kissed her cheek, leaving no doubt about how overjoyed they were. A tear trickled down Gracie's cheek as Brandon put his arm around her shoulders for a group hug.

Sometimes the Lord works in mysterious ways, Gracie mused. She'd already seen His work and been part of it at the Misty Harbor Inn.

She couldn't wait to see what else He might have in store for her here.

A NOTE FROM
the Editors

We hope you enjoy Nantucket Dreams, created by Guideposts Books and Inspirational Media. In all of our books, magazines and outreach efforts, we aim to deliver inspiration and encouragement, help you grow in your faith, and celebrate God's love in every aspect of your daily life.

Thank you for making a difference with your purchase of this book, which helps fund our many outreach programs to the military, prisons, hospitals, nursing homes and schools. To learn more, visit GuidepostsFoundation.org.

We also maintain many useful and uplifting online resources. Visit Guideposts.org to read true stories of hope and inspiration, access OurPrayer network, sign up for free newsletters, join our Facebook community, and follow our stimulating blogs.

To order your favorite Guideposts publications, go to ShopGuideposts.org, call (800) 932-2145 or write to Guideposts, PO Box 5815, Harlan, Iowa 51593.